The
Bum Magnet

by K. L. Brady

The Bum Magnet

Published by LadyLit Press
Cheltenham, Maryland

Printed in the United States of America

Publisher's Note:

This is a work of fiction. Names, characters, places, and incidents either are the product of the author's imagination or are used fictitiously, and any resemblance to actual persons, living or dead, business establishments, events or locales is entirely coincidental.

October 2009
First Edition

ISBN-13 9780615307046
ISBN-10 0615307046

This is dedicated to the Almighty Father.
Thank you for giving me the gift of writing—and forcing me to use it by refusing to let me find equal satisfaction in anything else.

Acknowledgments

I would like to thank everyone who gave me love and/or support throughout this arduous but thrilling process.

Thank you, Daddy, for all of your support. You were there for me in ways you never knew. Surprise, I'm an author!

Thanks to all of my family, the Bradys and the Browns, for being chock full of comedians who missed their calling—especially my mom, Francine Brady, who gushed over her daughter's work exactly as a mother should.

Thanks to Rhonda Erwin, Proofreader Extraordinaire, for your keen eye and bargain price.

To Editorial Consultant Marcela Landres, thank you for your advice, guidance, and expertise. You really helped me through the last leg of my journey.

And to all my girls—especially Lisa, Donna, Iris, Tonya, and Angie—for inspiring Nisey's character—a true best friend. Special thanks to Lisa for being the first to read it all the way through and giving me hope that I had a modicum of talent.

Thanks to my fellow writers and critics at The Next Big Writer and Amazon Breakthrough Novel Awards for all the helpful—and sometimes painful—feedback. You really helped whip this book into shape. Special thanks to Christy, LeeAnn, Isabel, Wiggy, and Bisi for being my second eyes and such supportive cheerleaders.

Thanks to J.S. and J.B., both at literary agencies I shall not name, for the feedback that moved me to keep going and make the story better.

And to anyone I've inadvertently omitted, my apologies and thank you too!

One

Self Therapy for Dummies

Her words played in my head like a scratched LP. "Charisse, a good man is like Santa Claus, believing in him feels real good until you find out he doesn't really exist." Although I ignored most of my mother's attempts at wisdom, this little gem stuck with me . . . like gum on my shoe. No wonder I was nearing the big four-oh and home alone on yet another New Year's Eve. No bubbly to pop, no confetti to throw, no love to kiss at midnight's stroke; only me, my remote control, and six goldfish—one in desperate need of a trip to the porcelain god.

Why was I home alone on New Year's Eve *again*? Because of Marcus damn Mathews—"the one." You know "the one," right? The one who *cheated*. The one who *lied*. The one who *broke my damn heart*. The one who kept calling my house begging me to take his conniving ass back. That "*one*." I had finally settled in for the night and tried to forget that I flushed three years of my life down the toilet of wasted time and squandered heart when my doorbell rang.

He's baaaaack!

"What do you want, Marcus?" I asked, exasperated by his unwillingness to accept that our relationship was over.

"I want you. I need you, Charisse," he pleaded, his eyes resembling those of hungry puppy dog begging for his next Scooby snack. I guess he didn't see the sign on my forehead—No Dawgs Allowed!

"No, what you need to do is go find that bitch I caught you with and ring her damn doorbell. Love don't live here anymore."

He let out a sigh of annoyance and aggravation as if *I* was the one ringing *his* doorbell unannounced and uninvited. "Why are you doing this, baby? You know how sorry I am."

"Yes, Marcus, I know how sorry you are . . . and that's *precisely* why I'm doing this. Now, you can leave voluntarily or I can call five-oh. In my neighborhood, you know they'll be here before you can back out of the driveway."

"Alright, Charisse. I'll leave for now. But this isn't settled, not by a long shot," he declared as I slammed the door in his face.

Damn! How could I let this happen again? I am suffering from a chronic case of Wrong Men-itis and it has to stop! I thought. Shaking my head in confusion, I walked back to the disaster area that formerly served as a family room.

Now, how am I going to entertain myself until I pass out in a drunken stupor?

I turned on the stereo determined to avoid any sappy love songs to send me deeper into my emotional upheaval, so R&B - out, Pop - out, Country - way out, nowadays you couldn't even trust Rock. Finally, the disco station, XM-83, what a relief. "Night Fever" by the Bee Gees played, a perfectly non-suicide inducing song.

Thought a gripping magazine article might help take my mind off my troubles, so I grabbed a few from the coffee table. My preferred subscription was Z: The Zaina Magazine, published by talk show hostess, Zaina Humphrey. Between hosting mind-numbing "hope you didn't come for the cookies" open houses; helping delusional "my home will sell for ten thousand above market price, even with the lime green carpet and Barney-inspired purple paint" sellers; and showing homes to unrealistic "will the seller spring for a Sub-Zero in this trailer?" homebuyers, my days were consumed. I kept her show on TIVO for occasions I needed my fix though.

Forty locked its jaws on me like a Pit bull, so my interests broadened far beyond the "Six Ways to Have an Orgasm While Balancing Your Checkbook" articles. I craved pithy, spirit-lifting, soul-feeding, personal-growth inducing, psycho-therapeutic edutainment in under sixty minutes or for less than five bucks an issue. Zaina delivered. She taught me how to improve my relationship with myself and the people forced to tolerate me.

After perusing a couple of editions and glancing at a few nuggets here and there, I decided to return my attention to the disappointing plasma if I didn't stop to read anything in detail. Near the last pages, I glimpsed an article that piqued my interest: "Stop Attracting Toxic Men: Five Steps to Unpacking Your Emotional Baggage."[i] I studied it with a level of focus I hadn't been able to muster in weeks.

Common Signs of Emotional Baggage

Do you have a difficult time opening up even when the new guy in your life makes you feel safe to do so?

No. No difficulty. It's none of their business.

Do you test him every chance you get or maybe try to catch him in the act to give yourself an excuse to remain emotionally distant or break off the relationship?

Eeeeh, that's a bad thing?

Do you carry around stereotypes and hang-ups? If all your boyfriends cheated on you, you assume all men lie and cheat?

Hmph, well if the shoe fits. . .

Do you avoid taking responsibility for your mistakes? You blame your partner for the demise of your relationship and for every bad thing that has happened to you.

So not true. I only blamed them because it was entirely their fault.

Do you have a lingering ghost from your past history you've tried to forget, but never put to rest?

Hmmm, maybe I better keep reading.

If any of the behaviors above sound familiar, you've got emotional baggage. Follow these steps to unpack your baggage for good.

1. Analyze every failed relationship you've ever had, but don't focus on what he did wrong, assess your role too. Use the information to decide what you need and don't need from a partner.

Every failed relationship? Jesus, by the time I'm done, I'll be too old to remember what I was trying to do in the first place.

2. You have faults too. Face them. Take responsibility for your own mistakes. Stop wasting energy on the blame game and conquer your "poor victim" mentality.

Piece of cake. I have no faults.

3. Take a little time off from dating. Give yourself some time to heal. Starting a new relationship without dealing with old hurts and bad relationships simply sets the stage for a repeat disaster.

When they say dating, I'm sure they don't mean sex.

4. Don't compare your current man with your ex-boyfriend, and don't burden him with sob stories from your past relationships. Resist the urge to tell him how your ex-boyfriend cheated, lied, or destroyed your trust in men.

Well, what the hell are we supposed to talk about?

5. Cut your new man some slack. Give him one hundred points and only deduct when he makes major mistakes.

I'll give them two hundred points, and they'll still find a way to muck it up.

Entertaining the prospect of dumping my bags and losing my bum magnetism filled me with excitement. But my stomach sank in fear of what might need to come out of the closet in the process. *That's a bridge I'm not quite prepared to cross.*

Two

Meeting Mr. Right?

I was back to work again and quite giddy because my pitiful New Year had passed. My office, located near the Washington Redskins' stadium in Largo, was situated on the street level of an office building that looked like an eleven-story Rubic's cube with mirrored windows. Just beyond the receptionist desk was a large, open space with thirty black laminate and steel contemporary desks positioned along four aisles. I was one of four top sellers who had been assigned a desk with space for an assistant. For the other agents—first come, first served. Our cheap ass broker refused to splurge on partitions, so one couldn't help but get into other folk's business, not always a bad thing if you wanted to keep up on the latest market news or office drama. When we required privacy, we used one of four conference rooms along a narrow hallway in the back of the office. Although our firm was relatively small compared to some of real estate's mega companies, we held our own in sales.

Unfortunately, the real estate market was a lot like me—overheated in the summer and depressed during the holidays. After spending a quarter of their life savings to make sure the kids had a Wii or PS 3, people weren't thinking about the single-most important investment of their lives. But I didn't care because the article had given me a new sense of purpose. I'd pore through my journals at bedtime to help recollect the nightmares of boy-friends past. There'd be no men, no dating, no sex *(who said that?)*, only many exasperating nights tackling the arduous task of analyzing my relationship disasters. That thought reminded me I was critically low on Grey Goose.

"Good morning, Nyla. What've we got going this morning?" I asked.

"I'm getting ready to pull leads in a few minutes."

"Okay, any phone calls?"

"Mr. Thomas called about his home inspection, and I think your mother called but she didn't leave a message."

Fantastic, just what I needed to start 2008 off on the right foot, a New Year's nag from my mother.

My assistant Nyla, a starving student from my Alma Mater the University of Maryland, handed me the daily new client file, and I sent them obligatory introductory emails and provided Web links to homes meeting their criteria. Nyla was as polite and perky as any twenty-something black woman I'd ever met—conservative too. Her small frame bounced when she walked and she exuded lively energy. She also wore a smile like vision-impaired people wear glasses. Although she could seriously pluck my nerves if I encountered her before nine a.m. or a cup of coffee, she presented the perfect image for my clients and knew how to handle her business.

Anyway, on that particular day, we only had one prospect.

Dwayne Gibson.

Already pre-approved for his loan, he was a dream client. Most of my clients went into cardiac arrest at the mere mention of pulling their credit report. I signed into Yahoo! to clear out my inbox and shoot him an email when my office phone rang. I hated answering the office phones—no caller ID. No telling what kind of nutcase I'd end up talking to.

"Hi, baby, I haven't heard from you since before Christmas. Is everythang okay?"

Great, my nutcase.

"Hi, Mom. Everything's okay. You know me, all work and no play."

"Well, you better stop burning the candle at both ends before you can't smell the roses."

Huh? My mom can seriously fuck up a good quote. She'd only been saying bizarre stuff like that since she hit menopause. I think the hot flashes burned her brain cells.

"I know, Mom, I know."

"How's Marcus and those bad ass boys doin'?" she asked.

I laughed; their reputation preceded them. "The kids are okay. They miss me, but what can I do? Marcus and I still aren't back together, but he won't go away, either. He took me to dinner a few days ago, but I sent him packing afterward."

"You know, baby, I ain't one to pry,"

Sure, you are.

"But sounds to me like even though y'all might not be together, y'all ain't exactly broke up either. If you want him to believe you're broke up, ya might wanna start actin' like ya broke up."

I hated those rare occasions when she made perfect sense.

She continued, "Well, he's a damn fool to go messin' around on you anyway. These so-called men these days I swear, don't 'preciate nothin' 'til it's gone. Can't live with 'em and you can't shoot 'em, not legally anyways. So, when you comin' home, baby? It's been so long since we've seen you. Your Aunt Jackie's been askin' about you, your cousin Lee too. He caught me when I went to the grocery store to pick up some watermelon and Viagra for James. Lee's managing the Piggly Wiggly. You know, he asks about you all the time."

I heard James and Viagra. *Ick!* And for poor James, Mom's partner-in-sin, watermelon became the sixth daily food group after the news reported it had the same effect on men as Viagra.

"God, Mom! That's such an over-share," I said, wincing while I finished typing the email to Dwayne. I hit the send button.

"What? You didn't know your mama was still gettin' her freak on? Ain't that what y'all say? Don't hate because I'm gettin' more than you," she said.

Ouch. Next time plunge the knife in a little deeper, why dontcha?

"Well, on that ugly note, please tell Aunt Jackie I said hi and I miss her. I've got bills to pay. So, let me get back to work."

"Okay, baby. Well, why don't you give your Aunt Jackie a call some-time, Lee too. Y'all were like brother and sister growing up. Shame y'all don't keep in touch anymore."

"I guess we grew up, Mommy, and went our separate ways. You know how it is," I said, brushing her off. She was easing into a taboo topic. And after skillfully dodging the Lee discussion for years, I wasn't *about* to travel that bumpy, dead-end road right then. "Anyway, let me get back to work. I love you. Talk to you soon."

7

I hung up the phone and stared at my computer screen until the words started to blur. A tornado of emotion welled up inside me at the mere mention of Lee's name. He's my cousin. Used to be an all-star quarterback in Winston Salem and all-around idolized and worshipped kind of guy. And when I say worshipped, I mean by *everyone*, including my mother and Aunt Jackie—and even me until I turned thirteen. His charismatic personality drew people to him like flies to a dead bunny. We all thought he'd be the next great football star, like O. J. Simpson—before that was a bad thing.

I adored my Aunt Jackie; she was like a second mother to me. But she was also the psychologist of the family—by trade. Every time we spoke, I had the sudden urge to lay on a couch and exaggerate insufficiently-tragic childhood memories, much (but not all) of which she already knew. Since the episode with Lee, I was a walking psychological study waiting for Aunt Jackie's special brand of wisdom. She made me feel like a freshly-Windexed slab of glass, when I wanted to be a door—a steel reinforced door with iron security bars. She saw right through me. For years, she tried to corner me and have "the talk," but I ducked and dodged her at every hopeless attempt. Suffice it to say, I needed to visit my mother. But between Lee and my Aunt Jackie, I'd delay my trip home as long as possible.

Thank God James kept Mom occupied. I didn't think she would ever date again after Dad. She'd been shacking up with James since I left for college, never desired to remarry. My father divorced my mother when I turned two years old, before I'd grown old enough to know the figure predestined to mold my image of manhood disappeared from our lives. So, she and I struggled through life together, just the two of us. Dad was in the Marine Corp when he married her; grandma dipslayed a picture of him in his dress blues on her mantel before she passed away. Tall and handsome, he looked freshly cut from one of those "The Few, The Proud" billboards. Mom fell hard for him, and, by the looks of him, it was easy to see why. Mom said he traveled to many ports and had *at least* one woman in every one of them. He moved to California after the divorce. Apparently, since the majority of his kids were from the west coast, he chose to live out there. I didn't have a father because I'd been outnumbered.

What the hell, I thought, *I'll just buy her a plane ticket so she can stay with me for a few weeks.* That'll end the "visit me before I'm dead" lectures. Just as Expedia's homepage appeared on my screen, my phone rang again. Mom always forgot to tell me something.

"Yes, Mommy."

"Uhhh, excuse me?" a baritone voice asked from the other end of the line.

"Oh, I'm so sorry. This is Charisse Tyson with Millenium Realty. How can I help you?"

"Hi, Charisse, this is Dwayne Gibson. I received your e-mail and checked out your website. You sent me some properties located in Fort Washington. I'm definitely interested in a few, and I wondered if we could meet sometime this afternoon to look at them."

Ka ching!!

"I'd be more than happy to show those properties to you, Mr. Gibson. May I ask how soon you're looking to move?"

"As soon as possible. I have a townhouse in Virginia but I want to live closer to my kids and they're in Prince George's County. While I'd like to sell my townhouse first, it's not critical. I want to get moved *yesterday.*"

"Okay, give me the MLS numbers, and I'll call you back in a few minutes to let you know where we can meet."

***

I pulled up to the first property and scanned the near-empty parking for anyone who might be him. Nothing. Although the frigid air pulled my "headlights" through my sweater, turning the heat on remained a last resort. Gas prices rose to nearly four bucks a gallon, and I had a twenty-three gallon tank—you do the math. I turned on my CD player and bounced to Jay Z's "Show Me Whatcha Got." *He's still got time*, I thought.

Fifteen minutes later, I looked at my Movado. *Ten minutes late.* I called to check his location. No answer. Sent a text message from my Blackberry, *I'm here. Let me know if you need directions*. No response.

I scrolled through radio stations for another fifteen minutes. Still no word. Then I started to get a little peeved. He should've at least picked up the damn phone and let me know he fell behind. Time is money in this business and although I didn't have to meet with another client later on, he didn't know that. Asshole.

Forty-five minutes later, a grey car zipped into the parking spot next to me. Borderline seething, I maintained my composure. I grabbed my electronic key to open the property door and jumped out. To my surprise, he too drove a BMW 760, steel grey with chrome wheels identical to mine. I was a little impressed; too bad his manners weren't as good as his taste in

9

cars. He might've been kinda cute had he showed up on time. But all I saw right then was a jerk.

Anyway, he didn't favor my usual "type" (as if *that* distinction had ever gotten me anywhere). He only stood about six-foot one, three or four inches shorter than most of my recent beaus. He was casually dressed in Dockers, a button-up, and a leather pilot jacket, neat but a little Urkel-esque. Ooh, but his remarkable dark brown eyes looked like black pearls set against white satin. Didn't matter. Mr. Dreamy Eyes already lost ten cool points, and we hadn't even said hello—couldn't be a good sign. He approached me as I flashed one of my business cards.

"Mr. Gibson?"

"Yes?" he said and then smiled.

Whoa, did someone turn on the sun?

Must not get distracted. He was forty-five minutes late.

"Hi, I'm Charisse, nice to meet you."

Not so much.

He grabbed the card and gave my hand a firm squeeze. "Hi, Charisse, it's nice to meet you too."

"Running a little behind, huh?"

Late ass.

"Yeah, look, I apologize. One of my project managers had a little crisis on the worksite. I own a home renovation company, so there's always something going on. Maybe I can make it up to you later, buy you a cup of coffee to help you warm up?"

"No, thanks. I appreciate the offer though," I said, politely declining. I shifted the conversation to friendlier ground. "You have excellent taste in cars."

"Same to you, nice rims," he responded. He grinned as his eyes traveled from my ankles to somewhere in the vicinity of my face.

I didn't appreciate the inspection, but he had a nice smile for a jerk.

"Well, let's go in. I think this is a foreclosure, so it may not be in the best condition, but we'll see how you like it."

I braced myself as we walked through the front door, most foreclosures were "tore up from the floor up," but we were both surprised. As we explored each room, Dwayne explained he'd separated from his wife—she kept the big house. Sick of sharing a common wall with a wannabe heavy metal drummer, he longed for the privacy and seclusion of a single family home. He'd been working with another agent based in Virginia near his company's main office, but she didn't have a Maryland license. Her loss, my gain.

"So, what do you think?" I asked.

"Well, it's not bad, needs new carpet, paint. The yard definitely needs some work, but it's mostly cosmetic stuff. I could work with it, but I'd like to move pretty quickly. I don't want anything that requires major renovations."

A home renovator that doesn't want to buy a home that needs renovations? What's wrong with this picture?

"We do have a few others to see today. They aren't foreclosures, so they'll probably be in better condition."

"I . . . I'm actually a little pressed for time today. Can we check out one more and then view the rest tomorrow?" he asked after glancing at the blinging gold watch on his wrist.

"Sure, Mr. Gibson."

"Call me Dwayne, please."

"Okay . . . Dwayne. Sounds fine, tomorrow then. So, you'll follow me to the next house?"

"Anywhere . . ."

Did he flirt with me?

"Okay, try to keep up. I can't have you getting lost," I said, volleying a subtle flirt back to verify whether his first pass was intentional.

"Oh, don't worry, I can keep up," he said with a smile and a wink.

Yep. Definitely a flirt.

Three

Low Down and Hooked Up

The next morning, Dwayne called and asked me to meet him at his townhouse. He wanted advice about issues he may need to fix before we put it on the market. He lived in Cameron Station in Alexandria, a picturesque, high-end, mixed-development community with luxury condos, townhouses, and single family homes. I paired my black Donna Karan pantsuit with a sexy silk chemise, pinned my thick, shoulder-length hair in a conservative up-do to save time, and jumped in my Beemer.

I hated driving the beltway during rush hour (think Daytona 500 with a bigger track and no checkered flag), but I obliged. Crossing the congested, dumb ass driver-ridden Wilson Bridge from Maryland into Virginia could test the patience of Mother Theresa. And road rage isn't just an attitude in the D.C. area, it's a way of life—and frequently involves heavy artillery. Thanks to my GPS, I drove straight to his driveway.

His lawn and shrubs looked perfectly manicured, almost too perfect, like an obsessive compulsive Edward Scissorhands stalked the bushes for uneven branches. *Great. It'll sell in no time.* I started spending the commission in my head when Dwayne appeared in the storm door wearing gym shorts and a wife beater that displayed the curves of his lean arms and chest. My mouth salivated as my eyes dropped to his thighs which were thick, toned, and flawless. And perspiration shimmered tantalizingly on his muscles. I credited him with five points just for being that fine. *Damn.*

"Hi, Dwayne, it's nice to see you again. Looks like I caught you in the middle of your workout," I said, trying my best not to stare at his body but failing miserably.

"Yeah, come in."

I stepped into the two-story foyer and glanced at the palladium window above the door as he closed it behind me. I turned to follow him into the kitchen and caught him checking out my ass.

I thought, *That's okay because I was sure as hell checkin' out yours!*

"I'm sorry, Charisse. I'm running a little late this morning, over-slept. Let me walk you through the house, and I'll jump in the shower real quick so we can get on the road."

"Okay. While you're in the shower, I'll wander around and take a few notes on the issues we need to address, if that's not a problem. We can stop by my office while we're out so you can sign your listing agreement."

"That'll work," he said.

We rushed through each room; the master bedroom, however, was eerily familiar. A king-sized, California poster bed sat dead center of the room, flanked by an array of Yankee scented candles strategically placed atop the nightstands, dresser, and armoire, and the smell of potpourri permeated into the hallway; the scent conjured up some vivid, unpleasant memories.

Dwayne looked fine, but he smelled damn funky . . . I ain't lyin'. If he hadn't gotten into the shower when he did, I might've hauled him out back and hosed him down myself. He went upstairs to shower in the master bedroom, and I trotted downstairs to note the issues he needed to address to get the house sold fast.

After poking around downstairs for fifteen minutes or so, I realized there weren't many fix-ups to complete—a little caulking in the basement bathroom, a few blown light bulbs here and there, minor stuff. His home was immaculate, for a bachelor pad anyway. It sorely lacked décor, but everything was in its place . . . or nearby.

I'd worked my way back up to the top floor, carefully eyeing the smallest of details; however, my mind drifted to thoughts of Dwayne, who I'd envisioned standing naked in the steamy shower with water trickling over his luscious body as I peppered his back with gentle kisses. *Lawd, lawd, lawd.* The attraction between us was both undeniable and unfortunate, particularly since I'd sworn off men in my determination to cure my lifelong case of Wrong Men-itis. But as I passed the open master bedroom door, Dwayne emerged from the bathroom, damp, with nothing on his body except a white terrycloth towel wrapped around his waist.

Oh. My. Gawd!

My feet adhered to the floor like I'd stepped in puddle of quick-drying super glue. He smiled as I stared at the towel, which was the only thing standing between my eyes and the massive bulge that taunted me from beneath. Drool surfaced in the corners of my mouth, so I licked my lips. While part of me hoped he would not translate the lick into an invitation, another part—sub-waist—wished he'd take it as an invitation, accept, and get the party started.

"Hi," he said casually, as if he was standing there in a three-piece suit.

I tried to respond, but I only conjured up enough vocabulary to sound like I'd been mute since birth.

"I . . . uhh. . . ummmm. . . .uhhhhh. . . "

Talk stupid.

"Whemmm. . . whaaa. . . whmmm. . . "

English, Charisse. English!

"See something that interests you?" he asked, teasing me. I wanted to say, "Yeah, can I measure your dick . . . with my mouth?" My ears warmed from the shame.

I regained just enough consciousness to feel my eyes staring at the towel—okay, the bulge—so obvious. But with my head locked into position and eyes fixed on the target, I couldn't turn my head or blink.

"Dwayne, I am so sorry. I was on my way to look at the other bedrooms and here you—we are."

"Yes, here we are. So, are you just going to stand there, or are you coming in?" he asked. He removed the towel and walked toward the dresser, exposing a full view of his ass—two heaping mounds of milk chocolate that made me want to eat myself into a diabetic coma.

Sweet Jesus, if I'm dreaming please don't wake me for thirty minutes.

Make that forty-five.

Without warning, my feet went on auto pilot, one foot in front of the other. My mind said, "Stop, slut. Stop!" But my body said, "To hell with you heifer, I'm horny!" I moved forward, damn the lack of consensus.

He met me half way, wrapped his hands around my face, and gave me *The Exorcist* kiss. You know, like he was trying to *kiss the hell* out of me. My clothes fell to the floor like dried leaves from an oak tree in November before he laid me on the bed, slipped on a condom (a heavenly Magnum), and commenced a bombing offensive that made my body explode in ecstasy.

Have mercy!

***

Lying in bed, next to a complete stranger, stark naked, dripping with sweat, and hair standing on all ends, I couldn't escape the feeling that something went wrong. Not "my life sprung a leaky faucet" wrong, you understand, but "my life needs needs a complete fucking renovation" wrong.

I came to get paid, and instead—I got laid.

So, so, so not the plan.

After thirty-nine-and-a-half years, you'd think I'd get a clue, learn a lesson. Nuh uh! In my world, repeating stupid mistakes came as easy as burning microwave popcorn—distractions always trumped experience.

Four

Score? Love Life One, Resolution Zero

I lay next to Dwayne hoping the hook up was a surreal dream sequence some over-zealous writer had edited into a cheesy B-movie screenplay resembling my life. But he and the moment were very real. I rolled on my side, propped myself up on my elbow, and leaned my head on my hand. As I watched him drift into a well-earned power nap, my brain replayed dismal scenes from the New Year's Eve I'd so conveniently forgotten.

***

New Year's Eve 2007

The crackling wood echoed in my Milano tile fireplace betraying the emptiness of my expansive colonial. I thought about adding another log to the dying flames, but in my depressed state, the five feet from the chaise to the fireplace was about four feet longer than I could bear to walk. I refused to budge for at least another two days. By then, the holidays would be over, and I could leave my house without suppressing the urge to rapid fire BB pellets into the spectacle of inflatable Christmas decorations adorning every front yard in the neighborhood except mine.

My house looked like Gale-force winds blew out the windows. I hadn't cleaned in over a week. The furniture exposed enough dust to grow crops, and the kitchen sink had all but disappeared beneath a mound of dirty dishes with a tilt reminiscent of The Leaning Tower of Pisa. Worse, I vegged on my chaise for so long the leather cushion resembled a foam memory pillow. But getting up was pointless, and I only had enough energy to R&R . . . rotate and reach for my snacks.

Critical life-sustaining provisions were positioned within an arm's length—one fresh box of Kleenex, a trash can, remote controls for all of the electronics, two bags of Ranch Doritos, one half-eaten bag of Cool Mint Oreos, approximately twenty-five dollars worth of Godiva truffles from a fifty-dollar box, an unopened bag of miniature Reese's Peanut Butter Cups (Hershey's versus Godiva—no contest), and an ice cold bottle of Grey Goose, also half empty. My electric cooler parked near the chaise stored water and the cranberry juice that accompanied my Grey Goose. The bathroom was just off the kitchen, so I pee'd during my trailblazing journeys to the Sub-Zero.

The remote to the fifty-inch plasma suspended above the fireplace became adhered to my hand as I surfed for a benign comedy to watch without being reminded how pathetic and lonely I'd been. Fan-freaking-tastic! *When Harry Met Sally, While You Were Sleeping*, and *Bridget Jones' Diary*. Jesus Christ. Once beacons of hope, those movies became sources of excruciating pain not unlike natural childbirth. If I endured one more boy meets girl, boy loses girl, boy wins girl back, joy of Christmas, and all live happily ever after fairytale, I might have slit my wrists and yelled, "Take me now!"

I flipped from channel to channel and paused to watch a Catholic Mass. In a true testament to my mental funk, only after ten minutes did I realize the priest was conducting mass in Latin. My exhaustive Latin vocabulary consisted of Semper Fi (Always Faithful) and Caveat Emptor (Buyer Beware), so I wouldn't find much consolation unless he mentioned one of the two.

At last, I settled on a rerun of Rudolf the Red-nose Reindeer and the Island of Misfit Toys. Now, that was a happy thought, my only happy thought of the day—an island somewhere between East Jabib and West Cucamonga to send my defective and unwanted shit. If only an Island for Misfit Boyfriends existed, I'd next-day-air Marcus's sorry ass there.

Before Marcus—and after my heart got stomped, trampled, and kicked for the umpteenth time—I prayed to God and asked Him, "Please send me a man who'll love me enough to never let me go." Ironically, I forgot to pray that he would make me happy. I forgot to pray that he wouldn't be a selfish, lying, cheating bastard. Oh, but God has a sense of humor, doesn't He? He answered my prayer with comical precision and sent my "blessing"—Marcus Matthews. A man who never made me happy, a man who always cheated and lied, BUT a man who wouldn't let me go. God mocked me, saying, "Don't tell Me how to do My job."

Score one for Him.

When God has a sense of humor, floating random prayers up there is risky business, especially when the small print on answered prayers includes a "No Refunds, No Returns" clause.

On Christmas Day, I snatched the small, well-deserved Tiffany & Co box containing Marcus's most recent guilt offering from his paws and told his dumb ass for the trillionth time our relationship was over, finished, finito, buh-bye, move on. His reply? "So, where do you want to go for dinner?" I wanted to scream, "Fool, is something wrong with your hearing? It's over!!"

Instead, I made him take me to Maggiano's for Italian.

I'm a full-figured, size fourteen; I don't pass up free meals.

I never understood the term full-figured. Are skinny women empty-figured? I guess *full* sounds better than *fat*. I stuck it to him though. I ordered two of the most expensive dishes: the manicotti for my right butt-cheek and the filet mignon for my left. Despite my size, I believed eating a balanced diet was important. Once upon a time, a yummy dinner would have earned him a coochie coupon, but those days were long over.

Marcus was my most recent "the one"—you know, the title all we desperate-to-be-loved women give to the one-in-a-million, once-in-a-lifetime, love-of-my-life superhero guy we hope God sent to rescue us from our miserable, single existence.

Yeah, I'd had five of them.

My best friend and sorority sister, Denise—well I call her Nisey (she calls me Rissey)—she introduced us.

Bitch.

I still loved her though.

Nisey's more sister than friend; we met over twenty years ago. She's my down-for-whatever partner-in-crime. You know, the friend that keeps you company at two a.m. outside your boyfriend's house because you suspect another woman is sleeping over. She's also the friend that'd let all the air out of his tires and dump five pounds of sugar in his gas tank on your behalf—despite your half-hearted protests—when you discover you're right.

She'd shared a box of Godiva with you when you were depressed so you didn't have to get fat by yourself—although cruelly, she never gained an ounce. She had the metabolism of a super model on Fen-Phen, but she maintained a respectable size eight figure. (Respectable for African-Americans in D.C., I should say. For us, a size eight is equivalent to a Hollywood size two. What can I say? Black men liked women with fat asses.)

She'd give you her last dime if she had one.

But more often than not she didn't.

She was always broke.

You wouldn't have a clue based on her Filene's Basement-sized closet though; she had more Chanel, Dolce & Gabbana, Marc Jacobs, and Prada than New York during Fashion Week. My wardrobe—mostly close-out buys from Knock-Off World—consisted of bona fide Channelle (a la ghetto), Dolcie & Gabbie, Marc Jacobson, and Tada!, a reflection of my hefty mortgage, Beemer payment, and non-existent benefactors.

Hey, I looked good too, just not quite as "authentic."

We were both real estate agents, but she was one of those high-fashioned, luxury-car driving Realtors who subscribed to the image over substance theory. She might not find you the right house, but damn it, she looked fabulous trying. I had to be fair though, about fifty percent of her inventory was guilt gifts from her boyfriends, lovers, and sugar daddies; she called them sponsors, whatever.

I'm sure she meant well when she introduced me to   Marcus. But, as the saying goes, the road to hell is paved with good   intentions.

Marcus and I worked for competing companies, and by all appearances, we were a match made in heaven. I was cute; he was handsome. I was a highly-successful top producer; he was a highly-successful top producer. I was tall; he was tall. I was honest, caring, and devoted to satisfying his every need; he was . . . tall.

Among our friends and family, he played the role of "doting boyfriend" who *couldn't* shower me with enough love and attention. And that was true, at least for the first six months. Then, like Jekyll to Hyde, he transformed into the self-centered jackass who *didn't* shower me with enough love and attention.

Somewhere in the back of my mind, I told myself to walk away. But I'd been in so many dysfunctional relationships that I thought suffering in relative silence with an asshole was normal, kind of like Stockholm's

Syndrome for love. In reality, we were a match made in hell, but I loved my jerk. In my mind, decent men only existed in movie scripts and romance novels.

He had three boys from a previous marriage—twins Mark and Mikey (age six) and the oldest, Malik (age eight)—whom I adored so . . . little cretins. Don't get me wrong, I loved them to death, but they were bad as hell, like three little Tazmanian devils whose diets consisted only of crack and Red Bull. Oh my God, they used to run my ass into the ground, always running, jumping, diving into something—often something rock hard, fussing over stupid stuff, constantly working my nerves until they couldn't work them anymore. And they knew it too. They'd ramp up the rowdiness anytime I was in the vicinity, which was quite often as Marcus worked non-stop . . . or so he said. But they quit giving me a hard time after I introduced them to mom's best friend—the switch.

Yeah, I went old school, made them pull the switch from the tree and everything. The fifty-foot walk from the deck to the Dogwood in my backyard was the longest of their little juvenile delinquent lives. They got to the point where they would straighten up if I even looked in the direction of a tree. I don't care what anyone says; even the *threat* of a good, old-fashioned ass whoopin' has lots of power.

Anyway, I thought we'd marry and Presto! Instant family. The marriage buzz among our friends spread like the flu. We'd even investigated a three-stone, platinum engagement ring at Jared.

So, can you imagine my shock and surprise when I caught that jackass lip-locked with some silicone-gorged, weave-wearing heifer in a parking lot? Oh, and did I forget to mention he kissed her in *my* car, parked in front of *our* restaurant? While I Christmas shopped for *his* gifts with *his* kids?

He had me, and I'd been had.

Looking back on the wasted three years of our farce of a relation-ship, he always looked for what I've termed the "BBD"—the Bigger and Better Deal.

Why? I don't know.

I brought home the bacon, served it up, and washed the dishes; spread eagle faster than a hooker on a countdown and licked the "lollipop" on-demand; knew the difference between a touchdown, homerun, goal, and a board; washed his dingy drawers, even the ones that looked like a nuclear fart blew a hole in them; left the toilet seat up; watched more football than John Madden; and quoted *The Godfather*.

I was a man's dream.

But Marcus, he was never satisfied. He wanted everything he didn't have and had everything he didn't want, including me.

His problem? He set the bar way too high, deluded himself into believing a Halle Berry/Martha Stewart/Oprah Winfrey/Virgin Mary/Vanessa Del Rio-type woman actually existed. He further conned himself into believing that—if by some miracle she did exist—she would want his sorry ass.

I, on the other hand, set the bar way too low. All a man pretty much needed was a pulse and a job—at least in the beginning. I admit the list lengthened as the qualities I billed as optional in the beginning - like considerate, thoughtful, trustworthy, honest, ambitious, respectful, big dick - became mandatory.

Hindsight's always twenty-twenty though, isn't it? After I kicked him to the curb, Marcus realized he didn't have it so bad after all. His constant, annoying calls and refusal to acknowledge our break-up were some futile expression of regret about his indiscretion, maybe even a deep-seated wish that I'd just play along, forgive and forget.

Well, he could hang that shit up.

I could never trust him again—or any of my ex-boyfriends for that matter.

Seemed a little scary when I looked back on my past relationships. I'd dated five versions of the same man, and married one . . . all bums. That clearly made me a bum magnet, and my bum detector was malfunctioning like a *mother*.

My heart became a revolving door, men in and out, in and out, because I couldn't trust them as far as I could throw them. You know how most women have "a type?" Well, I did too. They were usually the cheating type, every single one of them. All mouth-watering handsome, charming to a fault, and bedded more women than Sealy Posturepedic—before, during, and after our relationship.

During moments of quiet reflection, I often wondered which quality I possesed that drew "ho" men. My dilemma? A variation on the "which came first—the chicken or the egg?" question. Was I attracted to them? Or were they attracted to me? Did I come off too nice? Was my financial success intimidating? Couldn't be the sex, I'd all but installed a pole in my bedroom—it's on my list. Maybe I needed to tap into my inner bitch. Bitches always had the best husbands.

I left Marcus not long after I'd spent over half a million dollars on my dream home—a large, four-bedroom colonial in Woodmont, one of the more well-to-do subdivisions just outside of D.C. in Mitchellville, Maryland. After so many years of hard work and sacrifice, I'd arrived. I hobnobbed with the social elite in the nation's wealthiest majority-black county. I bought it, you know, thinking it wouldn't be long before I'd have a husband with whom I could share my life, the house, and the mortgage.

The joke was on me.

Nobody could've told me I'd be walking around a year later with a big ass house, a big ass mortgage, no instant family, and heartbroken by an . . . an amnesiac who refused to leave me alone. My friends and family kept asking me why a single woman with no children would purchase a McMansion in high-and-mightyville with no family to put in it. To them, it seemed a bit excessive, show-offish. But the answer was simple. I didn't buy the house for the life I had, I bought it for the life I wanted.

Cold winter nights snuggled by the fireplace with my ever-adoring husband, grilling burnt hot dogs on the deck in the summer, the pitter-patter of little feet from my boys getting into something that would lead to the fifty-foot walk out to the tree in the backyard. That's the life Marcus and I almost had.

I was robbed.

Or so I thought . . .

Five

The Inquisition

Dwayne stirred from his nap twenty minutes later. Eyes closed, his hands navigated layers of ruffled sheets and comforters, searching for the warmth of my skin. As he caressed my arm, a contented smile emerged on his striking face. My short-lived moment of bliss was dampened by the mortification from my "ho" moment; shame overcame me like a twenty-four-hour flu virus. And we were scheduled to look at *seven* houses later on, so I'd have to relive the wretched, but oh so satisfying, moment over and over again, *all day long.*

I'm officially living my nightmare.

"I didn't mean to come on so strong," he said, watching my eyes intently as if searching for a reaction. I tried my best to remain stone-faced to avoid displaying my embarrassment. "I hope I didn't make you uncomfortable. I'm not shy, and I was really feelin' you. You are so . . . irresistible, couldn't keep my hands to myself."

Oh, that's not all you couldn't keep to yourself.

"I've never done anything like that before," I said, covering my face with the sheet in a fruitless attempt to conceal my guilt and shame as my stone face gave way.

He laughed. "It's okay. I don't think either of us is going to burn in hell. It just happened; it was just one of those things."

I rolled out of bed and asked him if I could take a quick shower, didn't want to walk around smelling like booty all day. I emerged from the bathroom dressed and ready to go about twenty minutes later. Pensive, he rested on the edge of the bed in camel-colored pants and a black long-sleeved Ralph Lauren polo, smiling as if he was enjoying a flashback of our afternoon. I cleared my throat to get his attention.

"Uh, uh. We should, uhhh, we should get going. We've got properties to see, papers to sign . . ."

"Dinner to eat?" he interrupted as he stood up and walked toward the bedroom door.

"Dinner to eat?" I responded in shock, following a few steps behind. "You mean, *with me?*"

"Yeah you," he said as he stopped and turned toward me waiting for the answer he wanted to hear.

The moment felt almost surreal. He went from jackass to booty call to dinner date in Olympic speed. *How did that happen?* Must've been his naked, Hershey's ass; they get me every time. But all of a sudden—and at a most inconvenient time—I remembered my quest: discipline, determination, self-control. Oh hell, my willpower arrived like an hour past late.

"Helloooo . . . that was an invitation," he sang.

"I, uhhh . . . I don't know, I—"

"I won't take no for an answer," he interrupted.

"Uhhhh, well okay, dinner it is."

He twisted my arm.

"Great! Well, let me get my shoes on and let's go see some houses and sign some papers," he said, bounding down the steps like a child with one too many lollipops in his system. His mood was light—he joked, he laughed. Although I continued to wear my game face, my mood had turned somber when the gravity of the afternoon's events—and the realization at how miserably I'd failed my new life resolution—began to sink in. *How could I let this happen?* I thought.

Tomorrow I'm going to make a rule about not breaking my rules. I still had a small but improbable chance to redeem myself though. Okay, so I slipped—I could recover gracefully. I'd just select another rule to follow and get back on track the next day. The *little infraction* was a one-time thing anyway, right? It damn sure would happen again. So, I decided to follow rule number four. I wouldn't say anything about my past relationships at dinner.

Nothing.

Not one peep.

***

We dined at the National Harbor, which sat right off the Potomac River waterfront; the Gaylord Hotel was its architectural centerpiece. It featured an enormous eighteen-foot glass atrium looking on the water. Lush outdoor gardens were lined with cinnamon-colored brick walkways and water fountains, and an indoor garden housed a meandering stream.

Aside from hundreds of tourists and conference-goers, the setting was peaceful and calming. Though a stone's throw from the city, it felt like an oasis from the scurry and hurry. There were a few restaurants in the hotel, including my favorite sports bar, but I didn't want to eat dinner in the hotel—way too close to the hotel beds. Clearly, my defenses were weak. So, I suggested McCormick and Schmick's which was a block away.

I was starving by the time we were seated; thank God we had a short wait. But once we got settled, a wave of anxiety came over me. I wasn't sure if I could carry a conversation with a new man without mentioning my failed relationships. Why couldn't I have something easier to do, like end world hunger or solve a Rubik's cube in twenty seconds? My face wore concern like a bad haircut, I mean *ugly*. I hadn't been this worried since Marcus and I used a Mahatma Rice bag as a condom—long story. Anyway, we ordered our meals, the waiter poured the wine, and unfortunately, Dwayne was ready to chat.

"Are . . . are you okay? You look worried," Dwayne asked as he watched me fidget with my napkin.

Please don't ask me about my past. Please don't ask me about my past, I wished to myself.

"Oh no, I'm fine, I'm fine," I answered. My eyes scanned the table for alcohol. I grabbed the full wine glass to take a little sip, but before I could catch myself, the stem was pointed toward the ceiling, and the glass was empty. Dwayne's right eyebrow rose and wrinkles in his forehead emerged with a comforting grin. I tapped the linen napkin above my top lip to get rid of my Chardonnay moustache.

"So, uhh, what's a beautiful woman like you still doing single?" he asked.

God bless America, first damn question out of his mouth. How should I answer?

Ummm . . . because I'm a bum magnet?

"Hmmm . . . I don't know. Guess I just haven't found the right guy yet," I answered. *Good vanilla response,* I thought.

"Is that right? Have you ever been married?"

"Yes, I'm divorced. It's been about five years now."

"What happened?" he asked.

God, why dost ye test me? Let's see, I thought marriage meant we were supposed to stop screwing other people, and he didn't. Next!

"Ummm . . . well, I guess you could, uhhh, you could call it irreconcilable differences. Yeah, that's it, irreconcilable differences. End of story," I responded and exhaled.

Whew!

"So, what are you looking for in a man?" he asked.

Someone who doesn't make me want to cut his heart out with a machete. Will the questions never end???

"Someone nice, smart, good sense of humor. Someone who treats me well. You know, the standard stuff," I said as he nodded in acceptance. My major test was over, but I needed to turn the conversation around before disaster struck.

I continued, "So Mr. Fifty Questions, what are you looking for in a woman?"

"Good question," he paused and took a sip of wine. "Truthfully?"

"As close as you can get without going over," I responded.

"Well, if you must know, someone like you."

I laughed out loud. My first inclination was to cough "bullshit," but I resisted.

"That's pretty funny. You don't even know me," I said, sitting back in my chair and folding my arms in obvious disbelief.

"I know more about you than you think."

"Is that so? And how might that be? I haven't told you anything."

"I Googled you," he said.

"Oh really. You Googled me? And what interesting tidbits did you find out?" I asked, leaning forward and tilting my right ear toward him to ensure I didn't miss a lying word.

"Well, I confirmed that you're a real estate agent."

"As opposed to a deranged woman who breaks strange men into random, empty houses. Okay. I'm sure that's comforting. What else you got?"

"I know you graduated from the University of Maryland. Found an alumni roster with your name on it. So that tells me you're well-educated and shows you've got the stick-to-itiveness to finish what you start."

And your "full-of-shit-itiveness" is astounding.

"Hmmm, that's pretty good."

"I know you're beautiful, smart, sexy as hell, and you rock my world in bed."

"Good catch."

"I think you might be," he said, flashing a confident smile.

He's quick, gotta keep up with him.

"Is that all?"

"For now."

I wondered, *Does that mean there's going to be a later?*

"Well, I learned something about you too. So there!"

"And what's that?" he asked, looking at me as if he feared I'd knock him over the head with a skeleton from his closet.

"I know you're never on time for anything, you ask too many damn questions, and you like to invade people's privacy," I joked.

He appeared relieved and laughed as the waiter walked toward our table carrying our order. "Okay, okay. Well, it looks like our dinner has arrived. So, why don't we eat, and maybe I can finish the inquisition on our next date?"

Next date?

Six

On and Popping

Dwayne and I didn't speak a word during dinner, and the silence gave me a chance to collect my thoughts. As the most succulent, tender filet mignon ever to grace my mouth slipped down my throat like melted ice, I winced as I thought about my New Year's resolution. I'd retreated in the Battle of the Baggage and waved my big, white flag before the first cannon fired. My mind drifted back to New Year's Eve. I had a plan, I was certain of it. But, uhhh, what was my plan again?

***

New Year's Eve always seemed like a time to reflect, and some years I thought we had a God-given right to forget. I had a dream home, career, and my long-awaited 7-series Beemer (in my humble opinion, only the greatest thing manufactured on four wheels since the Ford Mustang), but no one to share my life with, whoopee!

Let's fucking celebrate!

Keeping it real, I mean, I had some unresolved emotional issues to deal with, but shit, who didn't? Should a little luggage preclude me from meeting a decent man? Show me one woman who didn't have some emotional baggage, and I'll bet she's a cartoon character.

I'm a self-aware kinda girl. To quantify my emotional baggage as a "shit-load" would've been a gross understatement. I was laden with it. Not just half-filled little carry-ons here and there, you understand. Uhn uh. I had the entire Diane Von Furstenburg Runway Collection, complete with expandable suitcase, rolling carry-on, boarding bag, garment bag, city bag, business bag, transit bag, lots of bags. Each piece packed to capacity with memories of mistakes and heart breaks. Over thirty-nine-and-a-half years, the weight had grown from pounds to tonnage.

There was a time when I tried to conceal my baggage from my new beaus, but it was like trying to hide a whale in a fish tank.

Pointless.

If we're supposed to learn from our past mistakes and apply the lessons, I'd be doomed to repeat mine over and over again unless I took drastic measures to empty my baggage—and with the quickness. My problem was akin to the scene in *The Godfather* when Clemenza said, "Leave the gun; take the cannoli." I had not yet learned to leave the bag and take the lesson.

I paused for a moment; the timing of the "Unpack Your Emotional Baggage" article felt a little uncanny. I wondered—*Is God trying to tell me something?* If I wanted to be in a healthy relationship, I'd have to learn to take the lesson and leave the bag.

I'd made it my New Year's resolution.

My new *life* resolution.

I peeled myself from the chaise to retrieve my journals from underneath my bed when I heard the woman's anthem boom from the radio as if on cue. "At first I was afraid, I was petrified, Kept thinking I could never live without you by my side. . . " *Woo!* I blasted "I Will Survive" and danced around my family room like I starred in a bad High School Musical video.

The time had come for me to take my emotional baggage to the mattresses, so to speak. I waged war, a war against myself. It required discipline, determination, self-control, prayer, and lots of chocolate, but I was well-armed—well, with chocolate anyway. I reached over and grabbed the bag of Reese's cups; I needed to build my strength for the difficult battles ahead.

***

As the waiter cleared my plate from the table, my mind refocused on the present, on Dwayne. Sex starved and vulnerable, I had no idea just how difficult my journey would be. Playing strong seemed much easier in the confines of my house, out of temptation's reach, than in the real world with Hershey-assed men like Dwayne walking around.

We left the restaurant and strolled to the car, both thinking much more than we said, I suppose. As I strapped on my seat belt and tuned the radio to the slow-jam station, I realized the depth of my insanity was baffling, even to me.

I chauffeured Dwayne back to his house but didn't want the night to end. *Drive slow*, I told myself as an eighty-year-old grandmother zipped past me at thirty miles-an-hour and flipped me the bird. An uncomfortable silence hovered between us as I suspected we both anticipated our imminent struggle to resist jumping each other's bones . . . *again*. But it'd been an exhausting day between the marathon sex, seven house tours, and two bottles of wine.

Neither of us made a peep while listening to the romance after dark Quiet Storm radio program in his driveway. "I Feel Good" by Stephanie Mills had just started to play. Truth be told, I wanted to drag him in the house, ram my tongue down his throat, and bull-ride him like a cowboy at a championship rodeo, but I thought better of it. To repeat my earlier performance would only reaffirm that I was the utter and complete slut he no doubt thought I was.

"Well, I guess you should be getting inside, and I should be getting home. I had a wonderful time with you today. Now that I have a better idea of what you're looking for, we'll have much better luck finding your house our next time out."

"Well, I enjoyed today too, Charisse. You make me laugh. I really like being with you. Honestly, I don't want the night to end. Why don't you come inside for a little while? I could start a fire, and we could sit and talk. *Just* talk."

I wanted to say, "Baby, it's too late, the fire is already started and if I walk in there we're gonna burn the house down." But instead I said . . .

"Look, Dwayne, I like you, but I can't come in. I mean, I want to come in, ummm, really want to come in but I can't. I . . . I really should be getting ho—"

Out of nowhere, Dwayne kissed me with the intensity of a convicted felon on a conjugal visit. He stroked his fingers through my shoulder length hair, caressed my face, and his tongue ebbed and flowed through my mouth like ocean waves. The tingling between my legs told me my ass wasn't going anywhere, and I was about to volunteer to be his ho for the night . . . *again*.

It was on like popcorn.

***

My eyes cracked open, blinded by the sun's light which poured through his plantation shutters like an interrogation lamp. My head was in Dwayne's arm pit and felt like a fifteen pound bowling ball. And if things couldn't get worse, the onset of a severe case of ho's remorse washed over me. My quest to reduce my emotional baggage had just taken its second major U-turn straight back to square one—although the trip was a lot shorter the *second* time. Dwayne was submerged in such a deep sleep, he didn't budge when I freed myself from his body.

I threw my clothes on, crept out of his house, drove home at warp speed, and took the day off to regroup. Nyla could handle my calls for the day.

After a long soak, I sat on my bed in a daze. The reality of my mistake set in, but I drew consolation from the realization I could turn a negative into a positive. I'd do what I should've done the night before instead of engaging in hot, steamy sex with tardy boy. I grabbed a journal from underneath my bed and checked the caller ID on the house line. As only family, close friends, and bill collectors called me at home, there was a sixty-six percent chance someone rang who I might want to talk to.

Turned out I was right; Nisey had called.

We hadn't spoken since before the holidays. She and one of her sugar daddies cruised to Bermuda. Nisey was the only person I could confide in about Dwayne. She'd keep it real without kicking me while I was down. "Welcome back. Did you enjoy your trip?" I asked.

"Girrrrrl, we had a ball. I for damn sure didn't want to bring my ass back here. Never seen such crystal clear water in my life, beautiful! If we hadn't got caught doin' the nasty in the ship's hot tub, the cruise would've been perfect."

"Oh my goodness, they didn't report you or anything?"

"Naaah, but trust me, nothing is more tragic than being on the brink of an orgasm and having some ninety-year old shuffle board champion jack it up. I started to ask for a refund. Anyway, how'd you spend your holiday? Did you do anything, or *anyone*, hopefully not Marcus?" she asked as if she suspected a "yes" answer.

"Well, how about you be the judge. I had a chocolate fest on my chaise for the better part of seven days and watched suicide-inducing romantic comedies until contemplating, albeit briefly, slitting my wrists. In a moment of near sanity, I read an article in Zaina's magazine, certainly meant for lucid people, and resolved to unpack my emotional baggage this year. I'm going to start analyzing my failed relationships. And you thought screwing in a hot tub was a good time. Ha!" I said, attempting to focus on what I was doing right before I confessed what I'd done wrong.

"Okay, Rissey, first of all, Freud couldn't analyze your failed relationships, so why bother? Secondly, chocolate, undoubtedly followed by a Grey Goose and Doritos chaser? You're definitely upset about something. What's up?"

I sighed. She knew me so well.

"I don't know. I'm teetering at a crossroads, with eternal happiness on one side and dating damnation on the other. I'm afraid if I don't fix what's broken, I'll be doomed to love purgatory forever," I said, sensing myself sink to a new level of pathetic.

"Well, I ain't gonna lie, Rissey, you've definitely got some baggage, but shit, who wouldn't after everything you've been through? You endured something that would break most women, yet your experiences only made you stronger. The problem is you're always so busy looking *behind* you, sometimes I get scared you're missing the blessings ahead."

I sighed. "You're right, but I've vowed this is my last year to look behind. I'm going to work out my issues and then I'm going to live, live, live," I said with all sincerity. I had a Herculean task ahead of me, especially since I'd just added Dwayne to the confusing mix. But I was determined to execute my plan despite my setbacks.

She laughed. "Newsflash, that's all well and good in theory, but honey, life isn't going to stand still and wait for you to catch up."

"Nisey, believe me, that is painfully clear to me, today more so than any other day. You . . . you didn't ask me about my life *post*-holiday," I said, preparing to drop the bomb I'd conveniently omitted in the earlier part of our conversation.

"Oh, reeeally, what happened? Did you meet somebody?" she asked with excited anticipation.

"Yeah, I did. His name is Dwayne; he's a client," I answered, pausing for her gasp. "I know what you're going to say, so don't."

"Awwww, shame, shame, shame. You of all people ought to know better. Mixing business with pleasure is dangerous," she said, no doubt as a subtle reminder of my ex-husband, Jason, and Marcus, both of whom are real estate agents. As if I needed her to jog *those* memories. You never forget your worse nightmares.

"I know, I know. Please don't remind me. He's so fine though. One minute I was cursing him out—in my head—for being late for our appointment and the next I was dislodging my head from his arm pit," I whined.

"So you fucked him?"

"Ummmm . . ."

"Did you?"

"Weeeeell, fuck is such an *ugly* word. Let's say we did some—genital gymnastics."

"Um hmm, whatever," she said. "That's okay girl. Honestly, you needed some with your uptight ass. Maybe now you'll settle down and stop thinking so damn much. Anyway, don't hold back now, tell me more about him."

"Well, he seems nice, you know. He's handsome, separated, has two sons, owns a home improvement business. He's intelligent, asks a lot of questions, and his kisses are like, mmmmm, like magic," I said, my mind flashing back to *The Excorist* kiss.

"Ummmmhm, I bet they are like magic, make your panties DISAPPEAR. Poof!"

"Ha, ha, very funny."

Very true

"You haven't Googled him yet?"

"No, not yet. I've been meaning to but haven't gotten around to it. Everything happened so fast."

"Ummhmm, okay. So, let's get down to the nit-tay grit-tay. How was the sex?"

"Girrrl, he put it on me, flipped my ass around like a pancake. I haven't sweated so much since I fell asleep in the sauna at The Ritz-Carlton. I woke up and pretty much ran out the door though, haven't spoken to him since. I felt like a total slut, don't think I'll see him again."

"You don't think you'll see *him* again, or you don't think *he'll see you*?" she asked.

"Six of one, half a dozen of the other. Take your pick."

"No, no, they're not the same. I think you ran because you're afraid he wants the booty and not the cutie," she said, easing into a motherly tone.

"But you've got to stop running. You don't know, he may not be a dog. He may well be a decent guy who couldn't contain his attraction to you. You, on the other hand? Well, you were a slut but who's to say that's a *bad* thing?"

Ever the voice of optimism.

"Okay, *this* from the hot tub Madam. C'mon Nisey, this thing has one night stand written all over it," I said as I suddenly realized a small part of me hoped our hook-up could turn into something more, despite my desperate need to break the cycle of bad relationships I'd fallen into. *I'm hopeless,* I thought, feeling torn between what my heart and body wanted and my mind and soul needed.

"Maybe, maybe not. For now . . . let's choose to keep hope alive."

I propped a pillow behind my back and began to read. My cell phone had started to ring off the hook, but I didn't want to talk to anyone else, not right then. I wanted to mourn my faux pas and start the work necessary to avoid future mistakes. I opened the journal.

It was October, 1988. And his name was Lamar. . .

Seven

Player for Life

O *ctober 2, 1988*
We finally crossed over. Hallelujah! I'm a Sigma! I've determined
there is a hell on earth. It's called pledging. I'm over it though,
back to my daily grind. I went for lunch today and caught this guy check-
ing me out. He's like the finest guy on campus, and I mean Billy Dee
Williams in Lady Sings the Blues fine. He's an Omega too. I ain't gonna lie,
I'm flattered. I mean, who wouldn't be? Nobody Lamar fine has ever been
interested in me. He's got the most beautiful eyes I've ever seen. But he's
married AND a cheating dog, a double no-no. The ONLY thing there will
ever be between us is air.

***

Lamar, without question, is one of the finest brothers I ever met—
or any woman ever met for that matter. He put the "OO" in smooth. At six
foot one, with fair, sun-kissed skin, juicy red lips, two of the most piercing
hazel eyes ever seen, and a smile that melted steel, he wasn't just fine, he
was *foine*.

I lost my natural mind over that man, not because he looked so
incredible—although he did. I lost it because he went through such
painstaking lengths to snag me—and not just for a few days or months—for
over a year.

Trust and believe—Lamar was not the snagging type. Oh no,
women snagged him, he did not snag women. He neither had the time,

inclination, nor the need. Women flocked to him like pigeons to Capitol Hill. So, why I had been an object of Lamar's desire remained a mystery to me. I guess it's true, some men will always chase what they think they can't have.

He and I went to the University of Maryland for undergrad; we both started college in our twenties. I majored in Economics, while I worked in real estate part time; he studied pre-law. Our paths might never have crossed if we hadn't pledged; he joined Omega and I, Sigma. We didn't interact much during our once-a-week Council meetings.

The Council—as I liked to call it—was an umbrella organization for black Greek-lettered societies, kind of like "The Commission" for the Five Families in the Italian mafia. We were all "made" when we pledged, but we had eight groups instead of five, and we represented philanthropic organizations instead of crime syndicates. Lamar and I were both chapter presidents—heads of our families.

Our first encounter outside The Council seemed unremarkable, a brief passing in the student union; I caught a glimpse of his hazel eyes, and his hazel eyes caught a glimpse of my ass.

Typical.

A bit later, I waited for my Big Mac at the McDonald's counter when he breezed by a second time. He circled me like a vulture. Stared at me like he'd been fasting for a week and I'd transformed into a four-course, porterhouse, T-bone steak dinner. He didn't swoop in because my chief cock-blocker sauntered in.

"Hey, Rissey, whatcha up to girlfriend?" Nisey asked.

"I'm waiting on my food, starving girl. Don't look right now, but do you see the guy next to those tables, in the black shirt, light-skinned with the hazel eyes? I'm not sure, but I think he keeps staring at me."

Of course, she looked dead at him.

Oh God, I'm so embarrassed.

"Well, if he sees you again, he damn sure won't be able to recognize you by your face. You might have to bend over before you say hello, good gracious!" she quipped. "Anyway, you better steer clear of that one, that's Lamar Jackson. From what I heard, his *wife*, you know, his *ball-and-chain, entitled-to-half wife*? She goes to school here too."

She always "heard" something, knew everybody—and stayed in everybody's business.

"Is that right? Uhm. He must be a serious player then because he's been on me since I walked in."

"Well, as long as you keep him from getting *in* you, you're doing better than half the sororities on campus."

She's so crass.

Clearly, I intrigued Lamar, but he was very married, so I kept my distance. Over the next year, I delighted in the frequent gossip of his most recent conquests, his divorce from his smartened wife, and his frequent romps with my sorority sisters—with everybody's sorority sisters. There was hardly an Alpha, Delta, Zeta or Sigma within a ten-mile radius who, at a minimum, couldn't locate the birthmark on his—. Well, no need to go there. Suffice it to say, they knew him well.

***

November 15, 1989
I broke up with Jay today. I will never ever date an athlete again in my life, especially not an unfaithful, stupid one. Nisey said the best way to get over your ex-boyfriend is to get under a new one. I don't know about that, but I'm a little lonely. And I miss dating, you know, kissing and having someone's arms around me. Oh well. That reminds me, I need to go pick up some batteries from CVS tomorrow.

***

Lamar sagas always made for entertaining dramedy, unless, of course, you were the lead actress. I vowed never to star in his show; he would never get in my head or my bed. Every time he asked me out, I shot him down like a clay pigeon. He was the king of stray dogs, and I was determined to be animal control . . . at least until we ended up in the same class after my break-up with Jay, a sorry ass ex-basketball player who needed instructions to button his shirt.

See, whether you majored in pre-law or Latin, *everyone* had a gym requirement. And as fate would have it . . .

"What are you doing here?!" I asked, eyeing Lamar as he approached the gymnasium door.

"Hey you! Well, I need this class to graduate like you do," he said. He dropped his book bag on the floor and leaned back on the wall next to me. "So, how are you? What's up with you and Jay? Y'all still kickin' it?"

I sighed, "No, we broke up a few weeks ago."

41

He craned his head toward me and revealed his pearly whites, a shabby expression of sympathy to say the least. "Sorry to hear that. You seeing anyone new or are you gonna chill for a minute?"

"No, I was trying to let the body get cold first. I think I need to chill for a while, you know . . . Anyway . . ." I said, shifting my legs nervously.

"I have to be honest with you. I was surprised to hear you even dated him, Jay, the sorry baller in the seventh year of his four-year architecture program. I thought you had higher standards than that. After all, you wouldn't even let *me* take you out," he said with a hint of disdain.

That's below the belt.

"Well, I heard you were busy with your double major, Pre-law and Pimpin'," I said, rolling my head with indignation. "What's your next class, Gigolo 101?"

"No, I tested out of it," he laughed. "You're crazy, for real. But look, Charisse, you've been turning me down for over a year. What's it going to take to get you to go out with me, *just once*?"

"Listen, when I met you, you were still married—"

"Well, now I'm divorced," he interrupted.

"And you've been dating Judy, she's my sorority sister, remember? I can't go out like that."

"First of all, I haven't been *dating* her. We hung out a couple of times, that's all. Second of all, what's the difference to you? You don't even know her like that. This isn't about me and her; it's about *me* and *you*."

"Yes, but—"

"But nothing. Do you think I have to beg a woman for a date? Hell no. I've been watchin' you, though. I see the kind of woman you are, and I want to know you better. You can't listen to the rumors and gossip. These people don't know me. You know, let me take you out, show you how a real man can treat you."

Hmmm, a real date, I pondered. After my disappointing experience with Jay, I longed for a little spoiling.

"Well, what's a real date to you?" I asked.

"Why don't you let me worry about that? I only need you to say yes."

I smiled half-heartedly and turned my attention to our tennis teacher who demonstrated his sad backhand.

Who taught this man how to play tennis?

I thought about what Lamar said and what I wanted. I had no misgivings about him or his intentions, but I was always intrigued by the man who seemed unattainable, emotionally unreachable. Lamar posed a challenge. He was insincere, a player, impenetrable. Didn't matter. Somewhere in the back of my crazy ass mind, I wondered if I could be "the one" who would change him, the one so "special" that I could make him fall in love with me.

Oh, I was "special" alright.

Short bus "*special.*"

After class, I handed Lamar a card with my phone number scribbled on it. "What's this?" he asked.

"Let's say your persistence finally paid off."

"For real?" he asked as pool-deep dimples emerged in his cheeks. "Damn, it's about time. But you'll see, Charisse, you won't regret it."

Talk about insanity. I had accepted a date with arguably one of the world's biggest players. *I must be nuts.* I later spotted Lamar at a Terp's basketball game, and he took the opportunity to confirm our date.

"So, we're meeting Friday at Union Station, right? Seven o'clock?" he asked.

"Yup, I'll be there. Make sure you bring your A-game."

"Is there any other kind?"

Eight

Dream Date

F riday approached and I wondered what Lamar had in store for me. I didn't expect everything to be all fire and music, but he aroused my curiosity. What kind of date would he plan given I'd turned him down for over a year.

Then panic struck.

***

December 1, 1989

I agreed to go out with Lamar. I have officially taken the term dumb bitch to a whole new low. What if he just wants to get me in bed? Or worse, what if this is all just a practical joke at my expense? He probably won't even show up, just wants to humiliate me for all those times I rejected him. Well, he's got another thing coming . . .'cuz I ain't goin'!

***

As I parked my car at Union Station, my stomach churned like I'd reached a peak on a rollercoaster, anticipating a two-hundred foot, ninety degree drop. I thought my lip quivered, so I glanced in the mirror to check it—nope, just my imagination. I fixed my lipstick and proceeded to the bar in the main atrium.

Will he even show up? I wondered. I rounded the corner from the Amtrak ticket booth and spotted him gulping from a Heineken bottle. He didn't appear to spot me approaching so I crept up behind him. I bent forward to whisper in his ear, and he said, "So you made it?"

"When did you see me?"

"I didn't see you, I smelled your cologne."

"Yeah, whatever," I said, laughing at an internal joke involving dogs and their senses of smell.

"You're wearing Chanel, right?"

I nodded. *How'd he know?*

"Check it, baby, I even know your scent. Pull up a seat and stay a while."

I dragged my stool closer to his and sat down. "Hmmmm. So, what else do you think you know?"

"Well, I know when the sun shines on your face a certain way, the light reflects the deep brown in your eyes. And I know when your hand brushes mine during class I get butterflies in my stomach."

I blushed, feeling thankful my cocoa brown skin wouldn't betray me.

Smooth, right?

I would expect no less from a player like Lamar.

After one Long Island Iced Tea, my nervousness disappeared into oblivion, and I was ready for the rest of the evening to begin. We talked for another hour before he drove me to a twenty five-and-over club in Northwest. It was a cozy, old-school spot on the bottom level of an office building.

We passed the security checkpoint, and he checked my jacket. I started taking in the ambiance when I noticed two Zeta's from The Council. I hoped beyond hope they wouldn't notice Lamar and I arrived together because I really didn't want any witnesses to my shame spiral. But as luck would have it, he stepped next to me just as they waved hello.

Let the gossip begin.

"Well, well, well, what are you two doing here . . . together?" one Zeta said, cocking her head to the side and pursing her lips.

"We're here to dance," he said. I kept my trap shut and nodded in agreement.

"Right, right," she responded. "You must really like this club, Lamar. Didn't I see you here last week?"

"Me? Here? I don't think so," he paused and grabbed my hand. "Well, anyway, I'm sure you two came over here to gossip. So, we'll be on our way and let y'all get to it. Charisse, shall we?"

He led me on the dance floor, and we danced for what seemed like hours on end. The DJ played all the old school hits, and we did all the old school dances. When "I Want Her" by Keith Sweat started, we both broke out in the Cabbage Patch. We followed that up with a playful rendition of The Bump when "Good Times" by LeChic played. I did the Running Man when I heard Chubb Rock's "Treat Em Right." That nearly killed me. Not to be outdone, Lamar followed that up with The Prep. I stole the show and claimed my crown when I did The Robot to "Dance to the Drummer's Beat."

By the time Cheryl Lynn's "Encore" played, we'd both run out of gas. We'd reduced our classic moves to a weak two step. Finally, the DJ announced he was going to slow it down a little bit. I started to walk off the floor when Lamar grabbed my hand and pulled me against his body. We stood face to face when the sweet melody enveloped my ear, *Ooooooooh Baybah!* "Adore" by Prince. *That's my jay-yum!* He held me so close everyone and everything around us faded into darkness. I closed my eyes as he leaned in and kissed me on each cheek, my forehead, the tip of my nose, and, at last, my lips. We swayed and caressed and never lost a beat.

"I'm having so much fun with you," he whispered in my ear.

"Me too."

"Baby, this is only the beginning."

After we left the club, he took me to an African spot in Adams Morgan, D.C.'s melting pot. It was a quaint, two-level Nigerian restaurant with a full bar, dance floor, and a live reggae band. We walked in and Lamar waved down a midnight black waiter who started toward us. The waiter shot Lamar a toothy smile as he reached out to shake his hand.

"Well, well, well. Back again, Mr. Jackson." He turned toward me, "He's one of our best customers."

I just smiled.

"Francis, how are you? Did you save a table for me?" Lamar asked, reaching into his pocket for his wallet.

"Yes, sir, it's upstairs. I left a reserved sign on it so it would be free when you arrived," the waiter responded. "The usual?"

The usual?

"Yeah. Thanks, man. Here you go," Lamar said. He greased Francis's palm with a twenty-dollar bill.

"I hope you and your beautiful date enjoy your visit tonight," Francis said, walking toward the kitchen.

Lamar grabbed my hand and led me to the dance floor, but my Via Spigas were kicking my ass. After watching me wince in pain once or twice, he escorted me upstairs to a candlelit table in the corner, where two over-filled plates of red stew chicken, Jollof rice, and plantains awaited our appetites. Two wooden chairs sat on either side of the table. He pulled out a chair for me and took a seat in the one opposite mine.

"Have you ever had African food before?" he asked. "I ordered a simple dish. With black folk, you can almost never go wrong with chicken and rice."

"Yes, I've had African food before, but you made a good selection," I said. "So, you come here often, huh? *The usual?* I'd hate to think I was a foregone conclusion."

He chuckled, "You're crazy, I swear. It's not even like that. After I joined the military, I served in the U.S. Embassy in Nigeria, so I came to appreciate the food."

"You served in the *military*?" I asked, swallowing a fork full of rice. All that grooving had me famished.

"Yeah, I'm a Marine. You know, once a Marine, always a Marine."

My rice stopped mid-throat, and I started to cough. "Wait a minute. You were a Marine? You, Lamar, were a Marine? A 'The Few, the Proud' Marine?"

His words jolted me. Lamar and my father were kindred spirits—Marines with women in every port. I wondered if I, like my mother before me, pinned my romantic hopes on a non-existent Santa Claus.

"Yeah, I, Lamar, was a Marine. See, I told you there was a lot you didn't know about me. Only a few hours into our date and you're already learning something new."

"Wow, you seem so, uh, how shall I put this . . . *free-spirited*? You hardly seem like the military type," I said. "Besides, I thought the Marines were looking for a few *good* men?"

I cracked myself up.

"Ha, ha. Very funny," he paused. "You're right though, I'm not. That's why I got out after four years."

"You're not a good man? Or you're not the military type?"

"Geez, do you ever let up? Not the military type, silly. I have too many bills, too many obligations. I didn't make enough money, so I decided to get my law degree."

"I guess I can understand that. I'm kidding with you, by the way. But all joking aside, before you catch me off guard—do you have anymore surprises I should know about?"

"Well, you might be surprised to know that ever since we sat down, I've felt like I'm sitting too far away from you. Would I be asking too much if I requested the seat beside you?"

I smiled. I hated it when he made me blush.

"No, come on," I answered, giving my eyelashes a seductive bat.

He sat down and scooted his chair so close to mine he may as well have sat on my lap. He slipped two fingers under my chin, turned my head toward his, and gave me a long, sensuous kiss. If I watched us from afar, I'd have told us to get a room.

"Wow," I whispered when we came up for air. "You are full of surprises."

"There's a lot more where that came from," he whispered back.

During the ride back to my car, I dozed off a little bit. It was nearly three in the morning, and my eyelids had grown heavy under the Sandman's weight. I heard the car stop and opened my eyes. I scanned the area for something, anything familiar. Nothing resembled Union Station . . . or my car.

"Uhhhh, Lamar . . . where are we?"

Nine

Player Gets Played

I stared at the front of a beautiful, brick-front townhouse as Lamar turned off the engine and opened his door. "We're at my place."

"At *your* place? May I ask why?" I bluntly queried, eyes wide open, ready to twist my neck and go ghetto sista on him. I hated to tell him, but dessert didn't come with *that* dinner.

"I know what you're thinking, Charisse, but don't. I just wanted you to know where I live, so you can stop by unannounced and try to catch me with another woman," he said with a chuckle. He didn't fool me. Lamar invited me to try and catch him in the act in an effort to thwart future spying operations. Poor, naïve, gullible little man. If I suspected him of cheating or other unauthorized extra-curricular activities, game on—let the spying commence. Superman himself couldn't stop that runaway train. So, he'd uttered those words for naught.

"Just come in for a few minutes," he continued. "I'll get you to your car. We're not far from Union Station. I can have you back in twenty minutes."

"Well, uhhh, okay," I hesitated. "Just for a few minutes, I guess."

Surprise, surprise, didn't look like a typical bachelor pad at all. It had an eclectic, contemporary feel—mahogany-wood flooring, black leather sectional, granite countertops in the kitchen and powder room, and a stone hearth surrounding the fireplace; and a smattering of Holston jazz prints adorned the walls. An obligatory framed print of Martin Luther King, Jr.

and Malcolm X shaking hands on Capitol Hill hung in a room just off the kitchen that appeared to be the office; his house looked like a place *I* might live.

"Wow, this is really nice, Lamar. Really nice," I said, scanning the room for evidence of the woman who decorated. "It's yours?"

"Is it mine? Of course it's mine. I used my VA benefits to get the place a few years ago. You really like it?"

"Yeah, who wouldn't?"

Our rushed house tour ended with a lengthier stop in his bedroom. Scented candles and potpourri-filled dishes covered the dressers and nightstand; the scent of vanilla-apple permeated the room into the hallway. A king-sized sleigh bed, the room's centerpiece, stood so far off the ground a step stool came attached to the frame. It oozed faux romance and one-night stand. He'd lured me to his love den, and I stood like a rabbit in a fox hole, vulnerable to his sly charm.

Lamar skulked up to my back and brushed his hand against my ass. The heat of his breath on my neck sent shivers to the tips of my toenails. His hands gently grasped my waist and turned me until his eyes locked on mine. The perceptible heat between us made my ass sizzle. I thought, *This is it.* His plot to screw me like a power drill was culminating in one surreal moment—and I didn't resist. He leaned in to kiss me, and said . . .

"Well, that's it, baby. We should get going."

Get going? I didn't see that one coming, but I played it cool. "Okay, sure, let's go."

I followed him back to the car and shook my head in confusion. I pulled my door closed and realized he was making a point. He'd made it clear he wasn't pressed to sleep with me. He had so many women, a substitution could be in his bed before we got out of the parking lot. I got the message *loud and clear.* I made it home, crawled into bed, and slept like I'd just finished my bi-annual workout at the gym. A knock at the door awakened me late the next morning. Lamar sent flowers, a dozen crimson Calla Lilies in a tall Mikasa vase. The card read, *Will you be my girl?* Beneath he drew three check boxes—*Yes, No, or Maybe So.*

***

March 20, 1990
There's only one bad thing about the love high. Eventually, you crash back to reality. Lamar hasn't called in days. I don't know about him but in my

world when people date they call each other . . . on the regular. Not bi-monthly . . . or quarterly. He's a fool if he thinks I'm gonna sit around here while he plays pimp daddy. I'll find someone else. In the meantime, I'll get my one and only faithful boyfriend off the closet shelf and feed him din-ner—two Duracells.

***

Lamar schooled me on one of the most important Manhood 101 lessons every woman should learn as early as possible. A man could be one of the biggest whore-mongering, philandering, slut, "ho-men" since the discovery of fire. He could get caught stark-naked, mid-stroke (no condom) with a 36-double D tit lodged so far down his throat he could digest it. But, if he even *suspects* his woman contemplated mounting another man, he will become engrossed in a psychotic, jealous rage not even Stephen Spielberg could orchestrate. That's why I believe women have become more adept at cheating than men over the years; we know the consequences.

They ain't pretty.

Lamar and I tried our hand at "dating" for a few months before I realized I'd been snookered into a relationship for one. He invited me to one more fairytale rendezvous at Morton's Steakhouse and our favorite groove shack before we devolved to VHS movies, lukewarm Guinness, and microwave Orville Redenbacher. He only initiated visits to my apartment when he wanted sex, but he played fair—he came over when I wanted sex too.

I endured about two months of unrepentant neglect before I met another guy—Roger. Nisey dragged me to the club during my extended funk and he rescued me from my emerging depression. Roger, who was built like a brick shit house and dumb as a stump, played semi-pro football. His biggest aspiration in life was to get selected for the Redskins' practice squad. Didn't matter to me though, I only needed a boy toy to occupy the vacancy left by my absentee, so-called boyfriend until common sense kicked in and I punted Lamar's ass to the curb. So, with mild trepidation, I invited him over to watch movies one night.

Roger came by my place the following Saturday, and no sooner than he assumed the position in front of the television with the remote control in hand did Lamar call—like he sensed a disturbance in The Force. When I picked up the phone, I was surprised to hear his voice, almost didn't recognize it.

53

"Hey Charisse, what are you doing? I thought we might go out later," he asked.

"Nothing, watching a movie," I responded, hoping he wouldn't ask if I had company.

"Do you have company?"

Damn!

"Yes," I answered before I realized I meant to lie.

Did I just say yes? A silence fell on the other end of the line. He was shocked—me too. I braced myself, expecting a massive fireworks show, but he only managed one measly firecracker.

"Alright, see ya," he barked and then slammed the phone in my ear.

Is that it?

What did I expect? He didn't care about me; I was just a booty call. As I started back to rejoin Roger, the phone rang again. I picked it up.

"What are you doing!" he said with a tone of genuine concern in his voice.

He had the *audacity* to sound astonished that I invited another man to the same house that he'd abandoned for two months. But nothing, and I mean nothing, would prophesy my astonishment at the next revelation. I shudder to think of it . . .

I felt *guilty*.

I'd spent more time on the mall escalator than he'd spent at my house, yet *I* felt bad. Goddamn Catholic guilt. His sparse phone calls and infrequent "hit and runs" led me to believe I was a booty call, maybe someone he liked a little bit, but our relationship didn't extend beyond the confines of my bedroom—or the hours of eleven p.m. and seven a.m. So, his reaction blew my mind. He asked me to excuse myself and walk to my bedroom, no doubt so he could convince me of the err of my cheating ways.

"So, why the fuck is he there?" Lamar asked as if he didn't know.

"Look, you have some nerve questioning me. Where the hell have *you* been?! You didn't treat me like a girlfriend; you treated me like a piece of ass. So, what did you expect? Did you think I was going to sit here with my nose pressed against the window hoping you would grace me with your presence? You need to start selling whatever you're smoking. That's some good shit," I said, peeking out of the bedroom door to ensure Roger couldn't hear me. Roger gave me a reassuring wave and returned his attention to the television. I sat on the bed.

"I expected you to be more patient and understanding," he said, still under the influence of some good smack.

"No, you expected me to be stupid and gullible, but you got the wrong girl. Maybe you should check behind door number three."

"Well, I want to be with you. Don't you want to be with me?"

"Yes, I did but—"

"Well, then what is *he* doing in your house?" he interrupted.

"He's here because I'm sick of sitting home alone while you get your jack rabbit on, jumping from hole to hole."

"Well, I have called you, like, last week."

"Whoop-de-freakin'-do. What about the other two months? Hello? Hello?"

The phone clicked, and a dial tone buzzed in my ear. *Did that Negro just hang up on me?* I turned off the ringer, turned down the volume on the answering machine, and proceeded back to the living room. I'd refused to allow him to disturb my date with Al Pacino—or Roger. Unbeknownst to me, he left a message I wouldn't hear until way too late.

That's fucked up! I can't believe you didn't pick up the phone. That's alright; I'm on my way to your place, so you can just bring your ass outside so we can talk.

Ten

The Perfect Man

R oger and I sat on the couch watching *The Godfather*. Just after Marlon Brando said, "I swear, on the souls of my grandchildren, that I will not be the one to break the peace we have made here today," Lamar banged on the door. Bam! Bam! Bam!

The peace had been broken.

"Lawwwwd . . ." I said as I cracked the door open and looked directly into a squinted hazel eye.

"Hi, Lamar."

"You need to step outside for a minute."

"Well, I—" I started.

"Let me rephrase that. How 'bout you step your ass out here right now or I'm gonna wreck everybody's night?"

"Alrighty then," I answered. Hey, I could take a hint.

I hadn't seen this side of Lamar before. No matter how idiotic he behaved at that moment, Lamar was too cool to completely lose it. To display the kind of jealousy that required law enforcement assistance was beneath him and would reveal a vulnerability Lamar's pride wouldn't tolerate. I turned to Roger, who was so engrossed in *The Godfather* he didn't realize the balance of his life verged on mortal danger, and announced I was stepping outside for a second.

As I closed the door behind me, Lamar wrapped his hands around my waist, pressed my body close to his, and leaned in to kiss me. I shoved his arms down and stepped back to a more easy distance.

"So why are you doing this?" he asked.

"Doing what? We're watching *The Godfather*," I said, a bit too glib for his tastes. He glared at me in silence, a bit too long for mine.

"You know what I mean. You're a trip."

"How am I the trip? You're the trip. Before today, you wouldn't come here if lightning set me on fire and only your spit could put it out. *You're* only here because *he's* here. So, why are you acting all incensed?"

"Look, Charisse, you know me. You know, I don't normally do this shit. I'm here because I want to be with you. I always kept two women. So, when some shit like this happened, I wouldn't care. But I care, okay? I care. I'll give you everything you want. Just send him home right now. I want Charisse."

Why is he referring to me in the third person?

I stared at the ground as if the right answer would appear carved in the concrete. *Damn he's fine*, I thought as my eyes roamed from his feet to the hazel twins. But I couldn't bring myself to trust his sincerity. I didn't know it at that moment, but what felt like misplaced doubt, would soon be revealed as first-rate instinct.

"You think the reason I'm doing this is because of your, uh, friend, right?" he asked.

"As a matter of fact, I do. Look what it took to get you out here."

"I decided last week to commit to you but—"

"Is that right?" I interrupted, folding my arms to deflect the bullshit about to be lobbed in my direction.

"Yeah, *that's right*, if you'll let me talk. This is the reason I planned to take you out tonight. That's why I got pissed when you said you had company. So, if you want to be with me, tell me now or else I'm leaving."

I shook my head in disbelief. His efforts to convince me of his sincerity failed, and my skepticism held strong and steady. What did he expect me to do, kick Roger out? In my heart, I wanted to, but I thought better of it. If Lamar was sincere, indeed, he'd soften in a day or two. If not, he'd leave me alone and my budding relationship with the dumb jock would prove quite timely. So, I turned to walk back in the house.

"So, that's it? You're just going to let me walk away," he asked.

"Yes, Lamar. Take care."

I closed the door and peered at him through the window as he walked away, his chin resting against his chest. Knowing the enormity of Lamar's ego, I didn't ever expect to hear from him again. I felt melancholy and wanted to affirm our relationship and give way to my feelings, but my change of heart came too late. Lamar had moved on.

Sleepless and clinging to my somber mood, I sat in my office the next day and replayed the episode over and over again in my mind, thinking about everything he said. I wanted to call, even picked up the phone and dialed all except the last number, but I thought he'd be cold and reject me, and my ego couldn't handle it. So, I hesitated before returning the phone to the receiver and turned back to my computer.

Then my phone rang.

No Lamar. My client, Mr. Johnson called to schedule a home inspection and wondered when I'd be available. I told him anytime the following Tuesday would be fine and hung up the phone disappointed. *He's never going to call.* Two seconds later, the phone rang again. *Must be Mr. Johnson again.*

"Mr. Johnson, sir, how can I help you?" I asked.

"You never answered me, Charisse. And the offer still stands," Lamar said.

It's him. I was astonished, not only that he called, but he didn't sound pissed. I didn't know whether to be happy or afraid, so I didn't say anything.

"You and I need to talk . . . this evening. Are you available or is your little friend coming back for more mafia flicks?" he said.

"You want to talk," I paused, "*to me?*"

"Yes, I do. I mean, I'm not gonna lie, you pissed me off. But I realized part of it might be my fault. I didn't make it clear where you stand with me. So, I'd like to clarify things tonight. Can I see you this evening?"

"I'll be home," I said with a slight air of self-righteousness.

"Okay, I'll be over as soon as I get off work," he said, chuckling a bit.

"Something funny?"

"When you said that, you know, 'I'll be home,' you sounded like me. It's a little scary."

He stopped by my apartment as promised and on time, dropped his brief case by the door, swaggered in like he owned the place, grabbed my hand and led me to the sofa. He stuck to the same lines he delivered during Roger's visit, claimed I hurt him, said he didn't realize how much he liked me until his fateful visit.

"I want to be with you, and I'm prepared to give you everything you want and need. The question is do you want Lamar?"

I hate when he refers to himself in the third person.

"What's your idea of a commitment, if I understand that's what you're asking for?"

"It's damn near like being married, without the ring and shitty sex. So, is that what you want? Do you want to be with me?"

I sighed and paused for a moment. *This is a great time to get out while I'm ahead.* So, I did what any bum magnet in my position would do—folded like a bad poker hand.

"Yeah," I answered.

"So, am I your man now?"

"Yes.

"I want to hear you tell me."

"You're my man," I said.

We smiled and hugged. Between kisses, he whispered, "I missed you," and we lingered in our embrace.

Each day, I believed in him a little more, though never completely. I suspected he might be setting me up for something—disappointment, embarrassment—something. I didn't know what. He offered his "commitment" with no reluctance—too neat, too perfect for a player like Lamar. It took me exactly two weeks and thirteen hours to realize that, despite my new title, I remained alone in my so-called relationship. I'd grown tired of the lonely nights and non-existent phone calls, but by then I'd become determined to get to the bottom of it.

This is where I learned another hard lesson of Manhood 101: A man may not want you, but he will say absolutely anything, he will sell his soul to the devil at a fifty percent discount, to keep another man out of your pants.

Eleven

Double-Oh Seven

Let's get something straight, I never cared much for Ronald Reagan, although I'm apolitical, but one thing he said should serve as the motto for all womankind—"Trust, but verify." Some women regarded spying on a significant other as a major violation of trust and a shameful act of insecurity that had no place in a healthy relationship.

I'd never been of that disposition.

No, to me, spying on a boyfriend was not only justified, it was a requirement. Hey, I keep it real. To ask me not to spy on an scheming boyfriend would be like asking a lion not to hunt, a dog not to bark, or babies not to throw up. "Verification" was as instinctive to me (and all womankind), as giving birth. It's what we did. Some were more adept at spying than others.

I was a spy's spy, no formal training, just raw instinct.

Chief consultant and co-conspirator in my friends' operations, I often considered developing a fee schedule to charge for my services.

Let's see, I picked pockets, while they weren't being worn of course; conducted many a code-breaking operation to get passwords for e-mail and voice mails accounts; spearheaded a few dumpster dives through trash for those carelessly discarded love notes and telephone numbers—it was a dirty business but somebody had to do it; instructed my friends to place voice-activated digital recorders near the "man chair" to capture any careless whispers that might be spoken while they were out of earshot—not admissible in the court of law but highly effective in the court of girlfriend; executed some stealth drive-bys past more than a few houses to identify unauthorized guests—in special cases, I had a friend in the police department who'd run the tags for a small fee; and I could shadow anyone in my Beemer within ten feet, all but completely undetected.

I didn't spy on all of my boyfriends, though; most of those jackasses weren't even worth the time and energy. No, I only spied on the really, really fine and sneaky ones, and Lamar's turn was up.

Lamar kept his pager turned off or on vibrate whenever he visited my house. Players are so obvious. He had something to hide, but what? I called his voicemail number and tried a couple dozen four-digit pin codes, you know, the usual variations: his birthday, license plate number, and the other easily remembered numbers, like 1234,1379, 1111, 2222, 3333, etc. In my experience, men generally kept their pin codes simple. The answer wasn't as complicated as it seemed at that moment.

That's when it struck me—the last four digits of his social security number. But how would I get them? The same method used by women for centuries.

Sex!

When he fell into his coma-like sleep after a night of high passion, I checked his wallet for his social security card.

I jotted down the numbers and tried them the next morning when I arrived at the office. Bingo! I hit the jackpot. The irritating, automated message said "You have ten saved messages."

Beep. Hi Lamar, it's Keisha. I just wanted to say thank you for taking me out to that African restaurant last night, the way you held me and kissed me, it was magical. I'm thinking about you. Talk to you later.

Bastard!

Beep. When are you coming to get your child Lamar? He needs diapers and I ain't got no money. Call me.

Son of a bitch! He didn't tell me he had a kid!

Beep. Hey baby, how you doin' today? I just called to say I love you. You know I do, boo boo. The twins really loved the bikes you bought them for their birthday last week; you know those boys ride them every day after school. I hope we're still on tonight; I got a babysitter. Give me a call and let me know by seven, okay?

Three kids?! Oh, hell no.

Beep. Hi Lamar. I haven't received the check yet this month. Please give me a call and let me know if we need to work something out. Your daughter needs school clothes. Call me.

Four kids?!

Beep. Lamar, it's Shaunte. I thought about what you said, and yes, Shaunte wants Lamar. I love you baby. Can't wait for our date Saturday. Call me later if you get some time.

Line up honey, hope you like African food.

Beep. Lamar, this is Dr. Lawry's office. Please give us a call and schedule an appointment so that we can go over your test results.

Tests?! I'm gonna die.

Beep. This is the nurse from Dr. Lawry's office again. We received your message. Everything's okay, we just want to discuss adjusting your cholesterol medication.

Whew!

Beep. Hi Daddy, it's Laila. I wanted to see if you were coming this weekend. I miss you. Can we go to the zoo? I got an "A" on my book report. Talk to you later, alligator.

Awwww... Wait a minute! Is that four or five?!

Beep. Hi, it's Judy; I just came back from the doctor. Sniff. The good news is I don't have the flu. Sniff. The bad news is that I'm pregnant. Sniff. What are we going to do? Call me. Sniff.

Judy's pregnant?! He told me they just "hung out" a couple of times.

Beep. Next Message: Hey, what's up man? This is Brad. Don't forget we have a frat meeting tonight. I thought we'd go have some drinks after, I ain't seen you in a minute.

Uhhhhh...Brad? The gay Brad?

Beep. You have no more messages.

To say I was a bit stunned by these revelations would be akin to saying Fat Albert's a smidge overweight. My stunned state soon gave way to anger, and the anger took a sharp left toward blind revenge. What's that saying about hell's fury and a woman scorned? Yeah, that was me. I wasn't normally the vengeful type, but determined to bring hate and discontent to every aspect of Lamar's miserable existence, I hatched a ruthless plot too ingenious not to execute. Karma had a new name—Charisse.

Twelve

Mission: Possible

May 16, 1990
That son of a bitch, what a damn dog (no pun intended)! I broke into Lamar's voicemail today. All those women. And all those damn kids. Jesus. No wonder he got into law. He's gonna need to save money on legal fees to afford the child support claims. And those poor women, they don't have a clue. That's okay. I'll share my clue with all of them.

***

I monitored Lamar's messages and pager, documenting each and every name and phone number. When all was said and done, I'd identified seven additional girlfriends, as many as six kids, a second ex-wife, and a possible down-low partner.

No wonder he never had time for me.

Over the following days, I called every gullible schmuck on my list; I didn't even entertain the prospect of calling Brad.

I always identified myself using the name of another girl in the harem, usually his baby-mama, Vanessa; my sorority sister, Judy; or Shante—his most recent conquest. They were unquestionably the most ghetto and would chew a second hole in his ass if he dared to accuse them. I started by recounting my recent discovery, you know, that Lamar had more kept women than Hugh Hefner. I followed that with "you deserved to know the truth about his extra curricular activities." I explained that I didn't want anyone to get hurt the way I had, said they might decide to stay with him but at least they'd know the kind of human scourge they were dealing with.

My contrived pleas turned out to be more effective than I'd ever imagined.

Brick by brick, Lamar's wall of lies tumbled down like Jericho. At school, gossip swirled like a Kansas tornado. He had no place to run and no place to hide. His car was keyed—on both sides, and Nisey told me someone cut all of the tongues out of his shoes. One of the more brilliant chicks tore every other page out of one of his most expensive law texts. Best of all, there was speculation that he spent an evening in the emergency room after someone put a "special seasoning" in his Jollof rice. A "stomach ailment" apparently kept him on the toilet for so long he went to the hospital to ensure his intestines were still intact.

Lamar triaged his victims enough to stop the hemorrhaging, a few stayed with him out of what I can only imagine was sheer stupidity or desperation. You know, like I'd been a couple of weeks prior. But he was bound and determined to discover his saboteur. In a wasted attempt to gauge my complicity, he called me a few days after my plot had concluded.

"Hey, Charisse, how are you baby?" he asked. I sensed a slight trepidation in his voice, like he didn't know what to expect.

"Well, I've had better days, I . . . I guess," I said, feigning sadness.

"What's wrong?"

"It's so funny you should call; I must've thought you up. I got a strange phone call last night from some woman who said she was involved with you. She said that she found out you were seeing me and several other women and thought I had a right to know the kind of man you really are."

"What! Who was she? Did she give you a name?"

"No. I asked her, but she wouldn't tell me. She said you knew who she was, and that's all that mattered. She did mention Judy, somebody named Shaunte, I think, and Vanessa? Do you know who these women are?" I asked, covering my mouth to stifle the laugh attempting to escape.

"Listen, baby, somebody is messin' with me. I . . . I don't know who they are, she's lying."

"I was sure of it, baby. I'm so relieved. I never believed you could do anything like that. I mean, what kind of *low-life snake* would you have to be to dog me and all those other women like that? It's just not in your character. I didn't believe it. I *couldn't* believe it," I said, realizing my stellar performance was easing into B-movie mediocrity. It was time to pull back.

"I'm just glad you waited to talk to me before you reacted. Right now, you're the only person I feel I can trust."

And the Oscar for Best Lead Actress in a Lamar Dramedy Goes to...

"You know, I'm here for you. You can always trust me. Anyway, I've got to go now love, I've got class. But I'll call later on to check on you, okay?" I said.

The more I thought about it, the more it became clear that Lamar wanted everyone to commit to him, but he committed to no one. I continued the joke we called a relationship for another three weeks to minimize the chances he'd figure out I was guilty. Then I told him that I couldn't see him anymore because I'd grown fond of Ron, which was a lie. I never had sex with Lamar again either, claimed I had been on my period—for over a month. No matter how ridiculous it may sound, men never challenge women on that issue.

Mission accomplished? For a while, I walked around like a peacock; I stuck my chest out with pride, like I'd beaten Lamar at his own game. But at the end of the day, all I did was waste months of my life dating a man whom I knew was a dawg before I met him, and a little more than a week of precious time and energy trying to unmask an unconcealed truth.

I wanted a challenge? Well, I got one.

I wanted to know, could I tame a wild dog? Well, I got my answer . . . no!

At the end of the day, only one truth mattered: I'd knowingly played with a vicious dog, so I only had myself to blame when he bit me in the ass.

Thirteen

Ex-Boyfriend Trouble

I arrived at the office the next day, after my foray into the world of Lamar, to find Dwayne waiting in the guest chair beside my desk. I never turned on my cell phone, so if he had called or left messages, I didn't get them. He smiled as I approached which I took as a good sign.

"Good morning, Ms. Tyson. What happened to you yesterday? You . . . you left *our appointment* abruptly," he said so my nosy co-workers wouldn't catch on. "Are you okay?"

"Everything is fine, Mr. Gibson, just fine," I answered and then laid my charcoal "I look *way* successful" Kenneth Cole briefcase on the desk. My heart began to pitter-pat. *Could the wish I'd suppressed actually be coming true?* I wondered. "What brings you in the office this morning?"

"Well, I wanted to make sure the, uhhh, *deal* didn't fall through because we moved too fast. You know, I like that property a lot and I definitely want to invest in it," he said. *Invest . . . in me?*

I smiled and plopped in my high-back leather office chair.

"Are you sure about that? I mean, the property needs some work. It's not in perfect condition, not even close," I cautioned.

He can't say I didn't warn him.

"Well, I guess that's a good thing because I'm not looking for perfection. I've got the tools to work with it," he said, his smiling eyes holding my glance. "I want the property that's perfect for me, and let's say I've got a good feeling about that one."

What planet did he come from?

"Really?"

"Yes, really."

"Well, I suggest you give the property a thorough inspection and close the deal as soon as possible."

"Oh trust me, Ms. Tyson, I plan to probe every nook and cranny," he said with a wink. We chatted about house hunting for a few minutes as I walked him outside to his car.

A sigh of relief, I thought. I stood in the nippy air and closed my eyes as I breathed in Dwayne. The sun beamed warm rays as if to celebrate my wish come true. He didn't plan to be a one-night stand after all, a cause for party and panic. I mean, eventually, if we hung in there long enough, we'd run into my weighty emotional baggage if I didn't get myself together—and quick.

Admittedly, I didn't have high hopes for any real longevity. After all, no relationship I started in bed ever ended at the altar. Just didn't happen. At least he'd be a good transitional person who could occupy my time, take me out to dinner, and perhaps substitute for chocolate on occasion.

***

Dwayne and I spent almost every day together in the following weeks. I started to think he rejected the houses on purpose. He may not be the next "the one," but I saw in him all the things I forgot to pray for.

He wasn't tall, ultra rich, or college educated but seemed to be a decent guy—at least on the surface. Not a man of grand gestures, he mastered the little things. He didn't cook every night, but when I was tired and needed to decompress, he came through like a champ. He rubbed my feet when they ached from showing houses all day. Like some freak of nature, he *asked* me to tell him what was on my mind—good, bad or indifferent—and listened with a receptive ear. He instinctively sensed when to respond and when to shut up, something most men didn't practice until after retirement—and only then because they were old and glad they could hear at all.

Dwayne seemed like a good sort of man, the best sort of man. He had a way with me, his presence and tone of speech calmed and soothed me; he took care of me, and he wanted to "get" me. The thought of trusting someone again never occurred to me until we met. If life couldn't get any better, Marcus hadn't called or stopped by in a while, only an occasional voicemail here and there. I rejoiced, *It's about time, he moved on!*

My patience wore a little thin with Dwayne and his inability to select a new home; we were on the road every morning. He made up for the tedious hunt by kissing me in every room of every house.

On one particular day, the last house on our tour was a foreclosure, a colonial adjacent to the Fort Washington Marina. He hated it. The enormous junior manor across the street with a "For Sale" sign planted in the front yard caught his eye, however, and held on for dear life. It didn't come up in my search, and I knew why. It looked somewhere in the range of a million dollars, more than Dwayne's loan would cover. He asked to see it, so I escorted him inside.

The basement, which was the only area he really cared about, featured a deluxe wet bar with three draft beer fountains, a home theater with a 100-inch projection screen, and a hot tub large enough to hold the Washington Redskins' starting line-up, offensive lineman included. His eyes sparkled as if he'd just won fifty-yard line seats to the Superbowl. The house was a winner but a dream just beyond his reach.

"Can I think about this one? I mean, I love it, but the price," he said, rubbing his chin, lips pursed. I knew he wanted that house, but I was also certain he couldn't afford it. I'd almost regretted showing it to him because no other house we saw in his price range would remotely compare.

"You'd have to come to the table with a lot of cash. The bank isn't going to increase your loan amount that much."

"How much do you think I'd need?"

"About a hundred grand."

"Wooooo! Well, let me see what I can do. Cash is really tight right now, but give me a couple of months to get the money together," he said, smiling almost too confidently for a man with *his* pre-approval letter.

"You serious?"

"As a heart attack. I want this house."

He didn't seem too concerned, so I chalked it up to good business. *Little did I know* . . .

When we returned to my office, like a hero from a Jane Austen novel, he stepped out of the car, opened my door, bowed his head as he kissed my hand, and said goodbye.

71

He was an angel, and I was in heaven. I felt like I was gliding on one of those people movers at the airport; I couldn't sense the motion in my feet, but somehow I arrived where I needed to go.

Nyla caught my cheesy grin and commented. "What's going on with you, Ms. Tyson? You look like you had an afternoon special."

I danced toward my desk and laughed. "No, no, Nyla. But I did have a *special* afternoon."

Not two seconds after I sat down at my desk and turned to my computer did Marcus storm in the main door. He tromped toward me and scowled. Steam rose from his ears. He was pissed about something, but I didn't know what. I only knew *I* hadn't done anything wrong, *unless* . . .

Fourteen

The Panic Proposition

"What the hell are you doing here?" I asked Marcus in a feeble attempt to head off his inevitable rant.

"I want you to tell me who the hell you were with this afternoon. I saw you getting out of that BMW. Who the fuck was that kissing your hand?"

Uh-oh.

I surveyed the office to check how many nosy co-workers were gawking. Of course, every eye was turned to an invisible ceiling crack or non-existent work on their desks.

"Listen, keep your voice down. This is my place of business. Let's go in the conference room," I whispered.

"Fine," he blurted as he followed me down the hall. I stepped in the conference room and walked to the opposite side of the room. I made sure I stood beyond his reach in case he lost his mind and started swinging. When he slammed the door, I sensed things might get ugly, but I didn't expect this . . .

"Answer my damn question, who were you with, Charisse?"

What to say? What to say?

Deflect, deflect.

"What are you doing here, spying on me now? We've been broken up for months, remember? I caught you with Ms. Boob 'n Weave. You don't have a right to ask me shit about what I do or who I date."

That a girl!

"Date? Oh, I see, you gonna play me like that, right?"

"Play you like what? You played yourself."

I'm on a roll.

"I thought we were still working things out, Charisse. How many times do I have to apologize? Whatever happened to forgiveness? Don't you have it in your heart to forgive me?" he asked, easing toward me, his eyes begging me to believe his sincerity. The delicious scent of his Boucheron cologne wafted through my nose. I had a hard time staying strong.

"Honestly, Marcus, I don't know what's in my heart. Every good feeling I had for you is buried under so much pain and heartache, I don't know what's there anymore. I know you had my heart, and I know you broke it. So, what the hell do you want from me?"

"I want you to give me a chance. I want you to love me again. I love you, baby. Can't you understand that? I can't see you with anyone but me. Not anyone. I can't," he pleaded.

He definitely tugged at my heart strings, but I hadn't found a way to forgive him. Someday I might but not *that* day.

"I'll tell you what I understand. I understand what it's like to love and adore your man, to want to make a life with him. I understand what it's like to be unable to imagine him with anyone else. I also understand the absolute misery it causes to watch his lips, which you thought belonged to you, kiss someone else, and night after sleepless night imagine him fucking someone else. You probably couldn't even comprehend that pain until Dwayne kissed my hand today. Welcome to *my* world!"

He closed his eyes, pressed his head against his fist and said, "Don't do this, Charisse. I'm asking you to please forgive me. I'm asking you to spend the rest of your life with me."

I must be losing my hearing, did he propose?

"Excuse me? What did you say?" I asked as I watched him drop to one knee.

"You heard me. I want to spend the rest of my life with you. Will you marry me?"

"You're serious?" I said, shaking my head in disbelief. His words paralyzed me, I couldn't move.

"Yes, I'm serious. I've never been more serious in my life," he said. He stood up, walked over to me, and grabbed my hand.

"Marcus, where is this coming from? I loved you with all my heart for three years and nothing! Why now? You're only saying this because someone else wants me."

"No, Charisse. I'm asking you to be my wife because I want you."

Damn. Good comeback.

I pulled my hand from his and took a step back so the smell of his cologne wouldn't confuse me anymore. It was like catnip for women. "I— I can't answer that right now Marcus. I can't. I need time to think about it. You've put me through too much."

"So, that's not a no then, right?"

"Not yet."

"Then I have hope?" he asked.

Keep hope alive.

"I honestly don't know. I need time," I answered sincerely. Oh, I needed time alright—time in a psychiatric ward.

As if on cue, his cell phone rang.

Saved by the bell.

He pulled his cell out of his belt clip, looked at the screen, and ignored the call. "Listen, Charisse, I've got to get going, I'm meeting a client. Please think about what I said. *Forgive me?*"

He leaned in to kiss my lips, but I twisted my head so it landed on my cheek.

"Okay, I'll try. Later."

I thought, *What the hell am I gonna do now?*

I returned to my desk in a complete daze. In a matter of weeks, I'd gone from not having enough men to having one too many. One broke my heart, and the other hadn't been around quite long enough to break it. Could I forgive Marcus and take a chance that he was reformed and ready for marriage? Or should I risk it with the new guy, whom I knew little about and could hurt me ten times worse than Marcus?

My conundrum called for a drink.

Many drinks.

I jumped in the Beemer and headed to the Gaylord at the National Harbor. I'd sit in the Pastime sports bar in peace, have a cocktail, or two, or three, and figure out what the hell I was going to do next. I pulled up to the entrance, gave my key to the polite valet, and took the elevator up to my destination.

The Pastime was an urban-contemporary spot. With mahogany wood accents and sleek furniture, the setting seemed more bar than sports, but enough flat screens and memorabilia adorned the walls to justify the name.

The main bar was nearly empty so I had my choice of seats; I selected one adjacent to the thirty-foot television screen. A Wizards game kept me distracted so I didn't sulk all night long. I ordered a Guinness from the sexy-chocolate bartender sporting dreadlocks and reclined in my seat while he made small talk.

"Looks like you're having a rough day," he said as he placed the full pilsner glass on a Budweiser coaster and slid it in front of me.

"You can say that again," I responded. I slapped a fifty on the bar, told him to put twenty in his pocket, and keep the beers coming until I said, "When."

He rested his elbows on the bar, leaned forward, and stared at me. Didn't say a word. I grew a little uncomfortable, thought a booger was hanging from my nose. So, I decided to break the silence.

"It's kind of empty in here tonight, huh?"

"Yeah, I think there's a National Bar Association meeting going on in the conference center, and they haven't let out yet," he said, still absorbed in my face. "So, you want to talk about it?"

"Talk about what?"

"Your day."

I snickered. "You're not one of those bartender slash psychiatrist types are you?"

"No, I wouldn't say that, although I did minor in psychology in undergrad. It's just there's a little sadness in that friendly face, and I thought I'd lend an ear, you know, if you needed it."

"Awww. Thanks, I appreciate the gesture. What's your name again?" I asked and then sipped from my glass.

"Ceasar."

"Nice to meet you, Ceasar. I'm Charisse. Anyway, thanks but I think I just need a little time to marinate, you know, just chill."

"Okay, sweetie, give me a holler when you're ready for your next round."

"I sure will."

I hollered at Caesar about three more times in the next hour, and none of the words included "When." All I could think about was Marcus, wondering if I'd been fair to him. After all, nobody's perfect; I certainly wasn't. Second chances and forgiveness were the Christian way, weren't they?

I'd never seen a reformed player live, in the flesh, with my own eyes, you know? Once a dawg, always a dawg. Men simply did not change—er—very often, at least not for the better.

The thought 'reformed player' had just breezed through my mind when someone crept up behind me. I paid no mind at first, thought they were just ordering a drink. However, I grew alarmed when the heat from their breath warmed the nape of my neck; I started to turn around when he spoke.

"All these years and you're still wearing Chanel. Some things never change, huh?"

I froze.

It couldn't be...

Fifteen

Bad Boy Gone Good

"Lamar?" I said as I turned to glimpse his face. "Oh my God, Lamar Jackson! How are you?"

He leaned in to kiss my cheek as I reached out to hug him. "I'm doing fine, Charisse. I thought that was you, still as beautiful as ever."

"Oh, thank you. That's very sweet," I said, inspecting him for gray hairs and a pot belly. He hadn't changed a bit, still mouth-watering fine fine fine. His navy pin-stripped suit and silk collared shirt looked tailored to his every bend and curve, as if no man on Earth could ever wear it except him. *Woo!* "What in the world are you doing here?"

"I'm staying in the Gaylord, attending the National Bar Association meeting," he said as he pulled a stool next to me. I glanced at his left hand. *Hmmm, no wedding ring.*

"Wow, so you went on to pass the bar, huh? Fantastic! How many years has it been?"

"Gee, I guess it's been about fifteen years or so," he said, rolling his beautiful hazel eyes up to do a mental calculation. "Seems like a lifetime ago, so much has happened."

Boy, he hadn't said anything but the truth. "So what's going on with you? You married? Got kids?"

Other than the six I know about?

"No, I'm not married. I had to step away from the relationship scene for a while, you know. I've actually been celibate for the last three years. I'm back into church though, regularly. Got my life back on track and praying I keep things moving forward."

"I'm sorry, I thought you said you'd been celibate for three years, as in the 'no sex' celibate."

"Is there another kind?" he asked, shaking his head as if to say, "She's still crazy."

"Wow, that's good. That's good to hear," I said.

"I mean professionally, I was successful, but spiritually I was a wreck. You probably won't believe this, but I often wished I'd run into you again someday, so I could apologize, tell you I'm sorry for everything I did to hurt you."

Definitely not the Lamar I dated.

"That's good of you to say but unnecessary. That . . . that's the past."

Who said that?

"No, it is necessary. See, Charisse, my life spiraled into hell—drinking, drugs, women, women, and more women. There was a lot you didn't know, and perhaps you knew more than I thought," he said, cutting his eyes at me, subtly casting suspicion. "But that's neither here nor there. I didn't have any respect for myself, for you, or for anybody. I made a lot of mistakes, a lot of enemies, and a lot of babies. But I've turned my life around. I'm saved, and I have eight beautiful kids who have accepted me as I am and allow me to take part in their lives. I am a living testimony to God's grace."

Eight? Damn, that's an African tribe.

"Eight kids? Wow, you kept busy, but I guess I kind of knew you were . . . uhhh . . . *busy.*"

"Oh, you knew a lot more than you let on," he declared. "But how could I blame you or the others for what happened then? I deserved everything I got and then some."

Does he know it was me?

"Well, what's done is done. I'm just happy to see this change in you. I always believed if you used your powers for good and not for evil, you would do amazing things."

He just smiled.

"So, what about you? You married, any kids?" Lamar asked.

"No, no kids. I was married for a couple years, but we're divorced now," I answered, avoiding eye contact. It hurt to even think about Jason.

"Oh, I'm sorry to hear that," he said, his voice sounding somewhere between empathetic and hopeful.

"Please, don't be. I mean, the end of that marriage resembled the sinking of the Titanic, slow, painful, and inevitable. So, anyway, I'm single now—sort of."

"What's 'sort of' mean?"

"Well, my boyfriend of three years, who is also my most recent *ex*-boyfriend, asked me to marry him today."

"Well, congratulations," he said as a reluctant smile emerged. It faded pretty quickly, however, when he realized I'd been sitting alone in a sports bar drinking more beer than a frat boy at a kegger. "I guess I jumped the gun. You haven't said yes?"

"No, I haven't. Let's just say he had an indiscretion, and I've had a difficult time forgiving him. And if that's not bad enough, I met someone new that I've only been seeing for a short while, but I like him. I'm not sure what to do," I said, taking deep gulp of beer. If he thought "lush," he'd be correct. Alcohol didn't really help . . . but it damn sure didn't hurt.

"Wow, that's got to be tough . . . but maybe it happened for a reason. Fate, maybe?" he paused. "Look, I'm not aware of all the particulars, but I'm nothing if not proof that a man can change when he's ready. Maybe not when *you're* ready, but when *he's* ready, anything's possible."

Lamar's words hit me like a Mack truck. I'd contemplated whether Marcus could change, when Lamar, the dog of all dogs (king dog even), had reformed. Still unsure, I questioned whether Marcus's proposal represented love or panic, but I did entertain the possibility that he could change. Yet, seeing Lamar again, sitting in his still-powerful presence, I couldn't help but wonder if something more than confusion had led me to the bar that night.

Anyway, Lamar and I exchanged business cards and vowed to keep in touch. He pressed his soft lips against my forehead and bid me farewell. *Uhn uhn uhn.* I shook my head in amazement. The thought *maybe now is our time* ambled through my mind. Talk about confused.

When I got home, I checked my voicemail. Marcus had left two messages asking me to give him a call because he needed to hear my voice. But Dwayne, dear sweet Dwayne, had asked me to dinner at his house the next evening. He hadn't been with me long but still he knew the most direct route to my heart ran through my stomach.

I called Dwayne back and accepted; Marcus could wait.

While at dinner, I figured I'd install the "for sale" sign in Dwayne's front yard and do a little home staging so his house would show like a model home when the buyers arrived.

***

Dwayne greeted me at the door with a colorful bouquet of store-bought flowers, and I handed him a bottle of Merlot; my mom said never show up to dinner empty handed. The food's aroma wafted through my nostrils and teased my tummy. Smoke rising from the deck suggested something tasty sizzled on the grill. I thought I must be pretty special for him to grill in this frigid weather. I resolved to let him do all the cooking if the food tasted as good as the smell.

He helped me carry the decorative furnishings inside. I brought a little something for each room: floral arrangements and vases, pillows, discount artwork, and coordinating fabrics from the stock I kept in my garage. I used props to decorate my clients' homes so they'd sell faster.

I started working upstairs in his bedroom when he yelled from the kitchen.

"Hey Charisse, I'm going to run to the grocery store for a minute, forgot to pick up the rosemary for the potatoes!"

I thought, *Well isn't he just a little Chef Boy-R-Dee?*

"Okay! I'm just going to rifle though all of your drawers, hack into your computer, scan through your caller ID, open your mail, and maybe run a credit check if there's time! See you when you get back!" I joked, astonished that he trusted me (or himself) enough to leave me alone in his house. Apparently, he didn't know he was dealing with Bond . . . *Jane* Bond.

He laughed. "Okay, baby, see you in a few minutes!"

Awwwww, he called me baby.

Just as he stepped out the door, his house phone rang. I started to run to catch him, but the sound of his car engine faded. I wasn't even tempted to look at the caller ID. Well, okay, I was tempted but I resisted. I reveled in my transformation into a new woman. I'd resolved to end the maniacal behavior; there'd be no more suspicion, no more spying, no more testing. I was determined to give his kind a fair shot. He still had two-hundred ten points, and I wouldn't deduct for anything until he did something really, really wrong.

After the fifth ring, the answering machine picked up.

Why anyone still bothered with answering machines in the advent of voicemail was beyond me. His greeting played; I just loved the sound of his voice.

After the beep, a woman spoke.

Hi, Dwayne, it's me. I just called to give you the good news. We're pregnant! Can you believe it?! We've been trying for so long and it finally happened. I know this isn't news I should leave on the machine, but I'm so excited I had to tell you right away. Call me as soon as you get in. Love you!"

My heart started palpitating like I'd just run a marathon. My mouth felt dry. I stood stunned for a few minutes before a few tears welled and trickled down my cheek, not because he hurt me, although he had, but because I'd finally decided to give someone an honest chance only to be let down yet again. My mind flashed back to the article, "Do you carry around stereotypes?"

Yes—men suck, all of them.

Yeah, I said it!

I didn't grab the furnishings, only my Coach bag. I jumped in my Beemer and sped home. I didn't even bother to lock his door, hoping someone robbed his ass blind.

By the time I pulled in my garage, my cell phone rang off the hook—Dwayne no doubt. I sent the calls straight to voicemail, and when that took too much energy, I turned it off. I cuddled up with my best friends forever: Godiva, Grey Goose, and Doritos. *Damn, I should've snatched the food off the grill.*

Oh well.

There'd be no work the next day, not so Dwayne could show up at my desk with the sad puppy look on his face and blowing lies out of his ass. Nope, I'd sit in the house and read my journals. Fortunately, Dwayne didn't know where I lived, and I never listed my number in the phone book. We'd spent all of our time together at his place. Confident he couldn't find me, I'd refocus on number one—me.

Needless to say, Dwayne's point balance went from two-hundred ten to negative two-hundred ten—with a bullet.

Sixteen

Surprise Visit

My projected one-day stint in the house turned into three; I'd sunk into a self-diagnosed mini depression. One of the best benefits of being a real estate agent was my office consisted of a laptop, a wireless printer, a palm pilot, and a cell phone; I could work from anywhere—including my bed, while cloaked in funky pajamas. I didn't want to talk to Dwayne and refused to listen to his messages or his lying, cheating voice.

Thoughts of Marcus had begun to replace Dwayne, although Lamar wasn't far behind. Even still, I made up my mind. I'd call Marcus as soon as I felt up to talking and accept his proposal. No more dating bullshit. Hell, marrying a jerk couldn't be any worse than living single in a jerk nation, but I planned to make our engagement a lengthy one—just in case. I went to Jared the night before to shop for rings; for all he put me through, I wanted to make sure the diamond was big enough to see from the space shuttle. I reasoned that perhaps God did answer my prayers by sending Marcus to me. Maybe He just wanted me to learn a little patience and forgiveness. Thinking back on those days, I'm of the firm belief that I needed some Prozac—*loads of it*.

I'd finally gathered enough energy to clean the house; I called an efficient Merry Maid named Maria who scrubbed everything from top to bottom. I'd get to bed and head into the office early the next day. My phone hadn't rung all evening, so I figured Dwayne probably stopped trying to catch me at the office. Perhaps he and his baby-mama were taking prenatal classes and were practicing breathing exercises; I hoped they both hyperventilated.

My doorbell rang as I turned off the lights and started up the stairs. I didn't have any idea who in hell would be stopping by unannounced at that hour. The days were frigid and short, so most people I knew didn't venture out in the evenings. Then I realized it probably was Marcus. He was the only person who thought he had license to visit my house whenever the feeling hit him, like he chipped in on the mortgage or something.

Well, his timing couldn't be better. There'd be no better time to wash Dwayne out of my hair and shift my attention back to Marcus. Fortunately, I'd taken a shower earlier or he might've been a little turned off by the swarm of flies that circled me a few hours before. I opened the door and to my surprise . . .

"Dwayne? How . . . how did you find me?"

"I've been trying to reach you for two days, so I can explain. Can I come in?"

"Hell no! You don't have shit to say that I need to hear," I yelled, slamming the door in a manner George Jefferson would envy. He pressed my doorbell for what seemed like an eternity, so I opened it.

"Alright, spit it out! You've got two minutes," I barked, annoyed at the imposition.

"Charisse, the woman on my answering machine is my sister. Well, she's my half sister, but she's my sister. She and her husband are pregnant," he said, waiting to see if I'd take the bait.

Nope!

"Yeah right, two days and that's the best you could come up with? You need to take that bullshit next door. She said, 'We're pregnant.' I heard it with my own ears."

"Yes, she meant her and her husband. They've been trying for two years. They live in Chicago."

I paused. "You never told me you had a sister. I've been seeing you a few weeks now. Why didn't you say anything about her?" I said as I crossed my arms and cranked my neck. I guessed I looked like Boo Boo the Fool because he said . . .

"Well, this is going to sound stupid, but you didn't ask. We'd been so focused on trying to find a house and *other things* that we just never talked about it."

He was right. It did sound stupid. But the truth is, I never did ask; the subject didn't come up. But then again, why would I?

"Is this the truth?" I said. I remained hesitant, but the icy wind whipped and swirled too violently to leave the door standing open.

"Yes, baby, it's the truth. If you bothered to listen to your voicemail, you'd know this already," he said.

"Yeah, I haven't checked my voicemail."

I remained skeptical, but his explanation seemed plausible. Still, I couldn't fight the feeling that I'd fallen victim to the Jedi Mind Trick.

"I figured that was the case when you didn't show up to work today, so I went to the courthouse in Upper Marlboro to search the land records for your address. I'm in construction, remember? I know these things," he said. "Now, can I please come in? It's *freezing* out here."

"Oh, I'm sorry, yeah, come in."

I closed the door behind him and took his coat. He scanned my house in amazement. My decor was an impressive sight, looked like it was cut straight from a Crate & Barrel catalogue . . . on an IKEA budget.

"Wow, nice place. Did you do the decorating?"

"Thanks. Yeah, I'm a little bit of an IKEA junkie," I answered, beaming with pride. I decorated like Bea Smith with on a tight budget.

"Did you get to keep the house? From your divorce, I mean."

"No, I bought it all by myself."

"This is pretty big. You don't mind living alone?"

"Well, to be honest, I didn't think I'd be living alone when I bought it, but uhhhh, things didn't *quite* work out as planned," I said, the sting of my break-up with Marcus still haunting me. Then it dawned on me that Dwayne was only man I'd invited into my home other than Marcus—there was a new sheriff in town.

"Oh, I see."

"Anyway, can I get you something to drink? You can have a seat, anywhere is fine," I said as I grabbed a glass from the bar.

"Yes, please. I'd like something a little stronger than a soda if you have it."

"Sure, Grey Goose and cranberry juice?"

"Perfect," he said, pausing for a moment. "Listen, Charisse, we need to talk. I mean seriously."

"Okay . . . talk seriously," I said as I handed him a half-filled glass of my favorite elixir. He gulped it down, a man after my own heart.

"I'm not sure what kind of men you're used to dating, but I'm my own man. If we're going to be together, you've got to learn to trust me, or shit, at least give me a chance to explain things when we have problems. Running away and staying out of contact isn't gonna work for me. I don't need anymore drama. I had a marriage full of drama, that's why we're not together anymore. Capiche?"

My eyes fell to the ground, masking my embarrassment. I couldn't make eye contact with him and was kind of ashamed by my behavior. Not many men could make me feel that way; it was usually the other way around—and much more satisfying that way I might add.

"I'm sorry. I warned you, the property isn't perfect. It still needs some work," I reminded him.

"I understand, and it's okay. I'm sure you've been through a lot too. That's why I'm here," Dwayne said.

"Well, I'm glad you came."

"Good. Does this mean we're okay now?" he asked.

"Better than okay," I responded. My heart softened like freshly-microwaved butter, after he flashed a reassuring smile.

"Now, if you don't mind, I'd like to take some time to give my property a thorough inspection. I mean, if that's okay with you."

"Is that right?" I asked. "Well, did you bring your *tools* with you?"

"Oh yeah, I say we go up to your bedroom. I'll lay them out on the bed, and you can do your own inspection."

"Awww, sookie sookie now," I said, scampering up the stairs with Dwayne tight on my heels.

***

Dwayne left early the next morning, and I woke up feeling revived and refreshed. My sex tank was full, and I was in a cheerful mood. I took a shower, got dressed, and was out the door lickety split. Worthy of a vanilla latte after my exceptional performance in bed, Starbuck's called to me on the way to the office. While waiting in line, thoughts of Dwayne dominated my mind.

I credited him with the two-hundred ten points I deducted and gave him five more for making the effort to find me. Not every man would care that much, especially given we'd only been involved for about a month. Most of my ex's wouldn't care enough to roll over and find me on the other side of the bed, let alone search the county tax records to find where I lived. The best part, though, was that he accepted me with all my faults. Isn't that what every woman wanted, someone who'd accept us for who we are, in all of our ugliness and splendor?

As I returned to my Beemer, my cell phone rang.

"Hey Nisey! How are you?" I asked with excessive cheer.

"Well, aren't you a ray of fucking sunshine this morning. What's up with you? You must've got some last night."

I hate her.

"As a matter of fact I did, *thank you very much.* These past few days have been crazy. You won't even believe me when I tell you. We definitely need a *tet-a-tet,*" I said. I could say about six words in every major language. That was my French.

"Yeah, I really need to talk to you. I'm in a little bit of trouble," Nisey said, her voice trembling.

"Trouble? What's wrong?"

"Well, I don't want to get into it over the phone. Do you think we can meet for lunch today?"

"Yeah, sure, where do you wanna go?" I asked, hoping she'd suggest a restaurant located in the 'burbs. I loved her but I refused to drive into D.C.

"Why don't we meet at Old Ebbitt's?"

"Nisey, you know how I hate driving into the city. You can never find a place to park."

"Well, I'm working downtown today, and I won't be able to take the extended lunch I'd like to take, so just park in the garage and I'll pay for it. This is *really* important."

She didn't fool me; I'd be paying for my own parking and lunch too. But if Nisey said she was in trouble, she meant it, and it was probably something major.

Seventeen

Baby Mama Drama

I arrived at the office, and Nyla told me business had picked up a little over the past few days. Apparently, a few homeowners called who urgently needed to put their homes on the market, trying to avoid foreclosure. Working with banks could be a real pain in the ass with all the bureaucratic red tape, but doing my job well meant helping them the best I could.

I called each client back and set appointments, so we could discuss their situations. Emotionally heart-wrenching at times, I just couldn't help but feel for people who struggled to keep a roof over their heads. Always wishing I could do more. I leaned back in my chair to take a short break when the office line rang.

"Hey, baby, it's Mom, how are you suga'?"

"Hi, Mommy, I'm fine. Long, long day already and it just got started. What's up?"

"Well, James went fishing this morning, so I was sitting here by myself when I got a surprise visit. Hold on a minute, they want to talk to you."

"Hello?" a man's voice spoke from the other end.

"Hi, who is this?" I asked. The voice was familiar but I couldn't place it.

"It's, uhhh, your cousin Lee. How are you, Charisse? Haven't seen you in a lonnng time."

Not *Lee*. I couldn't believe she put him on the phone, of all people. I remained silent not knowing whether to scream or hang up.

"Charisse? You there?" he asked.

"Ummhmmm, I'm here," I said, cold and agitated.

"Everything okay?"

"No, everything isn't okay, and I think you know why. What are you doing at my mother's house?" I snapped.

"I'm her nephew, remember? I stopped by to visit with her for a little while. She always invites me over when she stops in the store."

"I see."

"I hear you're doing big things in D.C."

"Don't believe everything you hear. Put my mother on the phone, All-Star," I ordered. That's what I called him—*all-star*. Trust me, there was nothing "star" about him, not anymore. An avalanche of failure had propelled him from Heisman potential to grocery store manager. I taunted him with the nickname because I knew the reference would remind him of everything he *wasn't* and all the dreams he'd never realize.

"Well, I'm so happy to hear everything is going well. Hope you can visit us soon. Let me hand the phone back to your mother. Take care," he blurted out, trying to play off the tension in our conversation for my mother's sake. He always was a good liar.

"Hey, baby, it's me. Well, I just wanted to let you kids talk for a minute. Been such a long time."

Not nearly long enough.

"Okay, Mom, well let me go. I need to get a lot of work done today. I've been out sick for a couple of days, so I need to get caught up."

"You okay?"

"Oh yeah, I'm fine. I think I was just a little run down, needed to get some rest."

"Well, don't work too hard baby. If you kill yourself, you won't be able to enjoy all the things you're workin' so hard to get. You understand?"

Desperate for any distraction, I glanced at my watch and wondered where the time had gone. I rushed to get on the road so I wouldn't be late for lunch with Nisey.

"Nyla, I'm running out for lunch. Send me a text if you need anything. My ringer won't be on."

"Okay, Ms. Tyson. See you when you get back."

The Bum Magnet

Hearing Lee's voice shocked me. We hadn't spoken in years, and it proved to be an eternity too soon. He and I were like brother and sister growing up. I tagged along with he and his friends during summer visits with Aunt Jackie before my mother left D.C. and headed back to North Carolina. Voices from near and far sang in unison like they did on "Cheers" whenever Norm walked in the bar. Everywhere we went, choirs of neighbors, friends, and strangers sang "Leeeeee!" I idolized him too, so much so I introduced him to my friends as my brother. Aunt Jackie had Lee, and my mom had me; we were all the sibling each other had. Even though he was four years older than me, we were thick as thieves, and he'd been the only male figure in my life. They treated him like his shit didn't stink, like he could do no wrong. I knew otherwise.

My mood grew somber when I thought about how our relationship had deteriorated, but I could never trust him again, not after what happened. My mom had no clue about why we didn't talk, and I couldn't be the one to tell her. It would break her heart . . . and Aunt Jackie, my dear Aunt Jackie. Dealing with what happened all those years ago was a bit more than I wanted to force on them and more than I could handle. I looked forward to Nisey's drama. It would be a much needed distraction from my own.

Nisey had already been seated when I arrived at Old Ebbitt's. As the hostess escorted me to our table, I couldn't help but drink in the atmosphere. Old Ebbit's, just around the corner from the White House, was home of the political power lunch. Some of the more saditty black folk dined there for the antiquely-rich marble and mahogany surroundings; most came for the shrimp and crab delights. My heart lept at the sight of a Grey Goose and cranberry juice awaiting me on our table.

My girl!

"So, what's going on?" I asked as I slid into the booth and rested my Coach bag on the seat.

"You might want to take a sip of your drink first."

"Big gulp or little gulp?"

"Oh, down the whole thing."

Uh-oh. A bad sign. But after my brief talk with Lee, I was more than happy to oblige.

"Okay, I'm ready. What is it?"

"I'm . . . I'm a little pregnant."

93

"Oh my God, that's wonderful! I'm so happy for you," I said. Her pouty lip and basset hound eyes told me my celebration was a bit premature. "Why aren't you smiling?"

"I'm . . . not . . . sure . . . who the father is?"

Holy shit! Stay calm. Stay calm.

"Wow, okaaaay. Hmm. So who are the possibilities?"

"Well, this is actually where it gets worse?"

"It gets worse?"

"One of the men is married."

"Okay, where is the waiter? I need another drink. Waiter!"

She chuckled. "Don't make me laugh, Rissey. This is serious."

"I know, I know. Okay, I only have one question to ask, and I'm not trying to pour salt on your wound because I know you feel bad. But what, on God's green earth were you thinking, having unprotected sex with two men?" I asked.

"I know, Rissey. You know that's completely unlike me, completely. I mean, I buy condoms by the case. All I can say is, I don't know. It happened, passion of the moment, alcohol, not thinking straight, etc. etc. And there isn't shit I can do to change it now. I'm mean, God, if we had the power to turn back the clock, I'd start a lot further back than six weeks ago, that's for damn sure," she said. Now, ain't *that* a superpower we'd all like to have, the power of the "do-over." Oh, the things I'd never do and the people I'd never meet.

"I know *that's* right. You told them yet?" I asked. Our waiter placed a basket filled with warm bread on the table and I went to town. I always craved simple carbs when under stress.

"No, I haven't. You already know David, the one I went on the cruise with, he's one. And I didn't tell you about the married guy, Robert, because I know you would've told me to end the relationship and I didn't want to listen, especially after the way I treated you when you were seeing Sean. Hell, at least you didn't know he was married," Nisey explained. "And to make matters worse, Robert's the one I'm really in love with. I get so lonely when he's at home with his wife and kids, so David became a distraction. We started hanging out, you know, just as friends, going to the movies and stuff. One night, and only one night, we both had too much to drink, one thing led to another and, voila, unprotected sex. I just don't know. How do you tell

94

the man you love the baby you're carrying may not be his?" she asked as her eyes flooded.

"Nisey, don't cry. You should've told me. I mean, you're right; I would have told you to end it but only because I've been there, done that, bought the T-shirt the soundtrack, and the collector's plate. If Robert's got you under some delusion that he's going to leave, I can tell you that he isn't. They never leave. Sometimes, they get kicked out, but they never leave. And I get the feeling he isn't getting kicked out. I would've supported you, no matter what. You know that, right?"

"Yes, I know," she said as she pulled the linen napkin from her lap and wiped her tears.

"So, what are you going to do? I mean, we're not getting any younger," I noted. Hell, our clocks were ticking so loud they could be heard from the international space station.

"Yeah, this baby is all I can think about. You might think I'm crazy, but I think I'm going to keep it. I know it won't be easy. I'm forty-two years old and just having my first child. I'll be fifty-two when he turns ten. Can you imagine me running around behind a ten year old in my fifty's? I'll be sixty-two, when he turns twenty. He'll be in college when I'm going into retirement. Can you imagine that?"

"Well, yeah, I can."

"Me too," she said through her tear-soaked smile.

"Nisey, you're not ancient. Women around the world give birth to beautiful, healthy babies in their forties. You'll be fine. You might be a walking Maury Povich episode, but you'll be fine. More importantly, I'll be Auntie Rissey, and I'll be able to be a mommy too . . . vicariously through you, of course."

"So, I guess not much is going to change, huh?" she said, letting out a chuckle. She was right though, I did more living through her than I did in my own life. Still, I couldn't let that slide.

"Ha, ha, ha, smart ass. Save the comedy for the big reveal show. How does Maury do it? Oh yeah, 'David, you arrre the father!'"

Her smile shrank but didn't disappear. "That was hurtful."

"Only because you know it's true," I said as I reached to pat her hand.

"You know, you're lucky I love you like a sister because I'd really like to kick your ass right now."

"Pregnancy hormones, dear, it'll pass," I said, still rubbing her hand. "Well, I hate to be the bearer of more bad news, but you've gotta tell them, preferably sooner than later. This isn't the kind of secret you can keep for very long."

"I know; I'll figure it out. I just need some time to let this all sink in. I'll deal with them later."

"Just don't wait too long. Mark my words, the longer you wait the harder it's going to get."

Nisey realized her new addition was more blessing than curse, so everything would be downhill after she broke the news. She might lose one or both of her so-called men, but she'd have her baby and a love for a lifetime.

When I returned to my office, seemed like poor Nyla was doing more work than I. So good to be the boss. I stayed at the office pretty late though, pulled together some market analyses for my foreclosure clients. They needed to know roughly how much we'd be able to sell their homes for up front. Home values in the D.C. area tended to decline a little more slowly than in other markets, but they still took a dip. Most homeowners who were forced to sell were generally not ready to listen to this sobering news. During our meetings, I had to be well-prepared to address their concerns and back up my figures.

By the time I got home, it was pretty late, nearly eleven o'clock. I used my last bit of strength to drive home and crawl onto my favorite chaise. I dozed off for about fifteen minutes when the doorbell rang. I thought Dwayne had returned for an encore performance. I hated to break it to him, but he'd have to get some in the morning; I was exhausted. I dragged myself to the door like I wore concrete shoes.

"Marcus, what are you doing here?"

"Can I come in?"

Eighteen

Goodbye to Yesterday

I debated whether or not letting Marcus in was a good idea, but we needed to talk. I couldn't accept his proposal now, not after Dwayne's visit. Dwayne deserved a fair chance, and I wanted to give that to him.

"Come on."

He headed straight for the family room, took off his coat, threw it across the arm of the sofa, and retrieved a beer from the refrigerator.

"Make yourself at home, why don't you?" I mumbled.

"You haven't called me, so I thought I'd stop by to find where your head is."

"It's on my neck."

As opposed to my ass where yours usually is.

"You know what I mean," he said.

"Listen, Marcus, this isn't easy for me to say," I started, feeling uncertain I could finish what I needed to say. "I love you, I always did. But unfortunately, that love just isn't the same as a year ago. I— I'm just not *in* love with you anymore."

Had I really said that out loud? I always thought that phrase sounded so cliché, never comprehended its gravity until that moment.

"How can you say that, Charisse, after all we've been through?"

"I can say that *because* of all we've been through. Sometimes we do things we can't take back. You can't make my pain go away or disappear with an emergency marriage proposal. I remember a time when I couldn't see anything except being your wife. Now? I simply can't see being your wife. I don't know, someday my feelings may change. But right now, I can't accept your proposal. It wouldn't be fair to you, and it wouldn't be fair to me."

"I know I hurt you, Charisse. If you need more time to work through your feelings, I can wait—but I'm not letting you go."

"Why, Marcus? Why not just let me go? Why not just find someone else who can make you happy?"

"Because I found her, you make me happy. You're a good woman, and I've always known it. My kids adore you, and the sex is off the chain. I don't know why I messed it up. I think I felt sorry for myself because business was slow; I wasn't making money like I used to make. I had you on one side saying, 'Get your ass out there and work harder,' which was what I *needed* to hear. I had her on the other side saying, 'You're the man, don't worry about it,' which was what I *wanted* to hear. I just got caught up. God, Charisse, if I could turn back the hands of time and start over again, I'd never hurt you. You have to believe me."

Sounded a lot like the truth, for a change. He should've figured it out *before* he kissed that heifer in my car.

"I know, Marcus, I mean wouldn't we all? Unfortunately, life doesn't always present us with chances for do-overs. Someday, I may get past this but I can't right now," I said. A sense of relief washed over me; the words had finally been spoken.

"So, what's up with you and old boy? Is he the reason you won't marry me?" Marcus had the nerve to suggest. It was clear the amnesia hadn't been completely cured.

"*No, you didn't.* Have you forgotten our break-up Marcus? Things between us went south long before I met him and you know that. I don't even know how you let that bullshit fall from your mouth."

His silence told me he'd finally acknowledged that truth. "So, what now?"

"Well, I'll go my way, you'll go yours, and in time, I guess we'll see if our paths lead us back to each other," I answered.

"Okay. I mean, if that's what you want," he said as he stood up to put on his jacket. "I need to say one more thing before I go."

"What's that?" I asked as Marcus grabbed me by both arms and stared into my eyes.

You'd better not ask for any goodbye booty, I thought.

"I love you, Charisse. I always will."

I escorted him to the door, hugged him goodbye, and watched as his headlights faded into the distance. Tears welled in my eyes at the thought that we might not ever be together again. My heart hurt, but the reality was that we had nothing if I couldn't trust him; it was that simple. Letting go had to be the right thing to do.

After taking a nice long hot shower and fixing a jumbo mug of Celestial Seasoning's Sleepytime Tea, I pulled another journal from underneath my bed and continued my relationship failure analysis. Talking to Nisey reminded me so much of my affair with Sean.

I only wished I could somehow convince her walking away was the right thing to do. Leaving a relationship with a married man wasn't always the easy thing to do, but without question, it was always the right thing to do, and you could never go wrong by doing the right thing.

It would've been easy for someone to tell me not to get involved with Sean, but the heart has a mind of its own. I've learned the hard way that the heart is an essential but *stupid* organ. It doesn't think, it doesn't reason, it doesn't rationalize, it doesn't contemplate, speculate, analyze, or deduce. The only things the heart does are feel, hurt, and break. That's it. Why any sane person would advise you to follow your heart, except to see you make piss-poor decisions and fail miserably at every relationship you ever attempt, is beyond me.

The truth of the matter was that if I could deign to control the circumstances that drew me to certain men, I wouldn't have been a bum magnet.

But, eventually, I took responsibility for my stupidity because the fact of the matter was that I could control whether I called, or saw, or screwed him. It's that simple. I didn't learn this lesson until a few years ago. Like all hard-headed, soft-assed women, I learned it the hard way.

So, during a conversation a few days after we had lunch, Nisey rehashed her relationship with Robert and, in excruciating detail, justified the relationship in her (delusional) mind. She requested my advice, and I summed up years of experience and knowledge into one word.

"Leave!"

"But Rissey, you don't understand. It's not all his fault. I stayed in the relationship too. You wouldn't say it's okay for him to hurt me, so why is it okay for me to hurt him?"

"Nisey, this isn't you talking. This is your hormones."

"It's not my hormones. It's me. You don't understand," she whined. Oh my God, there was nothing worse than a whiny forty-two-year-old woman with a hard head. I suddenly realized how she must've felt about dealing with *me* all those years.

"Okay. You're right Nisey, you're right. I've had a change of heart, shifted my position. I only have two words of advice." I paused for effect and then continued. "Leave *now*! Take it from me. If Robert wanted to leave his wife, he would have left skid marks on the floor of the so-called home he called a prison. It's as simple as that. He isn't shackled to the house like the dude on *Desperate Housewives*. He's a free-willed, philandering, want-to-have-his-cake-and-eat-it-too man."

"But Rissey—"

"Don't interrupt. Listen. Each day Robert stays with his wife is a day he has recommitted himself *not* to be with you. Period. Trust me, run fast, run far, and never look back."

She was in a difficult situation, but I had to be the same kind of friend and sister to her that she was to me when I played the fool.

After I settled in later that night, I took another deep dive into my journal. What a coincidence, Sean was next on the chopping block. I only hoped reminiscing about this relationship wouldn't prove to be as nightmarish in my sleep as it did in real life.

Nineteen

The Lion Pounces

February 7, 1996
I met a new guy today—Sean Grey, with E-Y. That's how he says it, so cute! Every time I look at him I get butterflies in my stomach. I haven't felt this way since high school. Who would've thought my bagel-a-day habit would lead me to the man of my dreams. He's handsome, intelligent, funny, and he can give me free food. He's the one, I'm positive.

***

On the "he's so fine" radar, Sean flew a tad below Lamar—but only a tad. He was the epitome of tall, dark, and handsome. He had the skin tone of Taye Diggs, finely-chiseled, model-esque facial features, and a smile fresh from a Crest commercial. He also had the boldness of a cunning lion in an urban jungle to boot. He preyed on me, and when I was most vulnerable, he pounced.

He caught me a few years after my break up with Lamar. I'd dated since, of course, but nothing serious. I wandered around unfocused, with my non-existent self-esteem and weak sensibilities. And like a clueless antelope grazing in the Savannahs, I left the scent of rejection and a perceptible desperation to be appreciated and loved, not even realizing he stalked me.

Sean emerged out of nowhere, sniffed out my emotional baggage, and sensed I was ripe for his pouncing. Under the pretense of being weak and wounded by his overbearing, under-caring wife, he wooed me with his sweet, empty words of love, admiration, and encouragement for the "wonderful, unappreciated" woman I was. At the end of the day, he feasted on me—an all too willing entrée.

He managed a little coffee shop I frequented when I worked in downtown D.C. A creature of habit and easily addicted to food (my crack), culinary experimentation was for food critics, not me; Italian food was the only exception. In my world, one could never go wrong with pasta and sauce, no matter the pasta, no matter the sauce.

Every day, I walked into his store at the same exact time and placed the same exact order: a cinnamon-raisin bagel with jelly and a hot chocolate. On the day we met, a short-staffed Sean helped on the cash registers, and I landed at his station.

"Good morning, ma'am, may I take your order?"

"Yes, I'd like a cinnamon raisin bagel with butter and jelly and a medium hot chocolate with whipped cream, please."

"I'm sorry we don't sell cinnamon-raisin bagels on Wednesdays."

"Huh?" I said as he waited for me to change my order. *Is today some weird religious holiday I forgot?*

He laughed. "I'm kidding with you, ma'am. Will that be all for today?"

I chuckled for a minute. "Okay, you got me. I thought 'what kind of dumb ass policy is that?'"

"You can pick up your order at the end of the counter but please wait for your receipt."

Wait for my receipt? Why doesn't he just stick it in the bag like they usually do? I walked to the end of the counter and picked up my order as Sean emerged from his office in the back of the store with a folded piece of paper in his hand.

"Here's your receipt. Have a pleasant day. Oh, by the way, my name is Sean, Sean Grey—with an E-Y."

"Okay, you too, Sean Grey—with an E-Y."

Why in hell would he take my receipt in his office? I thought as I exited the store. Did he need to print it on special paper? Recheck the math? I returned to my office, sat down at my desk, and pulled the slip from my pocket. The receipt contained a short note from you-know-who. It read, *You're beautiful. Please give me a call.*

Welcome to my nightmare. This is where it began.

Daily trips for breakfast expanded to breakfast, lunch, and sometimes dinner. Looking back on those days, the extra revenue was probably responsible for the store's expansion to K Street not long after we started "dating."

He treated me well in the beginning, like no man ever had before. He wined me, dined me, pampered me, paid people to pamper me, got my nails did, hair did, and he did me . . . and did me good too. We had the kind of sex that makes you ashamed to look at each other the next morning, that makes you scared to go church and confess your sins, the kind of sex that would make good fodder for a high-quality, homemade skin flick had we been so inclined—and had a fully-charged battery handy.

***

August 23, 1996
Sean and I are still going strong. He makes me perfectly happy . . . well, almost. I'm concerned that he's never invited me to his house. Every time I ask him if I can visit he blows me off or tells me he doesn't own any furniture. What do I care? We spend most of our time in the bed anyway. My spidey senses tell me something isn't quite right.

***

About six months into our so-called relationship, we took a trip on the Oddessy, a romantic night-time dinner cruise down the Potomac River. What a perfect night it was. The full moon illuminated the starry sky, and beams of light seemed to follow us as we danced outside in the spicy air.

We were both dreamy-eyed, cloud-hopping fools—well, make that singular. Only one fool was present—yes, that would be me. People stopped and smiled at us, said we were a beautiful, happy couple. I thought for sure we'd soon be engaged and ready to skip happily down the aisle to a life of never-ending bliss and off-the-chain sex.

"Charisse, I- I have something I'd like to talk to you about."
Ohhhh, this is it! He's going to propose. I just know it.
"What is it?" I said, caressing his face and stargazing in his eyes.
"Well, I just wanted to tell you how happy I am when I'm with you. I've never met anyone like you before. You're funny and understanding. You feel like home to me. I love you."
"I love you too, baby," I responded as I planted a gentle peck on his lips.

"I've been doing a lot of thinking, and I really think it's time to take our relationship to the next level."

Ohhh, here it comes.

"Will you. . . "

Say it. Say it.

"Will you. . . "

Come on, baby, tell mama what you feel.

"Will you give me a key to your condo?"

"Yes, yes. . . uhhhh, wait a minute." I said, pausing for a moment to reprogram. "Did you ask for a key to my condo?"

So close.

"Yes, a key, so I can come over whenever I want. I don't always want to wait outside for you to come home," he responded.

"Yeah, right. I think you want to scare away your competition."

"Do I have some?"

"Trust me, not in this lifetime. However, until I visit your house, you don't have a key either."

Most men who over-spoiled me were usually overcompensating for a pinky-sized dick, erectile dysfunction, or control issues. Sean didn't exhibit any of these issues early on—not to any alarming degree. So, I couldn't for the life of me figure out Sean's deal. The sex bordered greatness; he didn't act like intolerable asshole—although, like most men, he occasionally had his moments. The only time he raised his hand to me was to give me a pre-approved pat on the hinny, so what could the problem be?

Six months into our relationship, I found out.

Twenty

The Accidental Mistress

Nisey always asked me how I could not know for that long. I told her that his deception was a "convenient marriage" (no pun intended) of his crafty lies and my sublime ignorance. You know, when you suspect something is amiss but you don't know—and you don't *want* to know. And you don't want to let the sobering reality that the man you've fallen for is a deceptive bastard send you plummeting to earth from your lofty position on cloud nine. . . like a Boeing 747 jumbo jet with two busted engines and no parachute to break the fall.

We always met at my house. He said he didn't install a house phone and only used his cell phone. He frequently called me from home, probably when his wife worked or ran errands for a few hours. He covered the bases for as long as necessary—until my emotional attachment was such that I would not walk away when I learned the truth.

How did I find out? You'd think he'd *at least* have the decency— after six months—to make me beg him to tell me . . . or play charades . . . or something. Nope. No dramatic revelations, no extensive investigative operations, no stalking, no Google, no nothing.

I asked him and he told me . . . after *six* months.

"Charisse, I know I should've told you sooner but, after I got to know you, after I came to love you, how could I tell you the truth?"

"'Charisse, I'm married' would've sufficed. I'm usually pretty quick on the uptake."

"Sure, that's easy for you to say.

"It's easy for you to say too. You speak English as well as I do, most of the time."

"Charisse, why don't you try being stuck in a loveless marriage without the ability to see your way out, beyond the bills, the mortgage, and the kids? Now, I realize I never should have married her, but I didn't know love until I met you."

And there it was.

He had me at "until I met you." There were certain buzz words that appealed to most women, and any phrase that made us feel like we were one of a kind, one in a million, you know, special, we pretty much bit the bait.

Of course, he tacked on the old, "I'll understand if you walk away" at the end of his not-so-illustrious speech. But I'd bought the bill of goods, lock, stock, and barrel even though all of the above later turned out to be stone empty.

Like all rose-colored glass wearing mistresses, I had a glass-half-full optimism about Sean. His good wife wasn't leaving a bad husband; he was leaving a bad wife. It never occurred to me one woman's trash can be another woman's trash. While he was good to me in the beginning, nearly perfect in fact, I realized over time this Sean wasn't real. He *had* to play this role. It's hard to be an asshole and make someone fall in love with you, unless of course you were independently wealthy and could afford to purchase affection and loyalty with your platinum Visa card.

Let me phrase it this way, he managed *a coffee shop.*

Yeah, I was subjected to a performance of Shakespearean proportions.

***

September 3, 1996
I tried my best to break up with Sean today. I told him this, whatever we have, is against everything I was raised to know is right. He said okay and then stood outside my condo door for an hour singing "Because You Loved Me" in notes never meant for human ears. My neighbors called the cops on him though. Tough crowd.

***

Convinced he'd keep his promise to leave his wife, I stayed with him, but I suffered a major identity crisis as a result. No one gave me the mistress handbook. I didn't know a mistress was supposed to settle for substandard treatment. As a matter of fact, I fully expected to be treated like a real girlfriend; I expected all the perks, all the respect, all the time and effort. If he was going to pick someone who was going to offer him the path of least resistance, he should've picked someone experienced in the ways of "mistressing" because I was completely oblivious.

I didn't know I should only call when he left the house. I didn't know that spontaneously showing up at the store with a picnic lunch for us to eat on a nearby bench while we fended off overly-fed pigeons was off limits. I didn't know I should spend holidays sitting by the window hoping to see his car pull up in the driveway, as opposed to scheduling a full day of dining and forced merriment with my family. I also didn't know I wasn't supposed to get pissed if he didn't show up.

You know, someone needs to publish a handbook about these things because I couldn't be the only woman in the entire world duped into a relationship with a married man, who then remained too naïve to accept the second-class citizen, stepchild status. Others existed, I was certain of it.

Over time, I cut off communication with virtually everyone in my life except him, mostly due to guilt and shame. He became the center of my life, and I didn't think I could share our relationship with anyone without being called an idiot, fool, dumb ass, dumb bitch, stupid heifer—you know, all the synonyms for mistress. And let me tell you, if you're ever doing something inexplicably idiotic, you don't want Nisey for a friend. When she disagreed with your behavior or actions, she had a way of making stupidity both physically and emotionally painful.

"You know, Rissey, I think we should go out on a double date."

"Well, I don't think—"

"Ohhhhh, I forgot, you can't go because you're dating a cheater."

"Thanks, Nisey."

"You've been together for a while now, have you discussed marriage? Kids?"

"Well, I—"

"Ohhhhh, I forgot, he's already got a wife and kids, hmmmm, tough luck."

"Jesus, Nisey I get it."

"Do you? Do you get it? I know you, Rissey. I've known you since leg warmers were a major fashion statement, since the rise and fall of the

Yugo. This isn't the life that you want for yourself."

"You think I don't understand, Nisey? You think I don't want a husband and two and half kids, a house, two cars, and a dog? That's all I've ever wanted."

"Well, why in hell are you settling for less? Don't you think you deserve more because I do! Why do you do this to yourself? You get hung up in these relationships on a slow boat to nowhere. What I don't understand is why?"

Neither did I.

The thing is, she was right. I wasn't living the life I wanted to live. What Sean and I did was as wrong as two left shoes. Somehow staying with him seemed easier than not having anyone at all. And we'd moved beyond our trust issues. I already knew I couldn't trust him as far as I could throw him. I no longer needed to step out on faith and place my trust in him only to watch him disappoint me; he'd already let me down. And unless he reached some not yet discovered new low, we couldn't go any further into the muckety muck than we already were.

With someone new, I'd start up high again, I'd take the risk again, and I'd be vulnerable to the plummet. I hated the plummet. Nothing, in my mind, brought more disappointment than believing, trusting, and putting my faith in someone who let me down. That was a pain I'd felt too early in my life and far too often since.

So I stayed with him but not without making him miserable in the process.

"Swear, swear on the Bible that you're leaving."

"Charisse, baby, I'm leaving. I'm leaving, and it's not just because of you. I'm not—"

"I don't want to hear it. Put your hand on the Bible right now."

"Baby, why are you— Give me the damn thing," he said, snatching the Good Book from my hand and slapping it with his right palm.

"Go ahead, swear."

"Baby, I swear, with my hand on the Bible, I'll leave whenever the time is right. I'm not happy about this situation either. I want to spend my life with you, but we must wait. Think about the kids."

The kids . . . two little beings who held the cards to our collective fates.

The Bum Magnet

Whatever the consequences were for lying like a cheap rug while swearing on the Bible, I'm sure Sean suffered them in spades.

Twenty-One

Honeymoon's Over

After we emerged from the honeymoon phase—if that's what you call a honeymoon—the sob stories started. Not mine, his. I suppose his openness was a testament to the nature of our relationship. I mean, we had become good friends in addition to lovers. Our communication was excellent, with the obvious exception of his marital status.

Every time he visited me, he complained his wife accused him of cheating with another woman, and he had the nerve and the gall to be indignant about it.

"How dare she accuse me of cheating with my staff?"

I had to laugh because he sat with me, *his mistress,* relating how pissed he was his wife accused him of cheating. "Dear, I hate to break it to you, but you are cheating, remember?"

"Yeah . . . but with *you.*"

"And that makes it better how?"

"Because you and I are getting married, that's how."

"Well, why does she suspect you of cheating?" I asked.

"I don't know. She's crazy?"

Crazy, huh? All women are crazy . . . like foxes.

"I mean, I'm the store manager. The girl needs to call me," he continued.

"Uhn huh."

I wasn't the only one Sean had duped. No, he had been taken in by his own lies and deception. He didn't have a grip on his own reality, let alone the reality of our relationship. Meanwhile, the more he told me about his wife's suspicions, the more suspicious I grew. Her instincts were dead on because I represented at least one of the truths, but were there others? Did she know something I didn't? Or did she identify the wrong girl?

Soon after, our relationship went downhill. I couldn't trust him to volunteer the truth about anything—as they pertained to other women. So, I constantly questioned him about everything. It was like the inquisition on steroids and entirely his fault. The lesson I had learned from him? If I wanted to know the truth, I had to ask for it. He wasn't volunteering anything. So, I asked every question I could ask, all the time, for every stupid little thing.

"Why are you late, Sean? I've been waiting for over an hour. You couldn't call?" I'd asked for no good reason. I'd already come up with my own sordid conclusion.

"I had to work late," he responded.

"Work late? Since when do you work late?"

"Uhhhh, since you *met* me?"

"Okay, okay, who was there *with* you?"

"One of my staff."

"Male or female?"

"Female."

"Aha, your little girlfriend, huh?"

"She's sixty-two-years-old, Charisse."

"So you're into *older* women?"

"I'm going home."

"Ohhhh, need to get home to the wife, huh?"

"Listen, I want to be with you, but I hate jealous people and you're jealous. Every time I'm out of your sight, you think I'm out doing something wrong when I'm not. I'm here because I want to be here, not because I have to be. Stop acting so fucking crazy."

Oh, no he didn't. He used the "C" word—to me! No word will set a woman off like calling her crazy. We only acted "crazy" when we had to put up with men's bullshit. Talk about the straw that broke the camel's back; I jumped into his ass with both feet.

"Oh, wait a minute. You're right. How silly of me, what was I thinking? You're cheating on your wife, *with me* unless you forgot. Lying to her every time you leave to come here, and I should think you could never lie to me too? You're delusional. She suspects you're cheating with one of your staff, yet you want to get all self-righteous toward her because she got the wrong girl. I got news for you, you *are* cheating. So get off your high horse. I've got a newsflash bubba—I'm not jealous. I only want to know if you're playing games with me so I can leave your ass! If you don't like it, you can be gone."

He'd crossed the line, so he backed down with the quickness. He knew he'd better call me off the ledge or his little adulterous Camelot would come to a screeching halt.

"Calm down, Charisse, calm down. Just be easy, relax. I promise you, you're going to get everything you want. I'm going to leave and I'm going to be with you. You just need to give me a little more time."

Granted, I was paranoid, but I figured if he could cheat on his wife, he'd have no qualms about cheating on his mistress. What the hell was I going to do? Divorce him? Sue him for palimony? At the end of the day, I was no more than a piece of ass, devoid of power.

He continued, "I'll tell you what? Why don't we get out of here for a bit, maybe go grab a bite and hit Macy's. We can pick up the Coach bag I caught you eyeing the other day. Everything's gonna be fine, try to be patient. Please?"

There it was, the engine that made our entire relationship run. Anytime I got upset and ready to back out, he waved food and a shiny object in my face to distract me. I'll admit, it was pretty effective because when I got upset or stressed, like most women, I only wanted to shop and eat. My vices were Sean's enablers, but unfortunately, he wasn't the only one paying for it. I paid everyday, as little bits of my soul were chewed away, like it was infested with the termites of sin.

Anyone who sought out a relationship with a married man *must* be crazy. Being someone's mistress wasn't a life to choose, it was a life to lose.

***

November 1, 1996
Sean told me he was leaving his wife once the kids got out of school for summer vacation. I hope he keeps his word because he is coming real close to stepping on my last nerve. I love him and all, but sometimes he takes me

for granted, doesn't appreciate the things I do any more. If this is what marriage is like, I'd rather have a V8.

***

It was almost nine p.m. when I finally made it home. I'd been up since six a.m. and working since seven-thirty. I listed and installed signs on properties, showed fifteen houses—a personal best for a single day, wrote three contracts, attended one home inspection, and counseled one of my sellers on the ills of letting their dog Butch, which I not-so-affectionately nicknamed "Cujo: The Return," greet perspective buyers at the door bearing his fangs. I was exhausted, and though I hadn't eaten since breakfast, a hot bath and a good night's rest was all the nourishment I desired. As I walked into the bedroom of my old two-bedroom, third-floor condo located in Lake South, a "transitional neighborhood" (i.e., where black folks transitioned from ghetto to ghetto-fabulous), Sean called.

"Hey baby, what's for dinner? I'm on my way over."

"I'm exhausted Sean, it's been a long day. I haven't had time to cook anything. I walked in the door seconds ago," I said, kicking off my shoes and collapsing on the couch.

This is the part where my Prince Charming was supposed to tell me he was stopping by our favorite restaurant for carryout, right?

"Why not? You know I'm coming tonight?"

"Sean, I've been working all day."

"Working? You're a real estate agent."

"What the hell is that supposed to mean?"

"It means I'll be expecting dinner when I get to your house or else I'm going home."

Now, this is the part where Charisse—the bitch—who usually stayed buried, should have risen from her shallow grave, cussed his philandering ass out, and told him if he wanted dinner he should go home to Chez Wifey because cooking dinner is what she signed up for, not me. I, the mistress, was only with him to be spoiled and sexed into eternal bliss. Instead . . .

"Well, what do you want to eat? I don't know what to fix."

"You know what I like. Surprise me, baby."

In an instant, I'd relinquished my title as accidental mistress and became something a great deal more troubling.

Twenty-Two

The Alternate Wife

Sean had me right where he wanted me. Why did I put up with him? Because I had been duped, duped into believing that his wife prized him so dearly she'd employed the Kung Fu death grip to keep him from leaving; therefore, he was a valuable commodity that I must be petrified to lose if I didn't kill, humiliate, or exhaust myself attempting to satisfy his every need.

Meanwhile, Sean dangled the elusive carrot that promised my fairy-tale ending in which he would leave his wife and spend every waking moment of the rest of his life making me the happiest woman on the planet. Like a hapless bunny on a treadmill, I chased that damn carrot, always moving toward it but never getting close enough to eat it.

Oh, if that wasn't the all-time scam of the century, then I don't know what was.

Although the scam, in and of itself, was clever, something infinitely more sinister was afoot. Not only did slick Sean turn me into his mistress, before I knew it, I had evolved into the alternate wife.

"We never go out anymore. How about you peel yourself from the sofa, so we can go out for a night on the town, maybe dinner and a little dancing?" I asked Sean, who was watching a basketball game with his hand down his sweatpants . . . doing whatever men do when they stick their hands down their sweatpants.

"Baby, can't you see I'm watching the game? Let's go out some other time."

"Some other time? According to my calculations, this is some other time from the last time I asked you to go out and you said some other time."

"Okay, baby, you win. Can you hand me the TV guide, please?"

"What do you need a TV guide for?" I asked as I grabbed it from the end table and tossed it on his lap.

"I'm going to plan a date for us to go out. I need to make sure it's not a game night. See how much I love you?"

"You're kidding me right? You're going to plan our date around the NBA schedule?"

"Is that a problem?"

Aye yie yie.

Romantic, late-night dinners, dancing until three a.m., weekly just-because flowers, spur-of-the-moment getaways, and heart-stopping sex gradually and systematically transformed into routine honey-what's-for dinners, bi-annual Valentine's day and birthday because-I-have-to flowers, any-moment-now getaways, and heart-stopping sex—the one thing he didn't change. Shocker.

The worse part? His wife still had better benefits. His service to her was compulsory. His service to me? Voluntary. He didn't have to come home to me everyday—or make up a damn good excuse as to why not. He didn't have to check in with me to let me know where he was going or take out the garbage. He didn't have to mow the lawn (if I had one) or stop by the store to pick up an onion because I needed it to fix dinner. His credit rating wasn't tied to my mortgage. It didn't matter whether or not the electric bill was paid because he and I were usually in the dark anyway. He didn't have to do any damn thing he didn't want to do. I was on the bad end of a Nike commercial gone wrong—Just Do It . . . but only if you really, really want to.

And if I was disappointed, sad, mad, or pissed off, tough noogies for me. He didn't even have to endure my cranky face, pouty lip, teary eyes, or my highly-effective silent treatment. No, he could just go home to his wife and stay there until she pissed him off. By then, he knew I'd miss him so much that his wrong-doing would be forgotten, and I'd welcome him with open arms. Talk about the best of both worlds! And women wonder why men risk living double lives for so long.

"I miss you, baby. I hate it when we fight," Sean said after a particularly nasty argument when I'd threatened to leave him for the billionth time. Of course, he couldn't come and see me in person because he was "stuck" at home.

"Me too," I said.

"When we get married, let's promise never to go to bed angry."

"Okay, and let's also promise never to go to bed before hot make-up sex too."

"That's a deal," he responded and blew me a kiss.

"So, I guess you can't come out and play, huh?"

"No, my wife has some "thing" she wants me to attend with her."

"Some *thing*? What *thing*?"

"I don't know, some work function. It's for show, baby, so she can put on a good face for the partners at her firm."

"I'm sorry, wait a minute. *I'm* drowning in heartache because we can't be together and *you're* going on a date with *your wife*?"

"It's not a date per se. It's just a work function. Listen, I still live here. I can't just say no when she needs a favor."

"A favor, huh? Let me tell you what you can do with your favor! Stick it up your cheating black ass. It's over!"

Make that one billion and one.

Talk about rollercoasters. Every day, our emotions were up and down, up and down, mine were more down than up. But Sean's frolic through the meadow of infidelity didn't last forever. Why? This lifestyle had a few drawbacks too, the most important of which were the perpetual web of lies, cheating, and deception required to maintain it. No matter how Sean tried to conceal it, his wife and I were going to realize at some point that we only had half a man. He couldn't be everything he needed to be for everybody all the time. The only time a woman will ever settle for half of anything in a relationship is *after* the divorce.

***

December 22, 1996

I feel so ashamed, I can't stand it anymore. Damn Catholic guilt. I've always known I'd smolder in hell for every sin I ever committed, but adultery is a big one. I've sentenced my soul to eternal damnation, and for what? We're no closer to getting married now than we were the first day we met. Thank goodness my religion is sinner-friendly. As soon as I get the courage to go to confession and do my penance, I think I'll be okay. I wonder if God would be willing to hit the rewind button on my life. I could use a do-over.

***

It became harder and harder for Sean to make me believe he planned to leave and his wife believe he planned to stay. No man can promise polar opposites to two women with a modicum of intelligence—which I believe we both had despite appearances, come up empty-handed for months on end, and avoid the inevitable "blow up in your face" moment.

For Sean, his little world may as well have been 1945 Nagasaki.

"Charisse, did I tell you I have a business trip coming up tomorrow? I won't be here for your birthday next week. I promise I'll make it up to you when I get back, though," he promised.

"My birthday is tomorrow, and you told me you were going to take a trip, but you said you were going visit your mother. You said she was having some kind of in-and-out surgery."

"Your birthday's tomorrow? You mean, tomorrow, tomorrow?"

"Yes, the day after today—tomorrow."

"What were we planning to do?"

"You don't remember? Jesus, Sean, I can't believe you forgot. Sometimes I feel like I'm in this relationship by myself."

"Oh no, baby, don't say that. You know how busy I've been with work, managing the two stores and all. Refresh my memory."

"You said you were going to give me five hundred dollars so that I could have a full day of beauty at the day spa, then you were supposed take me out to Fogo De Chao's for dinner."

Fogo De Chao's, a fantastic Brazilian restaurant that served the finest cuts of all-you-can-eat meat, was the only place in the D.C. area where you could eat a cow for fifty-bucks.

"I said five hundred dollars? Uhhh, okay," he said as he reached in his wallet and pulled out the money. "Here you go baby. I want you to enjoy yourself and relax, but I'm not going to be able to take you to dinner. We'll do that some other time, if that's okay."

"That's fine."

"So, uhhh, which spa were you planning to go to?" Sean asked.

"I don't know. I thought about going to European Beaute."

"Oh, I wouldn't go to that one if I were you. I heard on the news that some women caught a virus because they didn't disinfect their spa areas."

"Really? It looks so upscale. I can't believe that."

"Trust me. You'll be better-off someplace else."

"Okay, I'll find another place. Thanks babe, you're so good to me."

Twenty-Three

A New Friend

Sean was a better man to me than he thought. Truth be told, my birthday was the previous month. Having an affair with a man who was tangled in a twisted web of lies he couldn't keep straight often had its perks. I'd already had three birthdays that year because he couldn't remember which day mine fell on. Because of my alternate wife status, birthdays were the only times he spoiled me. So, I claimed as many birthdays as I could get away with.

***

Of course, I ignored Sean's advice and hit European Beaute the next morning. The spa receptionist said she could squeeze me in if I arrived by nine. I'd driven by a gazillion times, but it seemed a bit too chic for my wallet.

I opened the door and crossed the threshold from Stressedville to Restville. It was absolute heaven, as glorious a place as I'd ever seen. The tension melted from my shoulders as soothing meditation music permeated the reception area. What was not to love? Five people would spend an entire day catering to my every whim. You couldn't even get that kind of service in a restaurant. Of course, Sean had paid a nice chunk of change, so it seemed worth every single one of *his* pennies. If I had to pay for it, I'd have been at home on the couch soaking my feet in the Dr. Scholl's foot bath Aunt Jackie bought me for Christmas six years ago.

The first stop in my spa day was the sauna; they said the steam helped open your pores for all the wonderful spa treatments. I entered the dressing room and noticed a woman gulping from a sterling silver flask. Envious, I wished I'd thought of it first. She was very pretty, about my complexion, but maybe ten fifty-dollar boxes of Godiva truffles smaller than me.

A few minutes later, I bumped into her again in the sauna. Tears streamed from her face, only slightly disguised by the sauna's steam. As I moved toward a bench opposite hers, she looked up and greeted me a slight grin and a feeble "hello." Then she sobbed like she'd just finished watching the *Bridges of Madison County* the day before her period.

I hoped she wasn't crazy. For some reason, I'd always attracted crazy people. Not eccentric crazy, but wear aluminum foil as a fashion accessory crazy. They always shared their life stories with me. Did I have an inviting demeanor or a friendly face? Perhaps. Although I had a deep-rooted fear that crazy people might just be naturally drawn to other crazy people, which would make *me* one of *them*.

Regardless, I didn't want to listen someone else's drama that day; I had enough of my own. If she could just keep her problem to herself, I only had ten minutes before my body scrub.

"You probably think I'm crazy, huh?"

Here we go.

"No, not at all. We all have our days. If you're stressed and upset, this is certainly the right place to be. Are you here for the full-day spa treatment?"

"Yeah, I think so. I don't know, I usually only come for manicures and pedicures. I figure they'll guide me around and kick me out when it's time to go."

"Yeah, just go with the flow."

I leaned my head back on the sauna wall and closed my eyes, hoping she would see I just wanted to meditate but no such luck.

"Don't mind my babbling; sometimes I find talking to complete strangers more comforting than talking to people I know."

I had no escape. I figured I'd better let her hurry up get her issue off of her chest so that I could enjoy peace and quiet sometime that day.

"Can I ask you something personal?" she queried.

"Sure, go ahead," I answered.

"Are you married?"

"No, sorry, I haven't had the *dis*pleasure."

She laughed. "Girl, you've said a mouthful. I'm going to give you a little bit of advice. If a man ever hoodwinks you into believing he wants to get married, and you even consider accepting his proposal, stop and go straight to your psychiatrist. Ask them to prescribe you something to cure stupidity, Prozac, Valium, morphine, anything."

I chuckled. "That bad, huh?"

"No, honey, it's much much worse, cheating bastard. Yesterday, I found out he's having *another* affair."

"Another affair? Oh no, how did you find out?"

"Well, it all started when our hospital bill for the baby arrived in the mail."

"Oh, you guys just had a baby?"

"No, we don't have any kids."

"Shit!"

"Umm hmmm. He knocked up one of the little cupcakes he manages. I want to ask him, 'Can you spell *P.O. Box?*' What a fucking moron."

"You must be devastated."

"More relieved than devastated. She's not the first; he's done it before," she said, leaning back against the wall, gazing upward as if she wished a hero would descend from the ceiling and rescue her from those pesky wedding vows. "We were so in love when we first got married, I mean head over heels. And we stayed that way for a few years, but over time I guess his love for me wore off, like headache medicine or suntan lotion. He started having affair after affair. I got tired, couldn't take it anymore, so I tried to cheat too. Couldn't go through with it though. For all of our big, fancy talk about being independent, modern career women, like the men we've emulated for so many years, they've still got one thing on us."

"What's that?"

"We still can't separate our pussies from our hearts."

"I know *that's* right."

"So many days, I've wanted to punch him in the face, you know, pluck his eyes out and flick them at the television. Hell, they spent more time on the plasma than they ever did on me anyway. He'd changed these past few weeks, though. He'd been on his best behavior, so I thought I needed to give it another try, give it my all. And now this. It's time to let it go, but I'm a little afraid of how he may react when I ask for a divorce."

"Whoa," I said, my mouth hanging open. "Honey, let me give you a hug. I see why you're crying. Jesus, I don't know what I'd do if I was in your position."

I walked over to her and put my arm around her shoulder, which only seemed to make her sob harder.

"It's going to be okay," I said. "I think you just have to listen to your heart, you know? I think you already know what you want to do. You're going to have to work up the courage to go through with it. And you're in luck, I know where you can find all the courage you'll ever need."

"Really, where? The Land of Oz?"

"No, not Oz, France. The glorious country where they make Grey Goose vodka. They export, you know. You can get yourself a thirty dollar bottle at the liquor store right down the street. Have a couple, no, four shots, call your husband, tell him you're too good for him and you're going to find someone worthy of you. Then tell him he can find what's left of his plasma on the front lawn next to the trash bags containing his clothes and get a good night's sleep. Everything will look better in the morning. That's my advice."

A laugh found its way through her tears. "Well, right now, it's better than anything I can come up with."

"Good, that's the plan," I said. "And I'll tell you what? I'll even treat for the Grey Goose. How about that? The store down the street delivers."

"Oh, I couldn't let you do that."

"I insist. I'm going to call and order a bottle for you and have them drop it off at the front desk."

"You know, you are an absolute angel. I really mean that, geez. I feel like I've known you forever, and I don't even know your name."

"I guess we haven't been formally introduced, I'm Charisse Tyson," I said, extending my hand.

"Hi, Charisse, I'm Stacy, Stacy Grey, with an E-Y," she said.

Did she say 'with an E-Y?'

She continued, "I don't know why I say that all the time. Something I picked up from my husband."

Oh my God, it's Sean's wife!

Twenty-Four

Dinner for Two

I'd always pictured Sean's wife looking like the Wicked Witch of the West, you know, only black. But she looked human, like me. What had I done? All I could think was, *Sweet Jesus almighty, please get me out of here.*

"Mrs. Grey," one of the attendants called, peering into the sauna door. "It's time for your body scrub."

Hallelujah!

"Well, Stacy, it's been good meeting you, and don't forget about your Grey Goose."

"Enjoy your day, Charisse, I hope we'll talk later. Maybe we can get together and do lunch? I'll leave my number with the receptionist."

Slowly, it sank in. *That bastard!* He'd been cheating with someone else all long, I mean besides me. Claiming he couldn't leave because of kids and they don't even exist. I sensed he might be lying, but to hear it from his wife? I knew at that moment fate led me to the spa for a reason.

Well, that was five-hundred dollars up in smoke, renewing my thankfulness that I didn't pay for my day of beauty. I couldn't even think about relaxing after that little development. I shriveled into a big ball of stress. Not even the one hour, therapeutic, Swedish and deep-tissue massage could loosen the knotted ball of ligaments I once called muscles. I was so tense that if I ate flour and eggs, I'd shit linguine.

At that moment—the moment at which I could attach a face to the anonymous persona he called wife—our relationship ended. It was one thing for him to have an affair on his wife, whom I could imagine was ball-busting shrew. It was quite another to meet her, see that she was as human as I, and actually think she was pretty nice as far as wives went. But it was another thing altogether for Sean to have an affair on me *and* her. Even a damned-to-hell mistress had to draw the line somewhere.

I picked up Stacy's phone number from the front desk and left the day spa, dazed, confused, and in desperate need of a bottle of Grey Goose myself. I should've ordered two. Didn't matter, I popped in the liquor store on my way home. While I stood at the cash register, Nisey called.

"You'll never guess what happened to me today," I said, feeling a bit despondent.

"I can't imagine too much interesting would've happened at the day spa, unless, of course, you had a male masseuse."

"Oh, if only. No, I made a new friend today."

"That's nice. Who?"

"Sean's wife."

"Sean's what!"

"Yeah, you heard me, Sean's wife, as in ball-and-chain, entitled-to-half wife."

"Oh shit, what happened? What was she like? She didn't know you, did she?"

"No, she cried because she found out Sean got one of his employees pregnant," I said.

"Shut up!" she yelled.

I explained that I advised her to throw his shit on the front lawn and leave him.

"Let me get this straight, you gave her advice on how to break up with Sean, the man that you've been having an affair with."

"Oh, and you're never going to believe this. He doesn't even have kids . . . well except the one with his employee."

"Ain't *that* a bitch? Well, he's going to come racing to you when she breaks it off. What are you going to do, Ms. Clean-up Woman?"

"Break it off before he gets his feet in the starting block."

"When?"

"I think I'll break it off over dinner . . . son of a bitch."

I avoided Sean's twice-daily phone calls and pop-up booty calls for the next week, barricading myself in the house like a band of Jehovah's witnesses were stalking me. I wanted him about as much as I wanted the chicken pox. But once I worked out my plan, I called him.

"Where've you been all week? I've been calling you like crazy, even stopped by your house a couple of times," Sean said.

"I've just been busy, Sean, working hard, even though I'm only a Realtor."

"Are you seeing someone else?"

"Don't be ridiculous, no. But I have been doing a lot of thinking. Can we meet for dinner? My treat."

"Your treat? This is a first. What's the occasion?"

"I want you to know under no uncertain terms where you stand with me," I said with a little extra sugar in my voice.

"Awww, baby. You're so sweet. Where do you want to meet?"

"How about M&S Grill on 13th Street? Say six o'clock tomorrow?"

"It's a date."

"Be there or be square."

***

I arrived at the restaurant at five o'clock as scheduled and got our table. The waiter delivered my Grey Goose and cranberry juice while I anticipated the evening's festivities. Just as my relationship with Sean had been my first affair, so would our dinner be the first of its kind. I'd finished downing my drink when my guest approached the table.

"Stacy, it's so good to see you again. Have a seat."

"I'm so glad you called. I hoped we'd stay in touch. And honey, you couldn't have called at a more perfect time. So much drama at home," she said.

"Oh, wow. So, how are things? You and your husband working things out?"

"I wouldn't say working things out. I'm trying to leave, and he's begging me to stay."

"Is that right? Well, it must be nice to be in the driver's seat," I replied. My words still hung in the air when I noticed Sean walk in the door carrying a bouquet of roses—just in time for Stacy to catch his glance.

"Oh my God . . . there's my husband. Right there, the one with the roses. Who the hell is he meeting?" she asked, waving him over to the table.

Let the games begin.

Sean avoided my eyes like a direct view of the sun as he made the long ass death row trek from the door to our table. By the time he reached us, beads of sweat had emerged from his forehead like perspiration pox; one dangled from the tip of his nose, holding on for dear life.

"Sean, this is my friend, Charisse," Stacy said. "She and I met at the day spa you treated me to last week."

"Oh, is that right? Nice to meet you, Charisse," Sean said, squinting his eyes at me as if trying to squeeze daggers from his pupils.

"Oh no, the pleasure's all mine," I said, bearing my fangs through a cheesy smile. "You know, you kind of look familiar. Have I seen you somewhere before?"

The dangling sweat bead lost its grip and cascaded toward the table.

"No, I don't think so," he said, still avoiding eye contact. "I think I have one of those faces."

Yeah, one of those cheating, lying son of a bitch faces.

"So what . . . or should I ask *who* brings you here?" Stacy asked. "And why are you sweating? It's not even hot in here."

"I, uhhh, I called your office, and they said you'd be here. I wanted to stop by and bring you some flowers. I decided to walk over from the restaurant, guess I got a little warm."

Stacy paused and scanned the restaurant. "My office, huh? Well, thank you. I'll take those," she said as she extended her open hand toward him.

"Well, I'm going to leave you two to your dinner. Sorry to interrupt."
Bastard.

"Oh, please, Sean, any husband of Stacy's is a friend of mine. Stay and have dinner with us," I said, dying to see the snake give one last squirm.

"No, no, I should get back to the store. It was, uhhh, nice meeting you though," he said, waving us both goodbye.

Stacy turned to me. "He's such a liar. I haven't even been in the office today. I wonder who he really came here to meet."

Whistle, whistle, whistle.

Sean knew I meant business. He didn't attempt to contact me again until years later and then only to ask for my friendship.

The Bum Magnet

So, my relationship with a married man didn't end in my favor. Rewind, I should take that back. The affair ended in my favor because he *didn't* leave his wife, not voluntarily anyway. The beauty of hindsight? After all was said and done, after I finally found the strength to walk away from that hopeless situation, my rose-colored glasses disappeared to expose all of Sean's flaws. He no doubt would've cheated on me the same way he cheated on Stacy, and I'd have been the one trying to find the strength to leave. Upon that revelation, I fell to my knees and thanked God that I narrowly escaped his wife's hell on earth before I was stuck with him myself.

Just because things don't work out the way you hope, doesn't mean they haven't worked out in your favor.

Twenty-Five

Kiss My Bumper

My cell phone rang incessantly. How I longed for the days when people hung up if you didn't pick up after three rings. When the cell phone stopped ringing, the house phone started. I groped my nightstand in the darkness to find the digital clock. Although the time was obscured by strands of my hair, which cascaded over my eyes like a mop, it *looked* like the time read six-thirty. *Who would be crazy enough to call me at this hour?* I looked at the caller ID. *It figures.*

"Heifer, do you know what time it is?" I asked, my voice sounding like Barry White on estrogen.

"I'm the worst friend in the world," Nisey said.

"Yeah, you are. Help me understand why you felt it necessary to remind me at *six-thirty* in the morning?"

"Rissey, you had news to tell me the other day, and I didn't even take time to listen to your drama. I feel so bad. So wake the hell up and tell me what's going on."

"Oh . . . yeah," I grunted as I stretched and yawned.

I wished I had my laptop so I could Google instructions on how to make my phone spontaneously combust if it ever again rang before seven a.m. I pulled myself up, leaned against the headboard, and searched through my grogginess for anything resembling the English language.

"Where to begin? Well, for starters, Marcus asked me to marry him," I announced, using my fingers to comb my hair back out of my eyes.

"What?! Are you shittin' me? What was he smoking?"

"Yeah, the day before yesterday he saw Dwayne kiss my hand in front of the office, and I guess it dawned on him that he really isn't the only man on earth."

"Whaaaaat? So, when's Dwayne getting out of the hospital? And more importantly, when's Marcus getting out of jail?"

I chuckled as I got out of bed and started perusing the closet for the day's outfit. "You're crazy girl. As much as I hate to disappoint, nobody went to blows. I think the only thing bruised was Marcus's ego."

"You didn't accept, did you?"

"Well, I almost did," I said, grabbing a navy Kasper pant suit from the closet. I promptly returned it when I remembered how big it made my ass look.

"Okaaay . . . what were you smoking?"

"I was over Dwayne's when some woman left a messaging saying, and I quote, 'We're pregnant.' Turned out, she's his half sister from Chicago; she and her husband had been trying for a couple of years."

"Hmmm, I see. You believe him?" she queried.

"Why, you don't?" I said, refusing to be swayed into doubting my way-too-hasty relationship.

"I'm just saying, isn't it you who always says, 'Trust, but verify'?" she asked. Why she only remembered the sensible stuff I said was really irksome. Nisey really had a knack for asking the right questions at the wrong time.

"I'm trying to turn over a new leaf. Spying only wastes time and breeds mistrust. I want to give someone a fair chance for a change, you know?" said the naïve fool—yes, that would be me.

"Okay, if you say so," she paused, "Well, how about you give me his information and let me check his ass out? I ain't turning over new shit; the old leaf suits me just fine."

"No, Nisey, at least not yet. Let's give the man a chance.Besides, I didn't even get to tell you the good part. After I heard the message, I left his house and didn't show up to work for the next two days. Since he couldn't reach me, he went to the county land records, got my address, and showed up at my front door. Can you believe he went through that much trouble?" I asked, still in a bit of disbelief myself.

"As a matter of fact, no, I can't. Something ain't right. He's only known you five minutes. Why would he go through that much trouble?"

"Two words: good pussy," I responded. In matters involving men, sex, money, and food were usually among their top three motivations for doing anything.

Nisey laughed. "Okay, okay, excellent point. So, you're going to kick it with Dwayne for a minute huh? What are you going to do about Marcus?"

"I mean, why should I go back with him after everything that happened? We decided last night that it was time for us to part ways and see where time takes us. Who knows what'll happen from here."

"How do you feel, I mean, really feel? Three years is a long time."

"I cried, of course. We went to our relationship funeral last night and buried it. Part of me will mourn for a little while, the other part will move on."

"I bet. It's gonna be okay though, sooner than later. So, is that all? Or do you have more news to share?" Nisey asked.

"I've got more," I said. "Are you sitting down?"

"Yeeaaah," she hesitated.

"Guess who I ran into at the Pasttime the other day? Here's a hint- hazel eyes."

She paused for a moment. I could almost hear the squeaky gears turning in her head. "Oh my God, Lamar Jackson!"

"Yeah, girl, the one and only. He's as fine as ever, and he's an attorney now. Not much changed since college, at least not until recently. He says he's trying to get his personal life together, even goes to church. And get this? He's been celibate for three years."

"Hold up, Lamar is *celibate*? We better bundle up because hell probably froze over. I can't even believe that. His ass was probably tired from all that sleeping around in college. His dick was probably like, 'I quit!'"

I chuckled. "And guess what else? He's got *eight* kids."

"Dayyum, that's like an African tribe."

"Yeah, that's what I said. He alluded to something that makes me think he knows it was me, you know, when all that shit went down in school. Surprise, surprise, he still wants to be friends, though."

"Well, you did a job on him, but he had it coming."

"Yeah, he said as much."

"So, is that all the news? I've got to pee but I'll hold it if you've got some more juicy tidbits."

"No, that's all from the peanut gallery. You go pee."

***

I got dressed, jumped in the car, and headed into the office. Dwayne settled his decision on the Fort Washington house with the mega basement, and we were scheduled to sign his contract. For some reason, traffic on Lottsford Road, high-and-mightyville's main thoroughfare, was inching along. I was a bit annoyed but it gave me the chance to think about what was next in my life post-Marcus.

I hadn't spoken to Dwayne in a couple of days, still felt a little sad about Marcus, but I thought our meeting that day might mark a new beginning. Perhaps Dwayne and I hadn't started on the right foot, but it was still early enough to get things on the right track if we wanted a relationship that consisted of more than a series of one-night stands.

No more bouncing from one relationship to another, I thought. No more sleeping together too soon and watching it crumble a few months later, after we realized we didn't take enough time to get to know one another. I thought about the article, "Take a little time off from dating . . ." Well, we couldn't turn back time, but it wasn't too late to take a step back.

I decided to ask Dwayne if we could put the sex on ice, take some time to get to know one another, and dare I say, date and talk. I figured if he opposed then I'd know what he wanted from me and I could keep on keepin' on. If he agreed, however, we would have a better relationship—or at least we could avoid wasting our time pursuing the wrong person. Filled with a sense of pride,

I took my decision as a real sign I was trying to change my bad habits.

My mind drifted to visions of Dwayne and me in non-sexual bliss, taking long walks in the park, dancing in front of the fireplace, and kissing in his new hot tub. I smiled from my imaginary fulfillment, when Bang! My Beemer thrust forward ten feet, just missing the Jaguar in front of me. My chest hit the steering wheel just before the seatbelt locked, jerking me back against the seat and jarring my head and neck. I was so deep in thought it took me a moment to comprehend what happened.

I've been rear ended.

Twenty-Six

North Carolina's Finest

J ust as I turned to open the car door, a handsome but concerned face appeared in my window.

Dwayne who? Hello, Daddy, come to mama!

"Hi, are you okay?" the friendly hunk asked. He tugged on the handle, trying to open the door for me. His warm smile helped ease my concerns that he might be a nutcase trying to attack me.

"I think so," I responded, yelling so he could hear me through the glass. I took a moment to collect my thoughts, unlocked the door, and stepped out to survey the damage.

Wow, he's tall, he's handsome, I thought as my eyes roamed first his body and then the car. My Beemer's butt looked like it had been hit by a truck—because it had. But my car fared a touch better than the front end of his Range Rover.

Oh great, he's taken!

I spotted an attractive, chesty, high-yellow black woman with long flowing hair behind the heavily-tinted glass on his passenger side. You know, every man's dream and every average-looking woman's nightmare. She appeared to look as annoyed as I felt. I waved her hello, but she didn't respond in kind, just rolled her eyes and looked into the distance.

Bitch.

See? They always get the nicest men.

"Are you sure you're okay? I feel terrible. I thought I was stepping on the brake and I must've hit the gas instead. It happened so fast I couldn't stop."

"Maybe you should think about labeling your pedals," I joked.

He chuckled. "Maybe you're right. Can I do something to help you?"

"Oh, I think I'm okay, it could've been worse. I guess we should probably exchange information," I said, digging in my pant pocket for a business card. Of course, when I needed one, I never had them on me.

"I can call emergency. Do you think you'll need an ambulance?" he asked as he started to dial 911 on his cell.

"Ummm, no, I don't think that'll be necessary. I do think I need to sit down for a second. Maryland is a no-fault state; the police wouldn't even take a report for something this minor," I said. I walked back to the driver's side and sat with my feet hanging outside the doorway. The pain in my chest from the steering wheel was piercing, but I figured it would go away in a day or two, nothing was broken; I was just shaken up. The towering, linebacker-shaped stranger with soft eyes and an inviting smile approached me wielding a sheet of paper and slipped it on my dashboard.

"You're sure you're okay?" he said, looking into my eyes intently.

Do people still swoon? I wanna swoon.

See, Charisse? That's why your life is a big fat mess now. He's got a woman. Let it go.

"Yes, I'm fine, just a little shaken up."

"What's your name, if I may ask? I'm Kevin, Kevin Douglass," he said, extending his massive hand. I looked down. *Hmmm . . . big feet too. Careful Charisse, he has a girlfriend.*

"Hi, Kevin, I'm Charisse. I would say it's nice to meet you but given the circumstances I'm sure you'll forgive my manners," I responded, extending my hand in kind.

"Uhh, yeah, consider yourself forgiven. Do you want to have your car towed? I have a friend who owns a shop not far from here."

"Wow, that's so nice of you but I think my car is drivable. My insurance will pay for my rental until I get it fixed. I probably need to get one sooner than later, my job depends on it."

"What do you do?" he asked.

"I'm a real estate agent. I was on my way to work and—. Oh my God, I almost forgot. I should call my client and let them know I'm going to be late," I said, slapping my forehead in disbelief. I forgot about Dwayne, but looking at Kevin it was easy to see why.

"Do you have a card?" he asked.

"Sure. If you'll excuse me for one minute, I'll make this quick, and I'll grab a card out of my glove compartment."

Kevin stepped next to his truck and spoke to the woman while I called Dwayne and told him what happened. Dwayne offered to pick me up but I told him not to bother, that I'd meet him at the office in an hour or so. As I reached to grab a few business cards, I noticed Kevin watching me; it seemed more out of concern than nosiness. His eyes fixed on me like he was trying to stare the pain away, which only seemed to add to the woman's aggravation.

"Here you go, some of my business cards," I said, my arm outstretched. When my hand touched his, a faint tingle stirred through my fingers, as if I'd been touched by a low-voltage tazer.

"I can't apologize enough. I know this will be a huge inconvenience for you. I'll do anything I can to help the process go as smooth as possible. You have my phone number and insurance information, right?"

"Yes, I've got it. I have to say I've never been rear ended by someone so gracious. People around here would usually curse you out for being in the way. You *can't* be from this area," I said as I smiled and walked toward my driver's door.

"No, I'm from North Carolina."

"Ohhh, that explains it. My family's from down there."

"Yeah, I know . . . I mean, it seems like everybody has family down there."

"I lived in Winston Salem for a couple years myself when I was much younger. Very nice people."

"Yeah, very nice. Well, take care and please call me if there's anything I can do," Kevin said as he waved goodbye.

***

Dwayne was waiting for me when I arrived at the office. He gave me a hug, then walked with me out to my car to inspect the damage. It amused me when the men in my life, who usually had the mechanical knowledge of a phone book, inspected cars like they had the remotest clue of what they hell they were looking at.

"How do you feel? Are you okay?" he asked.

"I'm a little sore, but I'm okay otherwise. I'm in one piece," I replied, wincing while I rubbed my chest. My brain and body were so not in sync.

"Well, I think you should go to the doctor. I've been in an accident before, and the real pain usually doesn't kick in until a few hours later. Judging by the damage, you'll probably be ready to offer your first born for a prescription-strength painkiller or muscle relaxer in the morning."

"You think so?" I asked. The thought of drugs had become more pleasing by the minute.

"I know so," he responded. "Give your doctor a call and see if you can get an appointment. You might want to call an attorney too. Dealing with the insurance companies can be more painful than whiplash, and the lawyer won't get paid unless you do. I'll come by your house and tuck you in later. I've got problems to deal with at the work site."

He always seemed embroiled in problems at the work site. I wouldn't say it to him, of course, but from what I'd seen, I wouldn't hire him to work on *my* house. Hell, I wouldn't hire him to build a dog house.

"Okay, I'll do that. But let's go ahead and get your contract signed and faxed first. I want to make sure you don't lose that house."

Dwayne's concern was comforting, even if a bit disappointing. It had been ages since I'd had a man even pretend to care about my well being, but I was kind of bummed that he didn't offer to go with me to the doctor. That gesture would've been "above and beyond"; Dwayne's effort had only reached "close and not quite."

I got back into my busted Beemer and started for George Washington Hospital which was on the lower northwest end of the city. I had a little bit of a hike to the primary care facility, but every kind of doctor one ever needed practiced medicine on one of its eight floors; it was a convenient, one-stop medicine mall.

I spoke with the nurse on the way; she said she'd squeeze me into the schedule, but I would have to wait. When I walked into the waiting room, I was surprised to see a familiar face.

Twenty-Seven

Chance Meeting

"Hi, Kevin?"

He was reading the Sports Illustrated Swimsuit Edition, so he didn't even notice me approaching. "Well, well, well, imagine meeting you here," I continued.

He looked up and hardly blinked, seemed much less surprised to see me than I was to see him, "Hey, Charisse, right?"

"I'm the woman who's going to sue you for everything you own, and you have to guess? How soon we forget. I see you're deeply engaged in some stimulating, intellectual reading. I'm sorry to interrupt," I said, occupying the empty seat next to him. The waiting room was packed with patients that looked to be in far worse condition than me. I settled back in my seat with an ancient copy of "Good Housekeeping" magazine and continued to chitchat.

He laughed. "Oh, this thing? I only read it for the articles."

"Yeah right, name one," I demanded.

"Uhhhh . . . Let's see . . ."

"Let me help you out, how about the one that starts thirty-eight, twenty-four, thirty-six, five feet eleven inches, one-hundred twenty pounds."

"Ohhh, you read it too?" he said, laughing like a mischievous ten-year-old.

"Was that supposed to be funny?" I deadpanned.

"I . . . I didn't mean to offend—" Kevin started.

"You didn't," I interrupted, flashing a wide grin. "I'm kidding. And you're easy. So what brings you here? Are you getting healed up so you can rear end another poor, unsuspecting driver?" I asked. Kevin was so easygoing, far more down-to-earth than I'd expected from a man married to an evil diva. We joked like old friends.

"Ouch, that hurt."

"I wouldn't go there if I were you," I said, dramatically rubbing my chest to make him feel guilty.

"You sure know how to make a guy feel bad. Is everything okay? Earlier you said you were a little sore."

"Yeah, I still am, but the pain is starting to intensify a bit. My, uhhh, guy friend told me that I might need some prescription-strength painkillers before morning."

"Boyfriend?"

"Aren't we nosy?" I responded. He had a lot of nerve for a married guy. But I figured he'd begun to feel at ease with me, just as I had with him.

"Not nosy. Just making conversation."

"Well, I guess you can say I'm between boyfriends right now. But I do have a . . . friend," I said, watching for his reaction. When someone said they had a "friend" in this day and age, you could pretty much add "with benefits" by default.

"I see. What's his name?" he asked. He spotted the skeptical arch that appeared in my eyebrow, reflecting my discomfort from his overly-curious probe. "I told you, I'm not being nosy just making conversation."

"Oh, okay. Well, his name is Dwayne since you must ask."

"Dwayne, huh? How long have you two been kickin' it?" he asked, apparently not knowing when to stop. I almost felt like I was being interrogated.

"Not long, a few weeks I guess. So, where's your wife?" I asked, shifting the probe to his life and out of mine.

"My wife?"

"Yeah, the woman that was in your truck earlier"

"Ohhhh, no, we're not married."

Ahhh, his girlfriend.

"She seemed a bit upset. Hope she's doing okay."

"Oh, she's fine. She and I'd had a long night. I think she just needed some caffeine. You know how the coffee fiends are, cranky when they need a fix."

"So, what's wrong with you anyway? Why are you here?" I asked, changing the subject to more neutral ground.

"I'm a little sore, thought I should get checked out. Besides, I'll use any excuse not to go to work."

"Oh, I see, a slacker too. What do you do?" I said, leaning forward to grab a magazine from the paltry selection sprawled across the table in front of us.

"I'm an FBI agent."

"No, seriously, what do you do?"

"I'm serious. I'm an FBI agent, been with the Bureau for twelve years."

"Is that right? Wow, a black FBI agent? You guys must be enigmas like the Loch Ness monster or Big Foot; sightings are probably very rare," I said, realizing why I felt like I was being interrogated. He was federal five-oh.

He laughed. "I've never heard it put quite that way before but I suppose there is a little truth to it."

"So, are you packin' heat?" I whispered.

"Yes, but don't say that too loud. There might be a stampede if people know there's a black man with a gun in here," he replied.

"Ahhh, duly noted," I laughed.

Kevin and I huddled together in the "bad kid" corner while onlookers giggled at our shenanigans. We had slipped into comfortable conversation about everything and nothing for about an hour before a nurse came out and called my name. I thought that was peculiar since Kevin had been waiting before me. I turned to him and extended my hand.

"Well, I would say it's nice seeing you again, but uhhhh, under the circumstances . . .," I said.

"Hope you feel better," he said.

"Same to you."

I disappeared through the double doors leading to the examination rooms and didn't see him again.

He was kind of nice and seemed well-mannered, funny, handsome and had a good job—of course he's taken. I thought, *Here I go again!* I'd been dating Dwayne who was perfectly single, so was Lamar for that matter. Yet, I couldn't stop myself from crushing on Kevin, the taken one. *Why?*

Why am I always attracted to unavailable men? Emotionally unavailable, physically unavailable, the more they shut me out, the more I wanted in. If only I could flip a switch and turn that shit off.

Besides, the notion that I, Charisse Tyson, could possibly meet two eligible men inside the same year would have a probability somewhere along the lines of a virgin birth, and since Jesus had already been born—girlfriend or no girlfriend—the chance that Kevin could me my next "the one" was slim to none.

He didn't seem all that interested in me anyway, a little overly curious maybe but nothing in a romantic sense. So I pushed him out of my mind and returned my thoughts to the man of the hour—Dwayne.

***

Dr. Jenkins prescribed me a Flexerill, Vicodin, and Motrin cocktail, which I filled at the Rite-Aid before I headed home. I'd always been skittish about taking too much medication, a feeling exacerbated by the bright yellow stickers on the bottles that read "Warning! May Cause Extreme Drowsiness. Do not take with alcohol. Do not operate heavy machinery." I resolved not to take them unless absolutely necessary. A warm bubble bath and some Grey Goose would be just as effective. As I pulled into my driveway, Dwayne called. His voice sounded agitated like he was stressed about something.

"What's going on? You don't sound like yourself," I asked.

"Oh, baby, it's just business. I had some problems with a client on the site today. She was a pain in the ass, but as you know, the client is always right."

"What was the problem?" I asked. Dwayne had more complaining customers than a crooked used car salesman.

"I don't want to talk about work right now. How did your doctor appointment go? Is everything okay?"

"Yeah, I'm fine. He prescribed me a bunch of stuff to knock me out, but I'm not for taking all this medicine at once, I figure a nice hot bath and some Grey Goose will do me just fine."

"Well, don't make a move. I'm on the way. I'll join you and give you a nice rubdown before you go to sleep."

"Okay, but listen, Dwayne, I need to talk to you about something important when you get here," I said. Hated to be a wet blanket given his

142

already sour mood, but if I didn't have "the talk" then, I probably never would.

"Concerning what?" he asked, shuffling papers in the background. He still seemed distracted and mildly aggravated by whatever business crises he'd become embroiled in.

"You and me," I responded, not quite able to bring myself to say "*us*." He and I didn't feel like an "*us*."

"My favorite topic. It's not bad, is it?"

"Well, I don't think so, but you might."

"You're not leaving me already, are you?" he asked. The papers quieted and he pushed out a long breath.

"No, nothing like that."

"Good because it's too soon."

"Too soon? What does that mean?"

"It means you should at least make me wait until after the honeymoon."

"Cute, real cute."

Twenty-Eight

Trouble at Home

Neck deep in bubbles and hot water, I didn't have much longer before Dwayne arrived. I thought it might be a bad idea to be butter-ball naked while convincing him of the benefits of nixing the sex so we could get to know each other better.

Reflecting on my crazy day, I thought Dwayne's idea about getting an attorney to deal with the insurance companies seemed like a good one. They were a hassle I didn't want to have to deal with, and I knew just who to call. I eased out to of the tub, slipped in my birth control pajamas, grabbed my cell phone, and stretched out on the chaise.

"Hi, Lamar, it's Charisse, how are you?"

"I've been thinking about you today. I'd planned to give you a call later."

Thinking about me?

"Oh, really. What's up?"

"Well, I was going to ask if you wanted to attend church with me in a couple of weeks. The Single's Ministry is sponsoring a dinner. I thought, with all the drama going on, you might need some spiritual uplifting. You interested?" he asked. *Spiritual uplifting.*

"Very. But you don't go to one of those churches where they make the visitors stand up, do you? I hate that," I asked. The mere thought of all those praying eyes focused on me made me cower in fear. Hey, I'm a "people" person, I'm just not an *"a lot* of people" person.

"No, you don't have to stand up if you don't want to."

"Okay, I'm in," I agreed as it dawned on me that Lamar was the first man to invite me to attend church. I'd never had a relationship founded on a common relationship with God. God had certainly been missing, but He'd never exactly been invited in either. Maybe Lamar's invitation was a sign.

"Great. Now, you had something to tell me before I cut you off."

"Yeah, well, I was in a car accident today. I was wondering if you can refer me to an attorney that handles personal injury cases. I don't feel up to haggling with the insurance companies."

"First of all, are you okay?"

Awwww, such concern.

"I don't feel too bad right now, although the pain seems to be getting progressively worse. My chest hit the steering wheel a bit before the seatbelt locked, so I got jerked around a bit."

"Wow, they must've hit you pretty hard," he said. "Yeah, I'll be happy to refer you to Jerry, another attorney in my firm. I'd take care of you myself, but I practice family law."

"Okay, sounds good."

His office line rang.

"Oh, I have a call coming in. I've got to take this, but I'll be in touch before our church date."

Date?

***

Just as I hung up the phone, the doorbell rang. In true Dwayne fashion, his half-hour arrival mushroomed to an hour. He came in, made himself comfortable, and asked me to sit on his lap and tell him what was on my mind. Truth be told, my feelings were conflicted—about Dwayne, Marcus, and Lamar. And I hadn't given myself time to sort them out. I hadn't given myself time to work on emptying my emotional baggage either—and the heaviness of my soul weighed me down. Sex just complicated everything. I believed that if I could just remove the sex complication, I could gain some clarity and sort the rest of my issues out. It would be *that simple*. I had no idea that I'd only scratched the surface.

"Here's the thing, I really like you, Dwayne, a lot. I'm happier than I've been in a while, but I think we may have moved a little too fast. I was hoping we might slow things down just a tad, you know," I said, biting my lip as he processed my proposal. Then it hit him.

"Slow things down? You don't mean the sex do you?" he asked, looking at me as if I'd asked for his kidney.

"Well . . ."

"Why?" he asked, his voice reflecting his twisted facial expression.

"I think we should take some time to get to know one another. Don't you want to make sure we're in this because we want a future with each other and not just because the sex is good, uhhh, really, really good."

He blew out a puff of air and dropped his chin to his chest, "For how long?"

"There's no time limit," I said, rubbing his shoulders to help ease the tension I'd caused. "We can take as much time as we need."

He lifted his eyes until they met mine. "You mean we can take as much time as *you* need. I'm straight."

"No, I want to do this for us," I said. I placed my finger under his head and raised it higher. "You don't really know anything about me, and I don't know much about you either."

He jerked his head from my finger. "But Charisse . . . I mean . . . Okay, you seem determined about it so, we'll do things your way for now. I'm not going to pretend I'm happy about it, but if this is what you want."

"Are you okay with it? I want you to be okay with it."

"Yeah, I mean, understand that I'm a man. We don't volunteer to cut the sex out of a relationship. It goes against our wiring. But things did get off to a fast start. It'll be better for both of us if we slow down a bit . . . I think."

Easier than I thought? Yeah, too easy.

"I guess you're ready to go now," I said, waiting for him to leave skid marks as he did the hundred-meter dash out the door.

"No, I told you I came here to tuck you in and that's what I'm going to do. You want me to make you something to drink, maybe hot cocoa or tea?"

"Tea would be great, Sleepytime if you don't mind," I said.

All I could do was smile. He was taking care of me, spoiling me, something I wasn't used to. I had never known a man to do anything for me without it benefiting him in some way. In my world, selflessness and men were like pork and Kosher food; they didn't mix, no matter how hard I tried to stir them together.

"So, what medicine did the doctor prescribe for you? When I had my accident, they gave me some powerful medication. I couldn't function."

"I think the bag is over there on the counter. They gave me a bunch of stuff too."

I heard the pills clang against the plastic containers as he opened the bag.

"Wow, Flexerill . . . Vicodin . . . Motrin . . . This is quite the pain-killer cocktail, huh?"

"Yeah, I'm not going to take any unless I need to."

The microwave beeped as I watched American Idol reruns. I loved the audition shows; they were hysterical. A few minutes later Dwayne handed me a jumbo mug of Sleepytime Tea, my favorite.

"Drink up," he said. "You need your rest."

I sipped the tea for about ten minutes before I my eyes began to close under the weight of my eyelids. I sat the cup on the floor next to my chaise, grabbed a blanket, and tucked a pillow under my head. My mind faded as I watched Simon tell some fat guy he sounded like musical wallpaper.

***

I woke up the next morning in my bed, groggy and finding it difficult to get my bearings. Although my body felt like Rip Van Winkle, awakened after I'd been hibernating for one hundred years, the clock said ten; I'd been asleep for twelve hours. *How did I get to bed?* If I didn't know better, I'd think . . . . No, that was too outlandish, wasn't it? Why would he do something like that?

Dwayne's pants and shirt hung on the closet door, so unless he left naked, he was still in the house. *Maybe he's gone to the kitchen to make some breakfast.* I brushed my teeth, walked downstairs, and heard a voice coming from my office.

"Yeah, I got the information we need," Dwayne said, speaking to someone on his cell phone. Normally, I can tell by the inflections in a man's voice whether he's on the phone with a man or woman, but this time I couldn't get a sense one way or the other.

"Oh she's asleep," he continued. "She's been knocked out for hours. She had a little car accident, so I gave her a *little something* to help her rest."

I watched his reflection in the office French doors. He pulled a disk from my CD drive and placed it in a manila folder.

"Don't worry," he said. "It'll be like taking candy from a baby. We'll have more business than we'll know what to do with. We've got to focus on doing what we can to keep the complaints to a minimum until we're done. What about your agent? Any luck there?"

He placed the manila folder in a black, leather portfolio, and the Windows log off tune played. He'd shut down my computer.

"Okay, well, keep me updated. I'm going to make her some breakfast. I'm sure she'll be hungry when she wakes up. Talk to you later," he said as he placed the phone in a pocket of his portfolio.

"What was that about?" I asked, agitated and concerned. He nearly jumped through the ceiling, startled by my unexpected appearance.

"Jesus, you scared the shit out of me," he said. "I thought you were still asleep."

"Apparently so," I responded, my voice dripping with accusation.

"I was taking care of some business, baby, that's all," he said. "You know how work is when you're self-employed, you don't get time off."

"Is that right?" I asked, arms folded and lips pursed

"Yeah, that's right. Why do you sound like you're accusing me of something?"

"Oh, I'm not accusing you of anything. I only asked a question."

"Well, uhhh, let's get in that kitchen so I can make you a hot breakfast," he said as he grabbed his portfolio and led me out of the office.

"You're making breakfast? You trying to kill me or something?" I asked, half serious and half kidding, watching for changes in his facial expression. Then I played it off. "I mean, I don't even know if you can cook."

He laughed but appeared calm. "Oh, I can cook. You're in good hands. So, how'd you sleep?"

"Like a baby," I answered.

I only hoped I wasn't the baby about to be robbed.

Twenty-Nine

Lamar's Confession

Lamar picked me up for church promptly at ten thirty a.m.; he arrived dressed in his Sunday best, a classic black suit accompanied by a silk tie that sported a color similar to the hazel in his eyes. Even if he was reformed, he still had player tendencies, for only a true player would coordinate his clothes to his eye color. My eyes gulped him down like an ice cold bottle of Gatorade on a hot summer day. *Dwayne who?*

As we engaged in some idle chitchat during our short trip to church, my discomfort swelled because of what I had done so many years ago, but this was our new beginning, a blossoming friendship, wasn't it? Should I confess my leading role in the anti-player plot that destroyed his Hugh Hefner-esque harem or just let bygones be bygones? After all, if I found it in my heart to forgive him, he might do the same, right? But feeling like I kept a deceitful secret, my conscience weighed as much as my ass. I had no choice but to relieve the guilt, and my reluctant confession had become unavoidable. Damn Catholic guilt.

"Look, Lamar, I need to tell you something. After I do, you . . . you might not want to be—"

"Don't," he interrupted, "I know what you're going to say, but you don't have to say it. I know you were my mystery caller. I've known for years, but trust me, I'm over it. I'm happy that you were going to confess it though. That tells me you're the decent woman I always believed you were."

"How'd you figure it out?" I asked.

"Well, you didn't make it easy. You covered your tracks pretty well. But when I thought about everything, I realized you were the only one who hadn't gone Fatal Attraction on me, you know, boil my bunny or stalk me from the bushes like everybody else did."

"Reverse process of elimination," I said, reaffirming his suspicions and continuing with my full disclosure. "You have to understand, you hurt me. I mean, you were a player; everybody knew it. I was just stupid enough to think you'd find it in your heart to love me. In some ways, I never really put the ordeal to rest until we talked at the Gaylord. I have to tell you I'm so glad to let go and forgive."

"Charisse, you *were* different. With everything the others did to try to hurt me, you were the only one who succeeded," he said, casting a sincere glance over his shoulder. "You shocked me. I never imagined you had it in you, but I was even more surprised when I felt hurt. My trust in you surprised me. This may not make a lot of sense, but in some warped way, I did love you. I mean, in the only way I could at the time. Like I told you before, my life was a mess."

"So, we're okay?" I asked as we pulled into our parking space.

"Yes, we're cool, Charisse, honestly. Let's get inside."

What a relief! I thought. *Truth good. Secrets bad.*

Church-goers from near and far herded inside like cattle. Fortunately, the First Baptist Church of Mitchellville, one of about ten or so mega churches in the county, looked to seat more people than the Verizon Center, but a sense of warmth and community permeated the sanctuary despite its enormity. I asked Lamar if we could sit in the back row, you know, where the Pastor couldn't spot me with his super-sinner vision, but he insisted we sit closer—dead center of the front center pews. Pastor Berry and his wife approached the podium in the front of the church sanctuary and began with the welcome prayer. No sooner than the Amens left our mouths, things went downhill just as I dreaded . . .

"At this time, we'd like to ask all of our visitors to stand up, tell us your name and your church home."

Oh no. It was worse than I dreaded, you had to stand up *and* speak. Not me! I had no intention of moving my ass until the service ended, that is until one of the ushers motioned toward our row, and an animated Lamar pointed his index finger at my head, like he just identified me in a line-up.

I only wished his finger would transform into the barrel of a revolver, so he could quickly put me out of my misery. I fumbled the microphone which let out a high-pitched squeal that only dogs should hear and glanced back at Lamar's mischievous grin.

So that's how you want to play, huh?

"Yes, sister, please stand up and tell us your name and church home."

"Hello, uhhhhh, I'm, uhhh, Charisse Tyson. My college friend and life-long sinner Lamar Jackson invited me today," I said as laughter erupted from the congregation. "If I may take one moment, on the way into church this morning, Lamar said he had a confession he wanted to make to the entire congregation. So, I'd like to hand the mic over to him. Lamar?" I said, thrusting the microphone in his face.

I hadn't heard a church that quiet since Aunt Jackie—a diehard, southern Baptist—caught the Holy Spirit and broke out in an epileptic holy dance during my first communion. Apparently, she didn't know the Holy Spirit was a little more sedate in the Catholic church; they almost called an ambulance for her.

Lamar snatched the microphone from my hand. His eyes narrowed and fixed on me like Uzis firing bullets by the dozens. Satisfied that I'd done my worst, I returned to my seat as Lamar said, "I, uhhh, I want to confess that, uhhh, I love my new church family. Hallelujah. Praise the Lord!"

"Uhhhh, well, thank you sister—and Brother Lamar. Welcome," the pastor's wife said, looking at me as if I'd sprouted two heads.

Lamar slouched in his seat like a fifth grader trying to avoid getting picked to solve the algebra problem on the chalkboard. His shabby attempt to embarrass me backfired.

He didn't know who he was playing with, but he'd better ask somebody.

Right then, a familiar, masculine voice boomed from a few rows behind me. "Hello, I'm Kevin Douglass. I'm visiting from Ebenezer AME church in Fort Washington."

I whipped my head around, forgetting I had whiplash. I grabbed my neck and grimaced as I caught sight of the distinguished gentleman speaking—it was my Kevin Douglass. Well, not *my* Kevin, but the very one who'd busted my Beemer. Unfortunately, his scowl-faced (but impeccably dressed) girlfriend, Evilina, rode shotgun. She donned a five-hundred dollar suit—and a five dollar attitude.

That's strange. Am I crazy or is the world getting considerably smaller? I thought.

My chance encounters with Kevin had become borderline creepy coincidences. First the accident, the doctor's office, and now church?

Is he stalking me?

I analyzed my suspicions. Hmmm, a stalker—an FBI agent stalker with a girlfriend no less—suited up to attend church on the off chance I decided to pop in and praise the Lord?

Okay, probably not.

After the service ended, everyone congregated in the massive church basement for dinner. The spread looked serious: fried chicken, candied sweet potatoes, macaroni and cheese, greens, potato salad, apple pie, and blackberry cobbler. Summed up in one word, *Yum.*

"Man, this food smells delicious. We don't usually eat like this in the Catholic Church, but we do have one advantage that you guys don't."

"What's that?" Lamar asked.

"We get to drink wine and beer at our church functions, so everyone is usually too tipsy to notice if the food sucks," I whispered.

He laughed. "Maybe they have some left-over communion wine in the back."

"You think so?" I asked. "I could use a tray or two after what you did to me."

"Why don't you go ask the Pastor's wife? She thinks you're crazy anyway."

"I wonder why," I said. "I think we're officially even, wouldn't you say?"

"Yes, we're even."

Thirty

Chance Meeting

About a hundred tables were set up to accommodate the Sunday singles, didn't know so many of us lived in the area. I recognized a few club regulars from my partying days standing along the walls, scoping out women like hawks. *Uhn, uhn, uhn.* They even hunted prey at church. Throw in a disco ball, a DJ, and half-filled glasses of Hennessey, and we could've been at the Platinum Nightclub.

Lamar led me to a table near the exit; I figured he'd want to make a fast escape after his earlier embarrassment. He pulled out my chair and sat down on my left. As I turned to grab my fork, Kevin sat down on my right and his girlfriend on his right. Sandwiched between fine Lamar and almost as fine Kevin, the only things that could've enhanced the moment were a king-size bed, cool whip, and baby oil.

"Well, hello there," Kevin said, chuckling. "You're crazy, you know that?"

"Well, *somebody* knew I didn't want to stand up, and he dimed me out anyway," I said as I watched Kevin rest his plate on the table. "Anyway, imagine meeting you. What are you doing here?" I queried. A good man and a church man—Evilina had a real winner.

"That's funny, because I was thinking the same thing. It's odd that we keep meeting this way. Or maybe it's just fate," he said. "I saw a sign in the front of the church that said 'Single's Dinner on Sunday.' I'm single and I like to eat."

Single? What about Cruella DeVille over there? Maybe he just means not married.

He continued, "So, here we are. Oh, this is Kristen, by the way."

"Hi, Kristen, it's nice to meet you," I attempted to say with some enthusiasm. She cut her eyes at me. *What does Kevin see in her?* The pussy must be *the bomb* because her attitude was funkier than a post-game NFL locker room.

"Hi," she responded in a terse tone and quickly returned her attention to her half-filled plate.

Stuck up heifer! Maybe she's cranky because she's hungry.

Then I remembered Lamar was beside me. "Oh, I'm sorry, let me introduce you two. Lamar, this is Kevin and his girlfriend Kristen," I said. Kevin smiled and cast a curious glance at Kristen. Kristen stayed focused on her plate.

I continued, "Kevin and Kristen, this is Lamar. Lamar is a college friend, and Kevin gave me whiplash."

"Hey, what's up man?" Lamar said, adding a little bass to his voice as he extended his hand to Kevin and waved at the witch. Her rude ass didn't even look up.

"What's up, man? Good to meet you," Kevin answered, his voice equally bass-enhanced.

"So, you're the one who gave Charisse whiplash, huh?"

"It was an accident," Kevin responded.

"Careful what you say, Kevin, Lamar's an attorney," I chimed in.

"Is that right? What kind of law do you practice?" Kevin asked.

"Family law," Lamar responded.

"You handle divorces?"

"Yeah, if you need someone give me a call." Lamar handed Kevin a business card from the silver-colored holder in his pant pocket.

"Thanks, man. I know someone who might be interested," Kevin said as he accepted the card and tucked into his suit pocket. He glanced at the wicked one and rubbed her back, as if consoling her. She somehow managed a slight grin.

"No problem, no problem. Oh, he's walking this way. If you'll excuse me, I'm going to speak to Pastor Berry for a few minutes," Lamar said, waving the Pastor down.

With Lamar out of earshot and Miss Anti-Social refusing to speak, Kevin turned toward me and smiled. "So, anyway, Charisse, how is business these days?"

"Not bad, not bad. I'm still waiting on you to send me some business, but Dwayne's contract on a house in Fort Washington was accepted, so that should be a nice commission. The house is enormous."

"Wow, he must make pretty good money. What does he do?"

"He's a home improvement contractor. Although, just between you and me, I'm not so sure he's a very good one. Every time I talk to him he's dealing with angry clients or site problems."

He shifted his body around to face me, and asked, "Oh, really? What kind of problems?"

"I really don't know, and I don't ask. He always blows me off when I ask so I just move on. He seems to make pretty good money though. He's got a nice place in Cameron Station that I'm helping him sell, but he's going to have to cough up a nice chunk of change to get that house in Fort Washington."

"Oh, yeah, how much?"

"Nearly $100,000 dollars."

"He's got it like that? Damn, sounds like quite a catch—for you I mean. That's not how I roll," he said with a light chuckle.

"I guess, ummmm, I don't know. You ever sense something isn't right about someone, but you can't put your finger on it?"

"In my line of work? All the time," Kevin responded.

"Well, I don't know. With Dwayne, something just doesn't sit right," I said. "I probably shouldn't speculate like this but something happened, something . . . I don't know. I'm probably just losing my mind," I said. Kristen looked over as if I'd said something that piqued her interest.

"What is it? Maybe I can help." Kevin said.

"No, I mean, it's probably nothing," I continued. *Why am I talking to him like this?* Something about him set me at ease. Had Cruella not been there, I probably would've confided in him, but I wouldn't want that evil heifer in my business.

"Well, I have a saying that I always remind myself of in situations like that, when I feel unsure about things," Kevin said.

"What's that?" I asked.

"Trust, but verify."

"You're kidding. That's pretty wild. I say that to my friends all the time. Maybe I should take my own advice."

"It's good advice," he said, adding extra emphasis on *good*. "Maybe you should."

"I hate to interrupt to you two, but we really need to get going, Charisse," Lamar interjected. He cast a sideways glance at me as if he'd caught us kissing or something. "I've got to make a few rounds today, to see my kids."

"Well, we really should hurry up or he'll be making rounds until midnight," I joked. "It was a pleasure seeing you guys again."

Well, Kevin anyways.

***

Lamar drove me home, and I smiled when I realized how at ease Kevin made me feel; he was almost familiar to me, like I'd met him in another time, another life. His eyes were so clear, so honest. He made me feel . . . safe, like I could share anything with him. Yet, I'd only met him a short time before. There were many men in my life who I'd known far longer and whom I trusted far less. I had nothing concrete to support my feelings, only a gut instinct, an intuition. But hell, what had my instincts gotten me in my life?

Lamar, Sean, Jason, etc.

On top of that, he'd already been captured by Evilina. And if *she's* his type, he'd certainly want nothing to do with me.

Ummmhmmm, moving on!

I noticed Nisey's car parked in front of my house as Lamar pulled into the driveway. Tears were streaming down her face; she trembled as she wiped them from her cheeks. My first thought was something was wrong with the baby, but she'd certainly be at the hospital if she didn't feel well. So, I surmised she must be experiencing problems with her sponsors, perhaps she'd decided to confess the truth.

"Nisey, what's going on? Are you okay?" I said as I closed the door on Lamar's S500 and trotted toward her.

"Yes," she said, sniffing and wiping her eyes with a soggy tissue that had seen better days. She craned her neck to look inside the unfamiliar Mercedes. "Is that Lamar?"

"The one and only. You wanna say hi?"

"Sure," Nisey said, motioning Lamar to wind down his window. "Well, well, well, long time no see stranger. I hear you're celibate now."

Oh God, kill me now.

Lamar chuckled. "Nisey, I see you haven't changed a bit. You doing okay?"

"I'm freakin' fantastic, Lamar. Just great! Well, it was nice seeing you again. I just wanted to say hi."

"You take care, Nisey," Lamar said. "Charisse, can I talk to you for a second?

"Sure, what's up?" I said as I walked over to his Benz and leaned in his window to ensure my dangly bosoms taunted him.

"I asked you to church today for a reason. I was hoping we could spend some quality time together. I thought maybe if you could see me in a different environment, you'd consider having dinner with me."

"Dinner? You mean like a *date* dinner?"

"Well, not a full-fledged date, maybe we could just go on a see-if-there's-something-there get-together."

Dates with Lamar mean trouble. I better decline.

"We have a lot of history, Lamar."

"I know. Trust me, if I thought we were going to repeat it, I wouldn't ask. I think we're both very different people now, don't you?" he asked, his eyes piercing me like x-rays and exposing my deepest desires.

Lord, why did you make this man so damn irresistible???

"Yes, I do," I said, flashing him a reassuring smile. "Okay, I'll agree to the get-together. You tell me when and we've got a date . . . but not a date," I said, stepping away from his car.

"Okay, in the meantime, you stay away from Kevin," he bellowed as he eased out of the driveway, "I don't like the way he looks at you."

"Looks at me? He has a girlfriend. Didn't you notice the angry black woman sitting next to him?"

"Trust me, men know these things," Lamar said.

Huh! Kevin seemed like a great guy, but he didn't have a damn thing coming. His girlfriend looked the type that carried Vaseline and tennis shoes in her Gucci bag on the off chance she could think up a good reason to kick somebody's ass. Wouldn't be mine!

"Who's Kevin?" Nisey asked.

"Long story, Nisey. We'll talk when we get in the house."

"I can't go in," Nisey said.

"Why?" I asked.

"Because I need to get back to my house," Nisey said. "Robert and David are fighting in my front yard."

"What! You left them at your house fighting?"

"Yup, I sure did. They got into a pissing contest, acting like a couple of nine-year-old brats fighting over who gets to play Superman, so I left. To hell with 'em, may the best man win."

"Oh my God, Nisey, you better get back home," I said, sounding like a mother hen. "I'll follow you. I can't believe you."

Thirty-One

Sumo Daddies

I shuttled Nisey into her car and followed in the Beemer. Nisey called me on my cell and explained she'd started to tell David about her pregnancy, when Robert popped up unexpectedly. One thing led to another and an argument ensued. Still, neither had been told about the baby; she hadn't had a chance to break it to them.

When we pulled up to her townhouse, Robert and David were locking heads in the front yard like a couple of underweight Sumo wrestlers, both stubbornly refusing to surrender.

"See, Rissey. What did I tell you?"

"Jesus, all they need is a mat and a couple of thongs, and we could charge admission."

"Robert! David! Break it up already. This is juvenile," Nisey yelled as she jumped out of her car. Each promised to let go if the other let go—so first grade. "Looks like my child is going to have the genes of a dumb ass no matter which one of you is the father!"

Well, that was one way to break it to them.

They released their grips, stood slowly, and glared at Nisey in stunned silence.

"Yeah, you heard me right, I'm pregnant. One of you is the father. I'm . . . just not sure which one," she said, her voice trailing off.

"Excuse me. Did you just say you don't know who the father is?" Robert snapped.

"Yes," Nisey answered.

"Are you going to keep it?" David asked, more concerned than angry.

"Yes, I am going to keep it. And let me say, regardless of who the father is, I'm prepared to go this alone. I care about you both. This isn't something that I wanted, but this is where I am. I don't want your money, your time, nothing. If you don't want to be in our life after today, I'm okay with that. My baby is the most important thing in the world to me, and we'll be just fine, with or without you. Now, you can feel free to stay and talk, curse me out, leave, whatever. I'm going inside. I have to pee . . . again."

Sullen and disappointed, they stared at Nisey for a moment that seemed an eternity and then walked to their cars and drove away. Nisey didn't know if she'd see either one of them again, but she made her position clear—the tiny life growing inside her belly had far surpassed the importance of the man who put it in there. I put my arm around her and walked her inside.

"Give them some time to absorb everything. I'm sure at least one of them will be back," I said, more hopeful than certain.

"I don't blame David for leaving," Nisey said while pulling a Kleenex from the floral-colored box on her slate end table. "I had feelings for him, and they seemed to be growing every day, but he's not the one who told me he was in love with me. He's not the one who said he'd be there for me no matter what. Robert was the one all full of words, now shit seems more accurate. I should've walked away a long time ago. You were so right, Rissey. You live and you learn, I guess."

"I'm sorry things worked out this way, but—," I started, interrupted by a knock at the door. "Looks like someone came to his senses pretty quickly."

Nisey opened the door. Her eyes widened and jaw dropped.

"You're back," Nisey said, motioning David inside. She closed the door behind him and plopped on the couch.

"I never left," David said. "I knew he'd never leave if I stayed, so I waited around the corner until he drove off."

"Oh," Nisey responded. "So, what do you want to say?"

"I want to say this. I know that this is a less-than-ideal situation. We agreed to keep this casual. You were honest with me; I knew you had feelings for someone else. The thing is, somewhere along the way I broke the rules. I started to fall in love with you. Now, more than anything, I want to be here for you, and the baby, no matter who the father is."

For the first time in her life, Nisey was speechless. An instinctive smile appeared on her face. She sat motionless, overwhelmed by surprise and relief.

"Well, you guys, I think I should get going. I think David's got things here under control," I said. I opened the door and glanced back at Nisey, still frozen, like she was fresh out of a cryogenic chamber. "Girl, close your mouth, you're letting the flies out."

A happy ending for Nisey—or beginning, depending on how you looked at it. I, for one, thanked God David appeared at the door and not Robert. I had always sensed he had a good soul in my brief interactions with him. He accepted Nisey and loved her, even though she carried a child who may not be his. Enough said. Robert's love proved to be all words; David's all action. I'd take actions over words any day.

On my way home, I decided to take a time out and assess my baggage unpacking progress. Life always had a way of sidetracking me as I pursued my goals. No matter what life threw at me, I had to keep them in focus. My future happiness depended on it.

***

I jumped in my pajamas, pulled out my journal, and started to read. Jason, my ex-husband, was next. That relationship was the most painful of my life. I was a size ten when it started and a size fourteen when it ended.

I literally haven't been the same since.

On the surface, I blamed Jason for the demise of our marriage but, in reality, our problems ran deep. I took it as a sign of major progress that I could acknowledge my role in my past pains.

Take Dwayne for instance.

I doubted his intentions after I deduced that he spiked my Sleepytime Tea, but there I was, still dating his shifty ass. I suppose I couldn't marry the two Dwaynes I'd observed: the incredibly affectionate, caring, sensitive man who I'd fallen for, and the sneaky snake who slipped medicine in my tea for some yet unknown reason. Did he want to make sure that I slept well because of the accident, or did he conceal a more sinister reason?

I didn't know.

The time had come for a little investigation.

Kevin's voice echoed through my head *"Trust but verify."*

Thirty-Two

Trouble at Home

I abandoned my journal and grabbed my laptop. I hadn't Googled Dwayne, but I figured there was no time like the present. I had hit the power button, watched the Google window load up, and typed his name in the search box—when my cell phone rang. The caller ID flashed "Mom."

"Hi, Mommy," I said, pushing my laptop onto the bed. *Dwayne will have to wait.*

"Hi, baby, it's not Mom. It's James."

"Hi, James. I haven't spoken with you in a while. How are you? Is everything okay?"

"No, baby, your mom is in the hospital. I think . . . we're going to need you to come home."

"The hospital? What's wrong? Is she okay?"

"Baby, she's going to be okay, but she had a stroke earlier today. I came home from fishing this afternoon in time to watch her collapse on the bedroom floor. She's in intensive care and stable now, but—" he paused as the sound of my heart pounded in my ears. "She's in a coma. The doctor says she may come out of it in a few days or few weeks, it's hard to say. She needs you here. I came home to pick up some things and make a few calls. I'm going back in a few minutes."

"Oh my God, oh my God," I said. My hand trembled as I covered my mouth. "Okay, James. I'll take the first flight out in the morning, the first flight."

"Okay, baby, let me know when you're coming in. I'll pick you up from the airport and take you on over to the hospital. I know it ain't gonna do no good to tell you not to worry, but your momma is a strong lady. She's gonna pull through this just fine. Just keep her in your prayers, you hear me?"

"Yes, sir, I'll see you tomorrow."

"Okay, try to get some sleep tonight too. Bye baby."

I laid back on my pillow as the grave news rested heavily on my heart and soon gave way to a flow of tears. I loved my mother so dearly, but the guilt of not visiting and calling as much as I should haunted me. I hadn't visited her in nearly two years, the last time I received news that Lee was on vacation for a month. I only visited when he wasn't in town, which was rare.

So unfortunate, I'd let the baggage of what happened so many years ago keep me away, but only God could keep me from North Carolina when my mom needed me. Lee was going to be at the hospital, no doubt putting on a stellar performance as the doting nephew. I'd have to face him . . . and he'd have to face me.

Mi Dios. (That's my Spanish.)

I needed reinforcements to get through it; I didn't know how long I'd be in Winston, but I wasn't leaving until she was out of the hospital. I called Dwayne, told him the news. He claimed he'd wanted to go with me but had too much going on at work. Depending on how long I stayed, he promised to come one weekend. I knew his answer before I called, but sometimes you just need to hear it. Next, I called the only person on whom I knew I could lean without falling.

"What time's our flight?" Nisey said.

"You're going with me?"

"Yes, Rissey, that's what sisters are for."

"I'm so glad. I don't think I could handle this alone."

"You don't give yourself enough credit," Nisey said. "Of course, you could handle it alone, but you shouldn't have to."

"I can't tell you how much this means to me."

"You can spew gratitude later. Right now, let's try and get some rest. We need to get out early, okay?"

"Okay. Goodnight, John-Boy."

She chuckled. "Take your crazy ass to bed."

I picked up my journal and stuffed my face with Reece's Cups as I read myself to sleep. My trip called for chocolate. Lots and lots of it. As a matter of fact, I fully intended to corner the market on Godiva and Reese's cups before I left for North Carolina.

Mommy. . .

Thirty-Three

Cradle Robbing

*A*pril 12, 2002
Mom called today asking for grandchildren. I told her I'd like to find a husband first. She asked if I'd considered mail-order since I'd apparently exhausted all possibilities in the United States. I told her that wasn't fair, just all possibilities east of the Mississippi. We've got a new guy at the office. He keeps scoping me out, but he won't even speak to me. He acts like I'm contained behind a deflector shield. Probably for the best though, I think I need to find someone more age-appropriate, he looks like he's still breast-fed.

***

Jason was a little younger than me.

Well, okay, a lot younger—ten years.

Yup, I was a cougar.

He looked like a Denzel Washington wannabe, six-feet-four inches of pure chocolate. Not Hersheys—Godiva. He possessed Denzel's air of coolness, you know what I mean? He was one of those brothers that didn't walk, he glided; he didn't talk, he conversed; he didn't flirt, he charmed. But he was low key about his business though, never overt, always subtle.

He carried himself like one of those contemplative brothers, you know, *deep*. Seemed like the kind of guy who pondered the meaning of life, the source of happiness, always insightful, poetic, and poignant. Well, I discovered he was deep in something; I'd wasted more than a year of my life before I concluded the "something" was shit.

I met him at the office. I usually adhered to my strict rule about not dating brothers from the office—with a broker being the only exception (owners never come to work). Otherwise that's a no-no.

Why?

Because you never want a man in a position to mess up your money. *Never*!

If we broke up, how could I cart my ass into the office and tolerate seeing his grill all day? Rumors would start flying, everybody would be whispering at the water cooler. I'd walk by and hear, "How about those Redskins?" And I'd think, 'You ain't slick, I know you were talking about me,' but I'd sing, "Gooood morrrrning!" Then I'd mosey around bitchy and rude, pissing everybody off, and end up hated and despised.

Or worse, I'd walk around looking pathetic and everybody would overwhelm me with trite pity phrases like "You're better off without him" or "Oh, you're pretty and smart, you'll find someone else in no time" or the ever dreaded "This will be a perfect opportunity for you to get some 'me' time." Treating me like I'm some emotional head case.

To hell with that!

If I worked with people like Nisey, we'd go out for a liquid lunch and plot conspiracies, like how to introduce a virus into his laptop and mess up his money. Suffice it to say, it's best to avoid all this madness from the get-go. As usual, I failed to heed the signs, failed to take my own advice.

Jason was an aggressive real estate agent, a rising star. He could sell an oak leaf to a pine tree—in the spring. For the first month, he flashed a cheesy smile every time he saw me but never said a single solitary word—not, hey, how you doin', kiss my ass, nothing.

Over the next two months, our relationship evolved; he followed the smile up with a little wave. I thought, *He must have a girlfriend.*

It took four months for him to say "hello" and an additional three weeks before he finally approached me in the copy room while I was printing out a contract.

"Hello," Jason said, hesitating for a moment. "You're Charisse, right?"

"Yes, I'm Charisse . . . right," I responded, wondering if our greeting would end the conversation as usual.

"I've been seeing you around. I'm Jason, new here. So, how long have you been working at Millenium?"

"Nice to finally meet you, Jason. Well, I think it's been a little over a year now since I started working in this office. I switched companies," I paused, "I've been hearing about you in the sales meetings, seems like you're doing your thing."

"I guess . . . you know, I'm just trying to pay the rent."

"Oh, you don't own?" I asked.

"No, I rent. I've got an apartment in Laurel. Haven't bought my first house yet, even though I seem to be pretty good at selling them to other people."

"Oh, okay," I said, thinking 'Can you spell priority?' "You're still young, though. Would I be prying if I asked how old you are?"

"Yes, you would be, but I'll tell you anyway. I'm twenty-five."

Too young for me. Let me put the brakes on this shit riiiight now, I thought.

"Well, it was really good meeting you, Jason. I really should get going. I need to fax this contract to my client; my fax at home is a little faster," I said as I started for the door.

"Hold up a sec. Uhmmm, can I get your phone number? I actually have a question about one of the forms, and I was hoping you could help me. I don't know many people here," he said, trailing me to my desk.

"That's what the broker is here for. He gets twenty percent of your commission, he answers your questions."

"Well, what if I just want to talk to you? Better still, what if I'd like to invite you out to dinner?"

Steak? Or milk and cookies?

"Uhhh . . . okay," I smiled. "Here's my business card; you can reach me on my cell number."

"Thanks. May I give you a call later?"

"Sure," I sighed, "That's fine."

I collected my belongings and dashed out of the office as quickly as possible. He called me a few hours later; I didn't answer at first. But when I heard the message he left on my voicemail, I sensed big trouble on the horizon. "Charisse, it's Jason. Look, I know I'm a couple years younger than you, but I hope that doesn't make you uncomfortable. To me, age is nothing but a number. I'd just like the chance to get to know you. Can you give me a call, please?"

A couple of years younger? Ha!

If only.

But damn, the bass in his voice played like a symphony in my ear, and when I returned his call an hour after debating with myself, we fell into a smooth and easy conversation.

Jason and I talked for five hours that night about everything; he revealed way more than I. Apparently, he liked the sound of his voice as much as I did. He enlisted in the Army and left active duty after four years. Still did the one weekend a month, two weeks a year thing. The short and tight haircut should've given it away.

Another damn military man, I mumbled.

"Did you say something?" he asked.

"No, nothing," I replied, making a mental note to use my inside voice when making smart ass comments. "So, anyway, what do you do for fun?"

"I hang with the fellas, play ball, go to the club sometimes. When I'm home, I like to read."

Like what? The Little Engine That Could?

"Wow, a man who likes to read. That's cool. Who are your favorite authors?"

"I read everything from Alex Haley to Frederick Douglass to Nietzsche and Jane Austen. And before you ask, I really did read Jane Austen. Pride and Prejudice as a matter of fact."

"What in the world made you read Jane Austen?"

"My mother. She reads everything. It was punishment for letting my grades drop during my junior year in high school, but believe it or not, I ended up liking her work."

"So what's your favorite book?"

"The Autobiography of Malcolm X. After reading it, I considered joining the Nation of Islam and becoming a Muslim until I realized they were serious about the whole no alcohol and fornication thing," he said, "And don't forget about pork. I ain't going to hell for liking honey ham."

At least he's committed to his principles.

"Yeah, seems like a high price to pay."

Thirty-Four

Chez Charisse

J ason's mother worked as a real estate agent before she retired. That's how he got into the business. Pretty typical. Most people didn't aspire to be real estate agents; they were usually recruited by family or friends. Anyway, she was a single mother, divorced from her much younger husband. *Interesting.* She carted him from house to house when she had showings or needed to get documents signed. He spent a lot of time in the back seat of mama's Mercedes.

I somehow managed to sneak in one critical detail about myself. "I'm allergic to nuts," I said, responding to his query for a little-known detail about myself. He'd need to keep that in mind when selecting a restaurant to take me out to dinner.

"Hey, you up? Time for bed sleepyhead," I said as I listened to him call hogs in my ear. Three a.m. had snuck up on us, and he snored like a Harley with a busted muffler. I played "Mary Had a Little Lamb" with the telephone buttons and woke him up.

"Charisse, can we sleep together?" he asked.

"Sleep together?"

"Yeah, on the phone, like in high school. Remember?"

Although I'm sure I had to search a little further in my memory banks than he did, I remembered those first-crush phone calls when my stomach felt overloaded with butterflies and conversations all about nothing lasted until the wee hours of the morning. I longed for that happy place and talking with Jason took me there.

***

September 3, 2002
Jason and I had a wonderful conversation last night. He made me feel young and excited and alive. Maybe dating a younger man wouldn't be so bad after all. But given that it took him over four months to have a conversation with me, I may be too old to hear him if he ever asks me out.

***

The next day, Friday, Jason had a major test to pass, at least in my mind. His behavior toward me, particularly after our long conversation, would show me whether I was dealing with a man or a man-boy. I'd expected him to behave like most men his age, a jerk with the attention span of a tomato. I thought he'd forget those five hours on the phone ever took place and treat me like an alien that just landed on earth, like he'd never seen *my kind* before.

True to form, he observed me from a discomforting distance without so much as a word to me all day. Hell, I could've worked from home. The only reason I showed up at the office was to give him a chance to ask me out on a date. By late afternoon, I'd conceded defeat, gathered my things, and headed out the door. He jogged outside behind me.

"Are you busy tonight?" Jason asked, a little out of breath.

"Well, that's a relief!"

"What do you mean?" he asked.

"Well, you *can* see me. I thought I was invisible."

"Oh no, I hope you didn't take any offense. I just thought it would be best to communicate outside the office to keep the gossip to a minimum. You know how people talk."

He had a good point. I used to think they operated a subsidiary of *The Enquirer* next to the water cooler. Lots of gossip passed through mouths and ears in that area.

"Oh, okay, I guess I can understand that," I said.

"So, do you have plans tonight? I wanted to invite you to dinner."

"Um, I guess dinner would be okay."

"How about I meet you at your house? About seven?"

"Okay, so where are we going?"

"To the best restaurant in town. You'll love it."

"What should I wear?"

"Whatever, it doesn't matter. Just make sure you're comfortable."

"There's no dress code?"

"Nope, no dress code. Come as you are."

The clock read four, and my house was a total mess. More clothes were on my bed than in the closet and more dishes in the sink than in the cupboard. I ran home and cleaned the house from top to bottom—sort of. Okay, so it wasn't a thorough cleaning; if he had opened any one of the closets, an avalanche of musky suits and lingerie would've buried him alive.

The butterflies in my stomach felt more like bats out of hell as I anticipated my date with Jason. People told me all the time that I looked ten years younger than my age but to actually date a man ten years younger was a new thing altogether. The drawbacks were serious.

First of all, despite his manly appearance, he was a mere twenty-five-years-old. According my calculations, twenty-five was approximately fourteen in man years. Age was one of the few ways men differed from man's best friend. While dogs reached adulthood within the first *two* years of birth, men generally didn't reach adulthood until the age of *fifty,* making Jason chronically under-aged.

Despite his intellectual level, he still played video games. He also ran to the clubs every weekend to prop up the walls and collect phone numbers at the end of the night in an effort to prove he still had "it"—whatever "it" was.

What on God's green earth could we possibly have in common?

Worse—and even more frightening—we could never have sex . . . together . . . in the same bed. I'd sooner hire a body double before I'd ever let him see me naked. No way! I carried thirty-four years worth of cellulite in all the wrong places—of course, cellulite had no *right* place—and an evil force had begun to tug both my tits and ass downward, further proof gravity was God's eternal curse to women for Eve and the apple incident. The more I thought about "us," the more I believed "we" could never work.

Just as I picked up the phone to call and cancel our dinner date, I heard a knock at the door. I peeped out the window to see Jason carrying two bags of groceries and a bottle of wine. I opened the door and an involuntary smile took my face hostage.

"What's all this?" I asked.

"I'm going to cook dinner, if that's okay with you," Jason responded.

"Cook? Wow, I don't remember the last time a man cooked for me."

"Well, believe me, it will be my pleasure. I just need you to point me to the kitchen."

"Sure, follow me," I said as I led him through the dining room. "Let me show you where everything is."

I showed him the cabinet where all the pots and pans were located. I'd just replaced the beat-up Walmart set that I'd owned since college with a new thirteen-piece Calphalon set. Since he seemed to be into cooking, I thought he'd be impressed by my never-used cookware from the kitchen gods.

"Wow, you have a nice kitchen here, lots of counter space."

"Yeah, well I like to have plenty of room for the pizza boxes."

"I see," he said as he started unpacking his bags. "So you don't cook much?"

"I know *how* to cook if that's what you're asking. I don't cook often, though."

"Well good, I love to cook. So I guess I'll be the chef in the family," he said, winking at me.

In the family?

"Geez, you sure came prepared. You brought your own seasonings, utentils, even a George Foreman grill. Have groceries, will travel, huh?"

"Well, you know, I've been known to do a little sumthin' sumthin'."

"A good cook and modest, gotta love it."

"Anyway, Ms. Tyson, why don't you let me pour you a glass of wine? You sit down and watch television while I get to work. Sound good?"

"You're perfect—er—I mean, sounds perfect."

Thirty-Five

High and Hitched

Dinner was delicious. He cooked basic man food—steak, shrimp, baked potatoes, broccoli, and brought cheesecake with strawberry topping for dessert. Being a meat and potatoes kind of girl, I was impressed. The meal was tasty but the best part of the evening had yet to come—the part when he refused to let me help clean up the kitchen. I pinched my arm to ensure I wasn't dreaming. I sat in the family room stuffed with steak and shrimp, suppressing a big satisfaction burp. Watching him stand barefoot in the kitchen, washing dishes and wiping down the countertops, wearing a World's Greatest Chef apron, I thought, *I'm going to marry that man.*

A glorious night such as ours would've usually ended in the bed—but not with Jason. No, I was terrified he'd run from the house screaming in horror if he saw me naked, so I held out for over a month . . . barely. Let me just say abstaining proved difficult because his kisses set me on fire—almost literally one day when he backed me into a lit scented candle. To use a baseball analogy, we went all the way to third base, but when it was time to slide into home, I called the game due to cellulite.

Oh, but when the time came to do the deed, I never imagined sex could ever be that good. Not only was he packing some serious heat (i.e. hung like a horse), he had the stamina of a marathon runner. We were a match made in heaven. I was a horny thirty-something with a voracious, insatiable sexual appetite, and he was a horny twenty-something anxious to keep me satisfied. Two weeks after our first encounter, I gave him a key to my house; I didn't want to let a little thing like a locked door block my midnight booty calls. And trust me when I say, the booty called and kept on calling.

One night, Jason told me I was so beautiful naked that he wanted to make love with the lights on—and I agreed. Love filled the air, your hear me? I mean, he used to just stare at me while I stood in front of the mirror getting dressed or doing my hair. And his expression wasn't one of disgust but lust. As his eyes traveled up and down my body, he licked his lips like I was a free bucket of Kentucky Fried Chicken. I figured we'd take the leap before long.

"I need to talk to you about something," he said one day after one of our marathon sessions. We'd had sex five times already, and the day wasn't even over.

"What's that, baby?" I answered, stroking his goatee.

"You know, from the first moment I met you I thought to myself 'I'm going to marry that woman'. I thought you were so beautiful, and you seemed like you had it all together."

"Stop lying! It took you four months to even say hello."

"Yeah, I know. I was kind of involved with someone at the time, and the relationship was complicated. But I told myself that once I ended it, I would ask you out. I had a feeling that when you and I got together, you were going to be it for me. Like I knew you were the one."

"Really?" I responded. A surge of pheromones drowned out the whole "I was kind of involved" part. All I heard was "I knew you were the one."

"Yes, really," he said, caressing my cheek. "These six months have been the happiest of my life. I don't ever want to lose you."

"So, what are you saying?"

"I'm saying I want to spend the rest of my life loving you and only you. I'm asking you to marry me. Will you be my wife?" he asked, pulling a Kay Jeweler's box from his pant pocket and opening it to expose a one-carat (at least) diamond.

Tears streamed from my eyes; he had good taste in jewelry. And I thought my dream had finally come true. Our relationship had evolved so slowly in the very beginning that it took me by surprise. We both thought we must be fated for each other. He had to be *"the one."*

So, as tears continued down my face, I answered , "Yes, Jason. I'll be your wife."

Looking back, I believe the continuous sex elevated my hormone and endorphin levels so high that I was legally intoxicated when I accepted his proposal. A few months later, we married at the justice of the peace. Neither one of us wanted to spend thousands of dollars on a wedding. He moved into my place, and we lived in matrimonial bliss.

***

April 6, 2003
I called Mom today and told her Jason and I got married. She said she wishes I would've invited her because no one would believe her unless she witnessed it with her own eyes. Typical Mom. No matter though. I've never known such happiness as I found with Jason. I have to admit that allowing myself to feel such joy makes me afraid. In my life, happiness is always fleeting. For once in my life, I hope it's here to stay.

***

We were annoying newlyweds of the worst kind. We had sex every night. He brought flowers home every day, and I cooked every night. We called each other pet names like "Schnooka Wooka" and "Pooh Bear" and "Snookums" when we got tired of "Baby" and "Boo Boo." We were so schmoozy that we got on our own nerves after a while. We saved money on that big expensive wedding, so we planned to take a trip to Jamaica. We planned to buy a bigger home in Woodmont. We were planning fools. But I remember a saying that went something like, "If you want to make God laugh, tell Him your plans." Oh, I'm sure He's still yukking it up. On the first Saturday of the month, almost eight months to the day after our betrothal, we got the joke, courtesy of the United States Army.

"Charisse, I have some news. I think you need to sit down," he said with a concerned look on his face. He'd just arrived home from his Army Reserve drill weekend.

"What's wrong?" I asked.

"I'm being deployed to Iraq for an eight-month tour," he said, unfolding the orders in his hand.

"Iraq?" I said, dazed and feeling as if the air had been knocked out of me. "Eight months? When?"

"In ninety days," he said. His face grew somber.

"You're kidding me right? We just got married. You can't go now. Can't you get out of it?"

"No, baby, this is what I signed up for. I have to go. There's no getting out of it. This is going to be hard for you, but it's going to be hard for me too. This is my first marriage and my first deployment. But we're going to get through this, okay? We're going to get through this together, I promise."

I thought, *How cruel can God be?* I get married after all these years, I'm over-the-moon happy, and He sends my husband to Iraq for eight months. The first damn deployment in his life, and it happened after we got married.

In retrospect, it's clear that God's biggest blessings can sometimes appear disguised as a curse.

Thirty-Six

A Digital Mess

*M**arch 8, 2004**
I'm pretty sure my marriage is over. Jason and I hardly spoke two words over the last eight months, at least it seemed that way. Something's definitely wrong, but I don't know what. Last night, I dreamed he asked me for a divorce, told me I'd been replaced . . . by his new boyfriend Pookie. Then I punched him in the face and woke up. I then realized it was just a dream because if he had brought Pookie up in MY house I'd have popped a cap in him.*

***

Jason had returned home after eight long months in Iraq. He claimed Baghdad was a hotbed for Iraq's insurgency, and he rarely had access to a phone or the internet. My instincts told me something was amiss. I'd all but given up on our marriage until he called me a week before, asking me to pick him up from his reserve unit.

The unit door swung open and soldier after soldier ran to the arms of their families. I imagined Jason swooping me up and smothering me with kisses like I'd seen so many husbands do to their wives moments before. But Jason didn't swoop me up. Just a smile and hug with an impersonal church pat, like he didn't want to touch me *too much*. I thought, *Am I his wife or his sister?* Oh, he came straight out with the I'm sorries, said our marriage meant everything to him and he wanted to make amends for the emotional distance that he'd put between us all those months. Said he was a soldier, he did what he had to do to survive. As an Army wife, I'd been briefed on what to expect from my husband when he returned. I'd prepared for Post-Traumatic Stress Disorder, depression, anxiety—not *Kendra*.

I'd sensed more excitement during an elevator ride, than I had from Jason. He didn't seem the least bit happy to see me. We threw his rucksacks in the trunk and held hands on the drive back to the house.

Who is he? I thought. *He's not the man I married.*

Jason was a familiar stranger.

We quickly retreated to the bedroom once we got home, but we'd lost our rhythm, and he seemed disinterested. He lay next to me because he was supposed to, not because he wanted to. I feared my Pookie nightmare might be more than a dream. Maybe during all those nights spent alone with a bunch of other men, Jason might've "switched teams."

Boy, did I get that one wrong.

The next day Jason returned to his unit to do some in-processing, and he left me alone to wonder what would become of "us." I sat on the couch and stared at the war gear scattered across the floor and realized that my time would be better spent cleaning the mess up than sulking.

When I picked up Jason's rucksack and began removing his uniforms from the overfilled bag, an object wrapped in one of his Army-issued t-shirts fell on the floor. I opened it to find a digital camera. It seemed clear he'd taken some pains to conceal it, wrapping it snug in the t-shirt.

Naturally, I powered it up to view its contents.

My heart sank as I scrolled through picture after picture of a fellow soldier, a familiar woman dressed in fatigues, holding, kissing, and laughing with him. My stomach burned when I realized she was the commanding officer of his reserve unit. I'd met her at Family Day the year before, along with her husband and two children. No wonder she'd been so cold toward me when Jason introduced us, coughed in her hand so she wouldn't have to shake mine. Some photos were dated before he departed for his tour of duty, one in his car, one in a nightclub. And in several, they wore nothing but smiles.

If I knew my husband, her smile, like her orgasm, was faked.

I cried for an hour. *How could he do this to me?* I thought. He told me we'd get through it together. He promised to love and cherish me forever.

I guess forever's only a year and a half in man years.

Distraught, I grabbed his camera, hooked it up to the computer, and opened each picture in Photoshop. On each, I placed a cartoon speech bubble near Jason's mouth that said, "Boy, I'm sure glad my wife wasn't here to see this." I printed them out and plastered them on the wall above our bed, packed enough clothes for to last me a couple of days, and then drove to Doubletree in Baltimore. I'd stay there until I figured out what to do next.

During the drive to Baltimore, a sudden urge to hurl intensified at the realization marriage had trapped me. I couldn't just pack up, walk away, and never look back like I'd always done before. We shared a mortgage, car notes, credit cards, bank accounts, gym memberships, everything.

I longed to drop off the face of the earth like Jimmy Hoffa and fly to some distant Caribbean island with my new friends: a horny cabana boy named Romone and an always-full margarita glass. However, my dream was tempered by the sobering awareness that I wasn't wealthy. So, if I had to eat *daily*, I'd only have enough money to survive for about a week. Any longer and I'd need to hitch a ride back to the United States on a raft with some illegal immigrants.

No, I had to stay for the moment, but I didn't have to like it—and neither did he. After a day passed, I'd reached the point where I could speak to Jason without beginning each sentence with "You moth*erfucker*...."

"How long have you been seeing her?" I asked with a supernatural calm as I sampled over-priced delights from the buffet I ordered from room service.

"Charisse, what good will this—" he said, pausing for my reaction.

"Don't patronize me!" I snapped. "Just tell me the damn truth for a change. How long?"

"Since . . . since before you and I met."

"Before we met? May I ask why in hell you married me? What, you needed to bring a little balance to your relationship? She was married, so you wanted to be married too?"

"She wouldn't leave her husband so I had to move on. We weren't together the whole time. We've been on and off for a couple of years. When I asked you out, we'd split up again."

"Oh, I see, and after we got married it was *back on*?"

"Listen, Charisse, I know this doesn't make a lot of sense, but some-times you just can't control your feelings."

"You're right, Jason. You can't always control your feelings, but you can control where you stick your dick, especially when you have a faithful wife waiting for you at home. That's something you *can* control."

"I know, and I'm sorry. I am so sorry. You're a good woman, and I never wanted to hurt you this way."

"Do you love her?"

"Yes, I love her, but I'm not *in* love with her. I'm *in* love with y*ou*. I would never leave you for her . . . not anyone. I swear."

"Oh, I'm sorry. Is that supposed to be some kind of consolation prize? 'Charisse, I planned to lie, cheat, and deceive you for the rest of our marriage, but I'll never leave you.' That's just great. 'Tell her what she's won Bob, a cheating husband who doesn't plan to leave.' Woo fucking hoo. Why not just leave Jason? Are you scared she won't make you happy or are you scared I might actually find someone who wants to make me happy?"

"You're twisitng things around. I swear, I told her that my relationship with her is over."

"Oh no, it's not over. It's just over for now, maybe fucking around isn't quite so much fun when you have to face the people you hurt, when you have to face the pain that you're causing to people that love you. I wonder how her husband would feel about all of this. Better still, I wonder what the United States Army's position would be on this issue. Hmmm, let's see. Can you spell dishonorable discharge?"

"Charisse, you wouldn't."

"You're right, normally I wouldn't. But if you so much as *fart* in her direction, I will. Are we understood?"

Thirty-Seven

Matrimonial Quicksand

I had Jason by the short hairs and he knew it. He'd served in the military, fraternized with a commissioned officer, and committed adultery. If I reported it, I could've made his life in the Army as miserable as we were at home. And while he deserved that and more, I didn't want to go there unless we were at the point of no return. The sad fact was that I still loved him. Lucky for him, I wasn't the type to hold his mistake over his head every waking moment, but I made sure it dangled in a visible distance—at all times.

***

May 21, 2009
My marriage to Jason would be perfect if I could stand the sight of his lying, cheating face. He's on the straight and narrow, but I just want to kill him for what he's done to us. I thought about tying him to the bed, dousing him with gasoline, and setting him on fire; cutting off his dick and throwing it on the side of the highway; slipping arsenic in his lasagna, but that's all so passé and overdone. If I'm going to jail, I'd at least like to be original.

***

As the months passed, Jason's pledge to maintain our marriage, no matter what, became more of a challenge than a promise. Every time I looked in his eyes, I saw flashes of the butt-naked pictures of him and his little skank. More and more, I became determined to make him leave. If he wasn't going to leave on his own volition, like he should've had the decency to do since *he* had the affair, then I'd have to force the issue.

I didn't want to be married to him anymore but, damn it, I didn't want to be responsible for ending my first (and perhaps only) marriage. So, I did what any vindictive, scorned wife would do. I made life as uncomfortable for him as possible at home and pledged to do so until he ran screaming from the house like the bitch-ass he was. Besides, as long as I felt dejected and riddled with self-doubt, why should he be allowed anything remotely resembling joy? He had no mistress, no cooking, no cleaning, no speaking, no sex, no-thing.

To make things worse, I grew pettier by the minute. Like I'd cook an entire pot of spaghetti, eat enough for myself, and then throw the rest in the trash can. If he wanted some, he could eat from there. He should've been used to it; all dogs ate from the trash at some time or another. I removed all of the super-quilted, two-ply Charmin toilet paper from his bathroom and replaced it with the industrial, one-ply paper that almost disintegrated when torn from the roll.

Over time, my plan to make him miserable went awry. Who knew a man would enjoy a junky house, frequent masturbation, and ordering pizza every night? What I intended as punishment turned into an extended vacation to nowhere. I still had one ace in the hole though, so-to-speak. I could do the one thing no husband could tolerate: screw another man.

At first, I pretended to have an affair, you know, left signs here and there, like random condoms and greetings cards, which I'd bet Jason avoided because they were stark reminders of shit he no longer did for me. He never said anything when I left condoms around either. He probably thought they were his. I got no perceptible response whatsoever, which offered me little consolation.

Un-vindicated and sex deprived, far longer than Jason (he'd actually gotten some ass while he was deployed), I decided to have a *real* affair. *Damn it, it's my right*, I thought. *I didn't break the vows first, Jason did.* I was entitled to get my freak on, and what could Jason possibly say or do to stop me?

I scrolled through my mental Rolodex to select an "affair-ee." I didn't want to "do it" with someone I didn't know. I feared what kind of deranged crazy person I might end up with or incurable, terminal disease he might carry. Or worse, he might dick-whip me and make me fall in lust again, been there done that. Love and I were mortal enemies, and I wanted no part of it. No, I needed someone safe. I needed a wham-bam-thank you ma'am, see you later alligator.

I needed Sean.

Divorced, still single, and in sporadic email contact since we'd split up, Sean was not only ironic but appropriate. He could rescue me from my marital melancholy. So, one day—under the influence of four margaritas and a shot of Patron—and after weeks of deliberation—I dug up the nerve to give him a call.

"Sean, how are you? It's Charisse."

"I'm fine, beautiful. Long time no hear from. How are you doing?"

"Uhhhhhh, I guess you could say I've been better."

"Now you know I don't like to hear that. What's going on?"

"Trouble at home. My husband had an affair with another woman. I'm afraid my relationship with you brought me some bad Karma."

"Charisse, you can't think like that," he said, "I mean, the truth is you didn't have a chance. From the first moment I saw you, I was determined to have you, and I probably wouldn't have stopped at anything until I did. Plus, you didn't go into it knowing I was married. I did a pretty good job of hiding that from you."

"You did, didn't you?" I said, more than willing to let him shoulder the blame. "Thanks for that. I guess it makes me feel a little better."

"Don't get me wrong, I'm happy to hear from you, but I'm very curious as to what prompted this phone call today."

"Well, funny you should ask. I actually called to, uhhh, ask you a *little* favor."

"For you? Anything, you name it."

"I'd like to have an affair with you."

"Excuse me?"

"I had an affair with you when you were married, so I'd like you to return the favor. I think it's only fair. It's *your* turn," I said laughing hard. The alcohol made the statement much funnier than it actually was.

"You sure know how to make an offer I can't refuse," he said. "But, why me?"

"Well, frankly . . . because I know that you care for me, but not *too* much, and the sex will be good, but not *too* good."

"You've been drinking, haven't you?"

"Just a l'il bit," I slurred as the Patron went into fourth gear. "Four margaritas and a shot of Patron to chase it all down."

"I'll tell you what, Charisse. Why don't you give me a call tomorrow, and we can talk about this when you're sober."

"You're pro-bally right, I've problably had too much too drink," I said as the slurs kicked in, "but I know what I'm saying, and I know what I'm doing. So, I'm going to email you an invitation, with the name of the hotel, time, and date. If you want to show up, you can. And if you don't, I'll understand. You don't even need to respond. Just remember I'm going to be there, waiting for *little ole you*."

Thirty-Eight

Tryst with a Twist

I hung up the phone and signed on to Expedia to reserve a room at the Pier V Hotel on the Baltimore harbor waterfront—one of my favorites, very chic. I sent Sean an Evite for a night of "dance, romance, and passion" as I recalled, scheduled for three weeks to the day from our phone call. The note lacked my usual witty brilliance, but it was the best I could do with four margaritas and a Patron shot coursing through my veins.

***

For the next three weeks, the guilt of my plans weighed on me, like I toted a fifty-pound barbell in a basket on my head—and I hadn't even done the deed yet. I wasn't cut out to be an adulterer and didn't even want to go through with it, but I refused to call off the plan out of pure, unadulterated stubbornness. If Jason could cheat for two years, I could certainly do it for a few hours.

I told Jason I was going to spend the night at Nisey's place; she was ready to cover for me if necessary. But my plan was to stay in the hotel only as long as necessary to do a quick hit and run with Sean. Afterward, I'd go to Nisey's place, so my cover story wouldn't be a total lie.

As I packed my overnight bag, Jason sat on the bed and stared at me, like he knew what I planned. Kind of freaked me out, made me nervous. I imagined a neon letter "A" (for Adulterer) flashing over my head. Eventually, I convinced myself that *damn Catholic guilt* was messing with my head and shrugged it off.

"So, you're going to Nisey's for the night, huh?"

"Yeah, she's been going through some changes with her boyfriend. She needs some girl time. We'll have a chocolate feast, a few drinks, and talk each other to death until we fall asleep."

"Well, I need some *wife* time," he said, grabbing my hand and pulling me on his lap. "How about you stay home tonight? Maybe we could just spend some time together, alone, watch movies, and snuggle up on the couch."

"Really? I don't remember the last time you asked me to snuggle up on the couch, maybe since our second or third date? What's bringing this on?"

"Things between us have been difficult, but I love you, Charisse. I want us to stay together. I want to make things right."

About ten months too late I would say. The timing of this speech was a bit off putting though. Seemed like he tried to give me a way out, but I didn't think he had a clue. Plus, after laying condoms and fake love cards around the house with no reaction whatsoever, I didn't think he cared enough to be concerned.

"Maybe next weekend, okay? It's Nisey, I promised."

"Okay, well . . . you have a good time, and I'll see you when you get home tomorrow. I love you, Charisse."

"I love you too, Jason," I said. Then it hit me.

I do still love him, damn it!

What the hell am I doing?

I didn't want to have an affair; who was I kidding? That's not the kind of person I wanted to be, no matter how Jason had wronged me.

Change of plans.

I'd still go to the hotel for a while; if I cancelled, I couldn't get a refund anyway. Rather than screw Sean, I'd chill for a few hours, maybe take a long hot bath. I'd tell Sean that I was backing out if he showed up. Hell, I didn't even know if he'd come; I hadn't heard from him.

After I checked in the hotel, I sat my bags in the room, plunked on the bed, stared at the ceiling until I drifted to sleep, and woke up about an hour and a half later. Guilt was exhausting. Sean still hadn't shown up or called. *What a relief.* I pulled out my laptop and checked my email to see if Sean had sent a note—nothing. Only an Evite reminder.

When I opened it, I realized I'd given Sean the right hotel name, but the wrong address, no doubt due to the loads of alcohol I'd consumed before I drafted the invitation. Either he was sitting at the wrong hotel or driving in circles trying to find me. Didn't matter, either way, there'd be no sex happening *that* night.

I sat in the Jacuzzi for about thirty minutes before the phone rang. I grabbed the telephone that hung on the wall next to the bathtub.

"Hello?"

"Hi, Charisse, it's me Sean."

"I figured as much. Where are you?"

"Well, I'm on the road. You gave me the wrong address."

"I know, my bad, but I think this mistake is for the best. I've, uhh, changed my mind about tonight. This isn't me, you know that."

"Yeah, I know. I'm actually surprised you showed up."

"I came to my senses late, so I figured I'd chill out for a while, take a nice bath, and head over to Nisey's house, which is where I'm *supposed* to be."

"Well, since I'm already out here, I'm gonna stop by for a few minutes before you go. Is that okay?"

"That's fine."

I gave him directions thinking a short visit would be harmless. "Okay, well I'm in room 712. Just come up."

Buried in bubbles, I soaked for a few more minutes; I had a serious "Calgon, take me away" moment and didn't want it to end. I jumped out of the tub, wrapped the jumbo Egyptian cotton towel around my curves, and started to lotion up when I heard a knock at the door. Unless Sean found a way to drive at warp speed, I knew it couldn't be him.

"Jason!" I said, startled and shocked. "What are you doing here?"

"What the hell are *you* doing here is the question?" he asked, pushing past me. The heavy door slammed shut and he glared at me.

"How . . . how did you know I was here?" I said, securing the towel around me.

"I found your little condoms and love notes sitting around the house, so I hired a private detective. He's been keeping track of you for weeks now, your emails, everything."

"What! Are you out of your mind! Why would you waste what little money we have on a private investigator?"

"Because I wanted to know what was going on with you. I wanted to know if you were capable of this, and it looks like I have my answer."

"You're crazy. This isn't even what you think—" I started.

"I don't want to hear it," he interrupted. "Get your shit and let's go. Now, you can walk out or I can carry you out, but one way or the other you're leaving this room, and you're coming home with me."

Oh, no he didn't. Ha! Joke's on him. I'd gained fifteen pounds since I found out about his affair. He couldn't pick me up, let alone carry me anywhere.

"If you'd just listen—," I started again.

"I don't want to hear it. You're caught and you know it. Don't try to talk your way out of it. Just get dressed, get your shit, and let's go."

"I ain't going anywhere! So, how ya like me now?"

Who said that?

"Oh, you're *not*? So, what? You wanna stay here and screw your old boyfriend, right? Damn our marriage, right?" he yelled, pressing his hand against his forehead as sullen tears flooded his eyes.

"*Marriage*? What *marriage*? You and I had a *wedding*, we *never* had a *marriage*. You want to sit up here and act all self-righteous and holier-than-thou because you think you caught me in something. You didn't catch anything. Now, if you'll excuse me, you can carry your black ass *right* back home. I'll leave when I get good and damn ready."

"So, that's how you want to play it."

"Yeah, we're gonna play it like Maxwell, 'Til the Cops Come Knockin,'" I said, feeling froggy and ready to leap out of my marriage. "You're not fooling me, Jason. You think I don't see what's going on here? You just wanted to get some dirt on me, so you can run back to your little girlfriend and I wouldn't have the grounds to report your relationship. You didn't have to go through all this trouble, though, you dumb ass. You probably spent, what, a couple thousand dollars? To catch me doing something I wasn't going to do in the first place, so you could do something I've been hoping you'd do for months. So leave, go on back to her. This so-called marriage is over!"

Jason brooded and stared at me as water leaked down his cheeks. He said nothing as he moped out the door. At last, I'd given him what he wanted—permission to leave. Damn soldier couldn't do anything without orders. I sat on the bed and cried myself into dehydration. Things weren't as they appeared, but I refused to explain. The truth: Our marriage ended before it began. I was door number two, and he wanted the prize behind door number one—Kendra. He never committed to us, always had one foot out the door. And you can't build a solid life together on such a faulty foundation.

I called Nisey and told her I would be staying at the hotel after all. I crawled into bed turned off the lights and stared at the harbor lights in the distance through the patio door, when I heard another knock. Part of me hoped Jason had come back to apologize, but another part of me sighed, relieved it was Sean.

"Well, your timing is impeccable. You missed the excitement."

"No, I didn't. I walked up to the door and listened to you two arguing. I only came back to see if you were still here and make sure you were okay."

"No, I'm not okay. I mean I ended our marriage and sent him back to his girlfriend."

"Come here," he said as he opened his arms and wrapped them around me. "It's going to be okay, Charisse. You're a survivor. You're gonna be just fine."

"I know," I said, sniffing as I walked toward the phone. "But since we're here, how about I order up some Grey Goose? Stay and have a drink with me."

**

Jason and I had built our marriage on overactive endorphins, a faulty foundation to say the least. We were doomed to fail because our hormonal high could not sustain our relationship through such trying lows—like war . . . or his love for another woman. As a matter of fact, we didn't have a lot in common and, had I taken a little more time to get to know him, I would've learned one simple lesson much sooner: *Never let what's between my legs select my man.* I want to be married to a good husband—not wedded to a sex partner who's good in bed.

Thirty-Nine

Date with Destiny

Nisey and I had been in Winston-Salem a week, and my mother remained in a coma. James, while glad to see us, was sleep-deprived and hadn't slept four hours together since they put her in intensive care. His face reflected a steady concern and love, a love I'd never known. The kind of love that makes a man stay with a woman year after year, even though she, the love of his life, refuses to marry him. A pain that keeps him up night after night because he feels half of him is missing. I don't know why my mother never married James; I strongly suspect she'd long succumbed to the fear of commitment I'd been indoctrinated with the majority of my life. But if ever my mother had a Santa Claus worth believing in, James was the one.

I didn't run into Lee once, thank God. A freak storm knocked the power out at the Piggly Wiggly for a week.

Dwayne called everyday without fail, once in the morning before I left for the hospital and once when I returned each night. He said he couldn't come to support me in my hour of panic-stricken anxiety because his sister was experiencing pregnancy complications. He'd been traveling to Chicago to help them out but promised to cash in his frequent flier miles for a weekend getaway for two when I returned.

Thank God for Nisey; she was my rock. I'd never seen that side of her. Then again, we'd never experienced a crisis of mother-in-coma magnitude. In the twenty-plus years that we'd been friends, we'd only lost a combined two relatives: my grandmother and Nisey's crazy Aunt Geneva who used to force-feed us fruitcake and chittlins' when we stayed with her during spring breaks in Atlanta.

Nisey held my mom's hand when I took bathroom breaks, talked to her, helped me massage and reposition her so she wouldn't get bed sores, lifted her so we could change her sheets, painted her toes and fingernails—said a coma was no reason for a woman to go without a decent pedicure—and we both read to her. I read J. California Cooper ("I know that if you want to find yourself some happiness, you have to get up and go out and work hard for it . . .") and Nisey read Zane's Sex Chronicles ("I wrap my legs around your waist, and you hold me up against the wall on the rear of the balcony. We begin to kiss again, but deeper this time. . . "). Nisey said we needed to read something that would wake her up—not put her to sleep.

Gradually, my mother regained consciousness; her eyes flickered a few minutes one day, her hand twitched the next. About three weeks after we arrived, she was alert, somewhat responsive, and her eyes fixed on me.

"You gave us a scare, Mommy," I said teary-eyed as her grip on my hand tightened. "James has been here day and night; he never left your side. Nisey's here too."

"I love you . . . baby. Glad you're . . . here," Mom muttered weakly, as her eyes scanned the room. "Where's . . . Nisey?"

"She ran out to get some food, she'll be—"

"I'm baaaaack," Nisey bellowed, placing the Burger King bags on a small table near the door. "Oh, look at you Momma Tyson. I'm so happy to see you awake."

"Come here, baby," my mother said, gesturing Nisey to come closer.

"Yes, Momma Tyson, what is it?" Nisey said as she leaned her face to my mother's and stroked her hair.

"I want . . . to . . . borrow that book . . . you been readin' to me . . . when I get better. Child, child, child," she said, winking at James.

We erupted in laughter.

That's my Mother.

The doctor said my mother would be fully recovered from her stroke after a few months of rehabilitation, and my relief soon gave way to exhaustion. Nisey and I jumped in the car and headed to my mother's house for hot showers, Grey Goose, and deep slumbers.

As we drove home, I stared out the window deep in thought and overcome by calm and angst simultaneously. -Although I'd tried for twenty-seven years to avoid my painful past, I sensed a confrontation with the truth and Lee was too close to avoid any longer. The blue sky hid behind heavy, ominous storm clouds, and the winds swirled relentlessly like the uneasy moments before a tornado strike. Even Mother Nature was more prepared than I for the intense drama that lay ahead that night.

***

I'd just stepped out of the shower and toweled myself off when I overheard Nisey barking at someone at the door. I cracked open the bathroom door and listened.

"Who are you?" Nisey snapped.

"I'm Lee, Charisse's cousin. I'm family," he said. "Is she here? I need to talk to her."

"Lee, huh? Oh, so all of a sudden you're family now, right? Well, you can just carry your ass on because she ain't got shit to say to you."

"And who the hell are you?"

"Don't worry about who the hell I am, you need to go."

"She told you, didn't she?"

"As a matter of fact, she did. Now I'm asking you nicely to leave before she gets out of the shower. And I promise you, you don't want to hear me ask *not-so-nicely*."

"Listen, I need to speak to her. It's important. There are some things she needs to hear . . . from me," he said as he pushed past Nisey and strode into the living room.

"Excuse me?" Nisey snapped.

Forty

Downsized

I stood near the door and slipped into my pajamas while I listened to Nisey and Lee banter. My rage boiled. The nerve of him to show up at my mother's house, acting like he was some kin to me. He was no family of mine and hadn't been for years. Families take care of each other, help each other. My mind flashed back to the cocky smirk on his smug face all those years ago, walking around like he owned the world and everything in it. He was my blood, the nearest thing I had to a brother (or father for that matter). He was supposed to protect me.

But he didn't.

He turned his head and walked away, like I was a stranger. The first man I ever trusted. And when I needed him the most, he showed me his ass. I vowed never to trust him or any man ever again. In my world, from father to cousin, men had become an unworthy lot.

Enough was enough.

"Get out Lee," I yelled, as I stomped out of the room, my anger almost beyond my control. "I want you to leave, now!"

"Charisse, wait, please. I know what I did was wrong, and I'm sorry. I have never been sorrier about anything in my life."

"Sorry, huh? You got that right. You're a sorry, pitiful, pathetic excuse for a man. You didn't even have the balls to tell Mama and Aunt Jackie the truth. You just lied, acted like nothing ever happened."

"I know, I know, but you don't understand—" Lee started before he was interrupted by the sound of the front door unlocking.

"Fantastic! James is home. Why don't we let James hear what I don't understand," I said, emboldened by my fury. I was in no mood to hide. I was in no mood to care. Lee's dirty little secret would finally find the light of day. There'd be no more cowering in the darkness of my shame and his guilt; I no longer cared who knew. He should've had the decency to stay away from me, leave me be. But no. He couldn't do that. That would've been too much like right. So, I set out to air the dirty laundry, right there, so our family would see him for the cowardly snake he was.

"Come on, Lee," I said. "You wanna talk, let's talk. Come on in, James, and listen to this story. It's a doozie!"

"Charisse, I don't think we should talk about this in front of James. I'll come ba—"

"Oh, hell no. You brought your happy ass over here to pepper me with your lame ass apologies, let's tell everybody the *big secret*. Maybe I'll call my mom and Aunt Jackie and put them on speakerphone."

"What's going on with you two?" James interjected.

"Lee has an apology he wants to make," I yelled as tears trickled down my face. "Go ahead, all-star, tell James why you're so sorry. Tell him."

"Charisse—" Lee said before I cut him off again.

"Tell him, Lee. Tell him how you took me to one of your little football parties when I was thirteen, tell him how you spiked my drink without telling me because you and your little buddies thought it would be amusing to see me drunk," I said, storming toward him with my hand opened and ready to slap the black off of his face.

"Tell him, Mr. All-Star Quarterback, how you were just going to let one of those bastards rape me," I shrieked.

My voice softened as my rage gave way to sorrow. "I was too drunk to fight. The music was so loud. No one could hear me over the music. But you saw your buddy pull me in the room, didn't you? You turned your back on me and walked out the door while I called your name. Mr. Popularity. So afraid to lose your lofty position in the 'in-crowd'. Tell him, Lee."

Nisey held her arms out to me with tears in her eyes, and I sobbed. After nearly twenty years, the secret had come to light.

"Is that true?" James asked.

"I—" Lee started, dropping his head in shame.

"Yes, it's true. Then he left me there alone. A stranger, a complete stranger, burst in the room and pushed him off of me. He sat with me until I calmed down enough to go home. I trusted you. I told everyone you were my brother, and you let them humiliate me. You never even said you were sorry. And who could I tell? Who would believe Mr. All-Star Quarterback would sit by and let that son of a bitch rape his own blood?"

Nisey wrapped me in a consoling embrace. "Haven't you done enough, Mr. I'm Family? Leave!" she snarled.

"Boy, you better go," James declared. "Get out before you make me do something we'll both regret."

Lee shuffled out the door in shame, too afraid to look back or say goodbye. Not even "I'm sorry" could help his black ass.

"Does your mama know about this, baby?" James asked.

"No, sir. I never told her. How could I?"

"Sweetie, come here," James said. He extended his arms toward me, then held and comforted me, like the father I'd always needed but had never known. Perhaps my father lived in California, but my *dad* lived in Winston Salem, and I was in his arms.

"I think we can all use a drink," Nisey said. "You got some Grey Goose in here Papa James?"

"In the deep freezer," he said with a slight grin as he kissed my forehead and looked in my soggy eyes. "I knew you'd be home eventually."

Forty-One

Everything is Everything

I woke up the next morning feeling hung over. Even though James had been the only one to hear it, a tremendous weight had been lifted from my soul, unnecessarily poisoned for so many years by pain, heartache, and mistrust. There'd be no more hiding, no more shame. I'd been liberated by something as simple as revealing a secret. And the world didn't come to an end. The sun still rose, the earth still revolved, the sky was still blue, grass was still green, everything was everything. Why I had given the secret such power over my life remained my only mystery. A secret untold had proved far more destructive than its truth.

The aroma of fresh coffee and crackling bacon yanked me out of bed. Nisey was one of the few bourgeois sisters that could throw down in the kitchen, and I was glad for it that day because all that drama worked up my appetite.

"How are you feeling this morning? Did you get any sleep?" Nisey asked. She slid some eggs and bacon on my plate.

"Yeah, I slept okay I guess, as well as can be expected under the circumstances. Is James up yet?" I said, cranking my neck to see if his car was in the driveway.

"Yeah, he left for the hospital about an hour ago," she responded.

"Ever faithful," I said.

"Yes, indeed. If we could all have such a man."

"Girl, I'll co-sign that!" Indeed to have such a man.

"I have to say, Rissey, I'm so glad that you found the strength to tell someone about what happened. You'd been keeping that to yourself for far too long. But I can't believe Lee, coming here like that. What did he think would happen?"

"I don't know. I don't know. I hope he avoids the hospital while I'm here. I don't want to bring any drama around my mother while she's trying to recover, you know?"

"I know. You definitely need to tell her, but now is not the right time. You don't think James will say anything, do you?"

"No, I mean, he knows it will upset her, she doesn't need that right now."

"Yeah, you're right about that," Nisey said as she sat at the table and scooped some eggs onto her fork. "I . . . I hope you don't mind me asking. You told me about what happened with Lee, but I was curious, did you ever find out who helped you that night?"

"No, I never did. He was like this caped hero who swept through like Superman, saved me from a burning building, dropped me off, and disappeared. My knight in shining armor. Back in the day, I used to daydream he'd appear somewhere, reveal himself to me, and we'd fall in love, get married, and live happily ever after. Ridiculous, right?" I asked rhetorically as my mind flashed back to that night. I couldn't remember his face, but I remembered his presence and feeling safe and secure. James, my mystery knight, they made me realize good men existed; they were out there. With my baggage gone, I might finally have some room to invite mine in my life to stay a spell—whoever *he* was.

"No, we all want to marry our knight in shining armor, don't we? Isn't that the bullshit they feed us in almost every fairytale ever written? I mean look at Cinderella, Snow White, uhhhhhh, Shrek."

"Yeah, it'll be just my luck I'll end up with the fat, green ogre," I said, laughing that I might've predicted my future. "You know, I just thought of something else too. When I saw Lee a few days later, I remember he had a black eye. I asked Aunt Jackie about it one time, and she said he got into a fight with a football player at a party he went to. I always imagined that ass-kicking was for my honor. But knowing Lee, he probably just talked shit to the wrong person."

"Yeah, I don't know Lee, but he seems like a shit-talkin' kinda guy."

"Anyway, we should get to the hospital. I know Mommy will be looking for us," I said before I stuffed the last piece of bacon in my mouth. "Nisey, thank you for coming. I don't know what I'd have done without you."

"Please, where else would I be?"

I knew in my heart that, like Dwayne, Nisey didn't *have* to be there. But I was oh so grateful and appreciative that she was.

***

We arrived at the hospital just in time to help Mom back in her bed. She'd just taken her first shower in weeks. I hadn't seen her that happy since the watermelon news came out.

"How are you feeling this morning, Mom?" I asked cheerfully.

"Much better, baby," she answered. "I start rehab on Monday. And listen, I know you've taken a lot of time to be here for me, but you can head home if you need to. James can take it from here."

"Oh, I see, trying to get rid of me already."

"No, I know you have a lot on your plate, a lot of bills to pay. And you need to go service your boyfriend before he run out and find somebody else."

I laughed. "Geez, Mom, you really are feeling better, aren't you?"

She had a point, although I didn't really miss Dwayne—not in the traditional sense. I mean, I missed having *someone* but not Dwayne so much. I don't know, perhaps I'd been over-thinking things again, but the feeling (or lack thereof) didn't escape me. Dwayne had been a good distraction and that's about it. I contemplated breaking off our "thing" when I got back to D.C.

I walked down to the gift shop to get myself some "I'm feeling better about life in general" chocolate. Chocolate is an all-occasion food, and any reason is a good reason to indulge. As I passed the hospital entrance, Lee approached the automatic doors. My eyes rolled in the back of my head just before I walked smack into a tall gentleman whose face was concealed behind an extravagant flower arrangement. He lowered it and smiled. I, on the other hand, freaked out.

"Kevin? What the hell are you doing here!" I yelled, a bit startled but, in an odd sense, comforted.

"Uhhh—hi, Charisse," he replied, thrown by my obvious concern.

"Okay, now I'm beginning to think there's something more to these *chance* run-ins."

205

"Look, I know this looks, uhhh, *strange*. But I'm not a stalker or anything. I told you I was from North Carolina. I'm here handling some business for my father's estate in Buena Vista. I called Lamar because a friend might need his help in their divorce and when I asked about you, he said you were here, that your mother had a stroke."

I paused to drink in his response. His eyes said "Please, believe me," so I obliged.

"Ohhhhh, okay. Whew! You scared me there for a second," I said, relieved that he wasn't some deranged serial killer the government had licensed to carry a gun. "Ahhhh, are these for her?"

"Yes, I hope they're not too much," he said.

"Listen, there are very few things in the world you can give a woman 'too many' of, and flowers are certainly not among them," I said.

I noticed Lee walking through the entrance door with a tiny store-bought bouquet. He glanced at me, then his gaze locked on Kevin. When their eyes met, they stared each other down like two testosterone-charged cowboys preparing for a high-noon gunfight at the O.K. Corral. Lee caved first and headed for the elevator.

"Damn. What was that about? Do you two know each other?" I asked.

"Ohhh, uhhh, he looked like somebody I played football against back in high school, that's all," he said, his eyes shifting to avoid eye contact. "Football rivals."

"If you say so," I said in disbelief. But he didn't seem to want to discuss it further so I let it go. "Well, do you want to come up and meet my mom? She's doing much better now," I said. Just then, Cruella Deville walked up behind him, her face snarled as usual. Kevin shot a glare at her, and she grudgingly waved hello and sashayed over to the water fountain, presumably to avoid contact with the rest of us humans.

"No, I better go. Please take these and give her my best regards for speedy recovery," he said as his eyes returned to the elevator doors that had closed behind Lee.

"Ohhh kaaay, if you say so," I said, confused by the sudden chill in his warm demeanor. "Thank you for stopping by. I hope everything goes okay with your father's estate."

"Please, no thanks necessary."

Forty-Two

Forgiven

On my way back to my mother's room, I saw Lee sitting in the waiting area holding his paltry bouquet. I paused for a moment to assess my feelings; I didn't want to create a scene that might land a second family member in the hospital.

I thought, *Hmmm . . . no detectable rage.*

Had I been so freed by telling James what happened that I could fathom holding a brief conversation with him, almost twenty-seven years later? Perhaps, the time had come to lay that horrible night to rest. It wasn't a secret anymore, someone knew, someone heard what happened and felt the same contempt for Lee's behavior I'd felt. So reaffirming. I'd shouldered the burden for far too long. By revealing the ugly truth, I'd transferred the burden from my soul to his. Had I known I'd be that liberated, I'd have placed an ad in the Winston-Salem Journal years ago.

"Lee," I said, sliding into one of the uncomfortable waiting room chairs adjacent to Lee. I sat Kevin's bouquet on the floor in front of me. "Hi."

"Charisse, I'm not staying. I only came by to say hi to Auntie. She'd be upset with me if I didn't show up to see her," he said, concerned a nasty scene was imminent. "I'll take these to her and I'll leave."

"It's okay, Lee. I mean, believe me I never in a million years thought I'd ever say this but, I forgive you," I said, almost catching myself off-guard. "After twenty-seven years, I forgive you. And I'm not doing this for you; I'm doing this for me. I've suffered enough. I've put myself through enough. It's your turn to live with this burden. I've lived with it long enough, and now I'm done."

He whipped his head toward me, and he glared in my eyes. "Do you honestly think I haven't lived with that night every single day? Charisse, I was an all-star quarterback, I had scholarship offers to seven schools, and now I manage the Piggly Wiggly—the Piggly fucking Wiggly, Charisse. Do you think everything just magically fell apart? I've spent so many years of my life trying to figure out how I could take that night back. I swear, it has haunted me, every single day. I always thought that if I could just go back and do the right thing, your life would've been so different—and my life too. I didn't just let you down and break your trust, I let myself down. I let everybody down."

"Yes, you did," I chimed but kept it brief. He was on a roll.

"But I want you to know that I sat my mother down and told her what happened last night after I left you. Watching you last night, in so much pain, I couldn't live with it anymore."

"You did? What did she say?" I asked.

"She cried. She said she didn't raise me to be that kind of man, and she didn't know I was capable of doing something so cowardly. She said I was a stranger to her."

"That must've been difficult for you to hear, you guys are so close. Are you okay?"

Who said that?

"I'm sorry. You're asking me if I'm okay?" he said, appearing astonished that I could find it in my heart to care for him after everything that happened. I hated to tell him that it wasn't me; that was nothing but God's grace.

"Look, we can't turn back the clock. All we can do is live in today and make the best choices we can from this point forward. That's all we can do. There's no magic to it. If there were, I'd have waved that magic wand a long, long time ago."

"I'm sorry, Char—," he started.

"No more I'm sorries," I interrupted, too tired and too free to feel sorry about anything. "It's time to move on. We both need to move forward. The slate is clean. We're still young, you know. Maybe you'll find life beyond the Piggly Wiggly. And maybe I can find the courage to trust again."

The Bum Magnet

***

When I walked in Mom's room, Aunt Jackie was standing beside my mother's bed, staring at her while she slept. She turned to me and smiled, tears clinging to the corners of her eyes.

I knew why.

"Wow, that's a beautiful bouquet," Aunt Jackie whispered.

"Isn't it? This guy who rear-ended me just happened to be in town and bought them for Mommy."

"What's up with that smile?" she asked.

"Was I smiling? I didn't notice," I responded.

"Uhm hmm, baby, let's take a walk to the cafeteria to get some sweet tea."

"Okay, Nisey, do you want anything?"

"No, I'm fine," she said, waving us off because she was engrossed in The Young and the Restless. She'd become addicted to soaps during our short visit.

Aunt Jackie grabbed my hand and walked with me down the hall.

"Lee told me what happened."

"Yeah, I know," I said.

"I've watched you for years, Charisse. I always said to myself, 'Here is a beautiful, smart, funny, successful girl. Why in heaven's name can't she sustain a healthy relationship?' Between what you been through and that mumbo jumbo your mama been fillin' your head with since you were old enough to understand the difference between boys and girls, now I understand why. What they tried to do to your body was a crime, but what they did to your beautiful soul, that's a sin," she said, leading me to a bench outside the cafeteria. "I knew something went wrong, but you are your mama's child. And I couldn't tell her how to raise you anymore than I'd let her tell me how to raise Lee. But now I think this family has had its fill of silence, don't you?"

"Yes, ma'am," I responded.

"I'm curious about something. Every time I've tried to talk to you before, you avoided me like the plague. Looks like you're fresh out of places to run, huh?"

"I don't know, Aunt Jackie. I've been doing a lot of soul searching this year and—"

"Baby, I'm glad you've been doing some soul searching, but you do understand that without dealing with what happened all those years ago, you could only gain insight into the symptom that something was wrong—not the illness and not the cure," she interrupted. "Looking at your life or your past relationships only scratches the surface. It's the alarm that tells you something deeper is wrong."

"Really?" I replied. "See, the thing is, I usually know when a man isn't good for me, I usually know early on, but I keep them around anyway, hoping I can change them, hoping they'll change on their own, hoping I'm wrong about them. Always hoping."

"I think it's possible you're hoping you're right."

"Hoping I'm right? What do you mean?" I said, confused that she could actually be suggesting I *wanted* these bums in my life. That couldn't be further from the truth.

"What happened to you scarred you, it would scar anybody. You committed yourself to not trust any man ever again. And you're not a gambler, never have been. So, you bring people into your life who you know you can't trust, that way you don't ever have to take a risk and open up to them. It's a defense mechanism, keeps you safe. You know they're no good for you from the beginning, so you don't have to gamble your heart. But, baby, you're never going to find the love you want, the love you need, if you don't step out on faith and take the gamble. Do you understand?" she said. A pleading in her eyes begged me to understand so I could change my life.

"Yes, ma'am," I said, feeling as if a shroud had been lifted from my entire being. She was right. On some level, dating bums gave me comfort in that I knew I couldn't trust them and never would. "I understand, maybe for the first time in my life."

"You can't lock your door and then wonder why nobody can't get to you. If you want to find a healthy love, and I know you do, you're going to have to let the bad in with the good—and then trust yourself to know the difference. And your mama and I, we made a lot of mistakes, but we didn't raise no fools, you hear me?"

"I hear you, Aunt Jackie," I said. "Trust myself."

I returned to my mother's house later feeling enlightened by my conversation with Aunt Jackie. She was right, I did choose people I knew I couldn't trust, but it wasn't a conscious effort on my part. I guess somewhere inside I knew, I just didn't understand why, never put two and two together. My bum magnetism was a defense mechanism; it kept my heart safe. I suppose I'd become fed up with being safe—safe equaled bum. Each day of my journey took me closer to a place where I was preparing to gamble.

Reading my journals had been as therapeutic as talking to Aunt Jackie, so I pulled one from my suitcase and collapsed on the bed. I'd blocked my relationship history out of my mind for so long, distressed by the failures, I never realized how much I had to learn from my own mistakes. Suddenly, the article that started my journey flashed in my mind. "Do you have a lingering ghost from your past that you've tried to forget but never put to rest?"

I smiled because for the first time in twenty-seven years, the answer was . . . No!

Forty-Three

The Man and the Mickey

I needed to support my mother, but enough was enough. Between rehab, James, and *Zane's Sex Chronicles*, my mother's life would be consumed for the next six months—at least. The time had come for me to get back on track and refocus on my own life—through a clearer lens, of course. Half of my extensive luggage collection was empty, and I began to really understand myself, my so-called relationships for what they were, and my choices in men for what they severely lacked.

Take, for instance, Dwayne. What kind of man prances around butt-naked in front of a complete stranger, besides the Chocolate Thunder, Rico Suave, Mick the Ruler, and the rest of the hung-like-a-horse crew down at the Strip-O-Rama? He had an agenda, and he caught me at a weak-willed, sex-deprived moment. But why would he slip me a *mickey*?

I decided to call Dwayne and have "the talk." I mean, putting the whole drugging incident aside for a moment, if I was keepin' it real with myself, the only thing I got out of our relationship was good sex. That's all. We hadn't really "dated" since the first few months. Our days and nights together were spent in my house or his. I may not be the brightest star in the sky, but that's the way you treat a piece of ass, not someone you want a future with. Sure, he bought me dinner and little gifts here and there but nothing that said "I'm working to make a life with you." Rather, they mostly said, "The only time I'm *into* you is when I'm between your legs, so I'm doing the *absolute minimum* amount humanly possible to keep the ass coming and you hanging on. And to be honest, I don't have any intention whatsoever of taking this *any further* than that."

He was scheduled to arrive at Baltimore Washington International airport from Chicago, his third trip since his sister had started having pregnancy difficulties. I couldn't help but feel a little miffed that, despite the fact that he contacted me frequently during my trip to Winston, he didn't go out of his way to support me. He didn't even send flowers; Kevin did that much and our relationship was built on a bent rear fender. If actions spoke louder than words, Dwayne was mute. It was time to clear the air, once and for all, and I'd start with the mickey.

"Hey, baby. It's so good to hear your voice. I was standing here at the baggage claim thinking about you," Dwayne said.

"Do you have a minute? I need to clear the air about something, something important."

"Shoot."

Don't tempt me.

"Why . . . why did you slip medicine in my tea?"

Silence.

More silence.

"Hello? Hello?" I asked.

"Yeah, I'm not sure how to respond. It sounds like you're accusing me of something."

"I am."

"Of what?"

"Of whatever it's called when you slip medicine in someone's drink without telling them," I openly accused. Emboldened by my new sense of "me," I flatly put it out there. No need to mince words.

"Okay, let me get this straight. You think, for some underhanded reason, I slipped drugs in your tea, helped you into bed. Stayed with you alllllll night long. Woke up the next morning and cooked you breakfast because . . . I'm what? I'm trying to kill you?" he asked facetiously. It sounded ridiculous but there was no mistaking he'd done exactly what I'd accused him of, so it was his case to prove—not mine.

"Well, uhhh . . . I didn't say kill."

"Or maybe so I could steal from you? Anything missing? Your wallet? Checkbook?"

"No, I didn't say steal either. I just—"

The Bum Magnet

"Charisse, I've been in car accidents before. I know how painful it is when you wake up the next morning if you don't take medicine. You kept saying you weren't going to take any, and I knew you needed it. I was just trying to do what was best for you."

"So that's it. That's all there was to it." I replied, a heavy cloud of doubt still towering over me. I remained conflicted, but the idea of Dwayne trying to drug me for no apparent reason still seemed unfathomable. I didn't want to believe what my instincts were screaming.

Do *good* men do *bad* things? Do *bad* men do *good* things?
Which category does Dwayne fit in?

"Of course, I know you're not stupid. I knew you'd figure it out. But I also knew you wouldn't wake up unable to move your neck the next morning too. That was more important to me than your suspicions."

"So, you did it for *me*?"

"Listen, we'll finish this conversation when I get there. I'm on my way."

I hated him. He always had a way of making me feel like a jerk when I knew deep down that I was right.

In one of my *many* less brilliant moments, I remembered that my fortieth birthday was coming up. I thought rather than put him on full blast, I'd use the "momentous" occasion to test him, gauge how he really felt about me. If he stepped up to the plate and treated me like I was his girlfriend, you know, took the lead to do something really special to mark my milestone, then I'd consider continuing our relationship. But, if he treated me like a piece of ass, you know, woke up the morning of and said, "Your *birthday*? *You were born*? I didn't even know you had a birthday. Well how about that!" I'd end it.

***

"Aren't you a sight for sore eyes," Dwayne said as he lifted me up in his arms like he'd returned from a six-year tour in Vietnam. "I'm so happy to see you."

"I'm happy to see you too," I said, planting a hesitant kiss on his lips. "How's your sister doing?"

"She's better, much better. I don't think I'll need to go back to Chicago for a while. Things are under control; the baby's doing fine. You and I just need to get to the closing table so I can get into my new house."

"You must be excited," I said.

"I am. I really am."

"Have you been able to pull the cash together? That was a pretty hefty sum. We can't close until you can get the money in certified funds."

"Don't you worry about that," he said, self-assured, "Cash is pretty tight right now, but I've got that under control, okay? Anyway, we have more important things to think about."

"Such as?"

"Such as how we're going to celebrate your fortieth birthday."

"You remembered?"

"I'm your man, of course I remembered."

My man, huh? Didn't quite ring true, didn't feel . . . *right*. I hoped but didn't expect him to do anything extra special for me. I decided to contain my enthusiasm until I was assured my big celebration wouldn't consist of three balloons, a number one, and a caramel sundae at McDonald's.

"Well, I thought maybe we could do a romantic dinner somewhere special. Maybe the Sky Dome at the Double Tree?"

Whoa, that's an unexpected gesture.

"The Sky Dome? Isn't that the rotating restaurant in Crystal City?"

"Yeah, that's it," he said. "The most beautiful views of D.C. in the area."

"I've always wanted to go there, but I hear it's pretty expensive," I said. I'd passed by the restaurant so many times and so longed to dine there. I always envisioned dancing and swaying to music while the restaurant slowly turned my dream man to reality. It was the crème de al crème of romance and fantasy—a perfect place to celebrate my fortieth birthday with "the one". But was Dwayne "*the one*"?

"So what! You're worth it. You only turn forty once, right?"

"Right," I said.

"Well, then it's a date. The Sky Dome for dinner on your birthday," he said. "But, uhhh, can I have my dessert *now*?"

Typical man, never something for nothing. My body was craving some attention and fair exchange was no robbery, but I couldn't help but feel sleeping with Dwayne again, before I'd resolved my misgivings and concerns, would be a major step backward. And I'd begun moving forward. No, that was the perfect time to demonstrate *my maturity, my evolution*. I'd be *direct*; I'd tell him *straight up* that I didn't want to have sex again until my reservations about him and our relationship were alleviated. And he could deal with that or bounce . . .

"Uhhh, well, I'm uhhhh . . . I'm on my period, sorry. How about a movie?"

Okay, so I punked out. Rome wasn't built in a day.

Forty-Four

Friend Isn't A Four-Letter Word

I'd been away from the office for so long that I actually looked forward to getting back to work. Nyla was an absolute lifesaver; she managed the paperwork for the sale of Dwayne's house which, by the way, sold one week after I arrived in Winston Salem. Nyla told me the buyer's agent said her client loved the décor and wondered who'd done the interior decorating.

C'est moi!

"Good morning, Nyla," I said. "It's good to be back."

"It's good to have you back , Ms. Tyson. I'll let you get settled in and get you up to speed," she said, shuffling papers on her desk.

"No, that's okay, shoot. What's going on?"

"Well, you know Mr. Gibson is scheduled to close on the Ft. Washington property on Monday. You also had two calls from the clients who were trying to avoid foreclosure. Apparently, they are ready to list their homes; they received the Notice of Default from the bank."

"Oh no, please do not let me forget to call them later. But back to Mr. Gibson for one moment, have you spoken with the settlement company? Is the title work done?"

"Yes, ma'am. They've advised him how much money he needs to bring to the closing table. As long as he has the funds, everything should go very smoothly."

"Okay, that sounds good. Anything else?"

"Yeah, a Mr. Jackson stopped by to see you early this morning. He was here when the office opened."

"Mr. Jackson? Lamar Jackson?"

"Yes, that's it. Lamar."

"Did he say what he wanted?"

"No, he mentioned something about an insurance settlement. I told him you'd be in before noon."

I rang Lamar to find out why he didn't call me. He said he *happened* to be in the area, so he thought he'd drop off my check and take me out to breakfast, no big deal. I invited him out to lunch at Jasper's that afternoon; we needed to talk.

My stomach dipped a little as I anticipated our lunch; I didn't feel quite ready to discuss our future. I couldn't believe Lamar and I would even contemplate a relationship with each other after so many years. If he still had dawg tendencies, there'd be no debate. But he wasn't the super fine, pounce-everything-moving Lamar anymore. He was the super fine, new (and much improved), successful attorney, church-going, S500-driving Lamar. Unfortunately, he was also the "Eight is Enough" got a basketball team and three substitutes Lamar.

Damn, I wanted kids but *eight* of them? And not one of them the result of my surviving twenty-four hours of excruciating labor pains? (Wait, that's not a drawback; they're coming.) I was a bit prejudiced, but I couldn't help myself. What about Christmases? We'd have to take out a home equity line of credit just to keep them clothed. And birthdays? Oh my God, child support? I'd just heard about a case in which a judge ordered a newlywed wife to pay child support for her husband's three kids because the dead beat dad was out of work . . . again. What kind of shit is that? I envisioned eight ghetto baby-mamas dressed in Jimmy Choos, carrying Gucci bags, and wearing the super-sized gold hoop earrings with their names spelled out in cursive (so I'd know whose name to write on the check) lined up outside my house like the family credit union. The kids were a huge stumbling block to come to grips with.

Okay maybe not huge.

Colossal would've been more accurate.

And uhhh, well, maybe they weren't a stumbling block per se.

More like . . . *the Great Wall of China.*

We arrived at the restaurant and were seated at our table. I hoped that he wouldn't bring up the relationship issue at all. I didn't think I could give him the straight answer. There weren't many nice ways to say, "I think you're nice, but you've got too damn many kids." I don't know, maybe there was a nicer way to say it. "Uhh, Lamar, I like you, but I could only be a good mother to three, maybe four, of your kids. You might need to find someone else to love the rest." Or maybe "Lamar, baby, I think we could make this relationship work, if we could be parents on a rotating schedule, maybe two kids each year?" Mmmm . . . but to wake up to those hazel eyes everyday and feel his arms around me. We could manage, couldn't we?

"May I get you some drinks to start with," the waiter asked.

"Uh, yeah, I'll have two Grey Goose and cranberry juices on the rocks. He doesn't drink so I'm having one for him too, thank you."

Lamar laughed. "Iced tea for me, please."

He continued, "So, how are things going? If I recall correctly, your fortieth birthday is coming up right?"

"Wow, you remembered. Yeah, can you believe it?"

"That means I've known you, how many years? Let's see—"

"Stop right there," I interrupted. "Don't forget you're older than me. Any attempt to make me feel old will only make you feel ancient."

"Good point," he said. "So, what's up with you and that Kevin guy? You know, he called me looking for you while you were in North Carolina?"

"He did? He told me he called you about his friend's divorce, and you mentioned that I was away."

"Well, that's partially true. He did call about his friend's divorce, but he asked about *you*. He asked if we were seeing each other."

My heart fluttered in a pleasing surprise before I was cast back to Earth at the reality that he and I couldn't be together as long as he stayed with Evilina. I'd officially colored myself finished with bums and unavailable men. The only thing Kevin could do for me is introduce me to his *single brother*—if he had one.

"Oh, really? What did you say to that?"

"I told him no, that we were college friends, but I was hoping for more."

I sipped that down with my Grey Goose. *Why is Kevin asking about me?*

Lamar smirked and continued, "Are you *sure* something isn't going on with you two?"

"Not that I know of, unless we've entered a relationship without my knowledge . . . besides you saw his girlfriend."

"Yeah, I *saw* her alright."

"I see. You were checkin' her out, huh?" I said, studying his expression to see if he'd try and squirm his way out of this one.

"No. Don't get me wrong, she's fine as hell but she seems a little too evil for my tastes."

"Oh, get outta here. You men *looove* the bitches."

"So, what does that make you?" he asked with an elevated eyebrow and sly grin.

I couldn't do anything but shake my head. "Okay, touché. You got me there. Anyway, I'm actually pretty surprised he said that—and to you of all people."

"Me too," he said as he reached in his pocket and pulled out an envelope. "Oh, before I forget, here is your settlement check. I ran into Jerry in the hall, and he said he was going to deliver this to you himself. But I told him I'd do it, since I'd be seeing you later today."

"Is that right? So, you *knew* I was going to see you, huh?"

"I didn't know, but I hoped. Anyway, I've got one more question to ask you before we eat."

"I'm almost afraid to ask," I said. "What it is?"

"What's up with you and Dwayne? I know he's still in your life. Are you two getting serious or what?"

"Or what. I honestly don't know how to answer because I'm just not sure about him. You know, how you get a feeling about someone, but something just doesn't sit right? On the exterior, he seems okay. Every time I think I've found something concrete against him, he pulls a Jedi Mind Trick and makes me feel like a paranoid idiot. Do you know what I mean?"

"Yeah, I know exactly what you mean," he said. "Can I tell you something and ask you not to take offense? I'm only saying this to be helpful, not hurtful."

"Okay," I said, bracing myself. "What is it?"

"Well, I've known you for a long time, and from what I've seen, you don't seem to trust yourself anymore than you trust men. Once upon a time you had 'a bad feeling' about me, and guess what? You were absolutely right," he paused to take a sip of tea and continued. "You know, you kind of remind me of the sorority girl in the horror flick who knows a deranged murderer is lurking in the woods, but when she hears the leaves crackling beneath the footsteps, she stops to say, 'Who's there?' and gets her head chopped off, rather than running like hell to safety. Sometimes, Charisse, it's alright to run like hell and assess what happened later."

"I hear what you're saying. But in my world, everyone is a deranged murderer. I feel like my 'good man' detector must be broken because they can't all be bad. Can they?"

"Yeah, they can. Maybe you feel like they're all deranged murderers because they're all deranged murderers. Well, let me ask you this. Search your deepest feelings and tell me, in your heart of hearts, do you feel like I'm the same person I used to be? Or do you think I've changed?"

I closed my eyes and searched my deepest feelings. Lamar was not the same man he used to be. He was different. He had a new spirit. He'd grown up and become a man . . . a real man and father. He understood his place on life's stage, and he'd taken his final bow in his role as player. He'd given it up for the role of . . . Lamar.

"No, you definitely feel different this time."

"Well, that's because *I am* different. I'm not the same Lamar I used to be. So your instincts are right."

"You don't count."

"Why not? Fifteen years ago, you had it right."

"Well, if that's the case, then you would be the only man I've had a positive feeling about in fifteen years. That's a little scary."

"Are you sure about that?" he said, appearing optimistic that he'd proven his point and that I'd realize he was the man for me.

I closed my eyes and searched my feelings again. Sean, Jason, etc., all flashed through my mind. Until . . . He was right, that wasn't quite accurate. There was one other man in the last fifteen years that I truly had a good feeling about—from day one. And when his face appeared, all I could do is smile.

"Hmmm, maybe you're onto something there," I said as the waitress placed our food on the table. "Maybe I do need to trust my feelings."

"I think you should," he affirmed.

"Listen Lamar, I need to say something," I said, pausing to draw the courage I needed to continue. Making the speech to Lamar was hard, but I had to follow my instincts. And my instincts told me that although Lamar might be a *good* man for me, he wasn't *the right* man for me. "I am so glad to have you back in my life again. Lord knows, I have given serious thought about the possibilities for us. In so many ways, you make me feel like you did when we were in school . . . but in a good way," I said.

I took a gulp of my drink and continued, "The thing is, I think that you and I have a beautiful future . . . but as friends."

"Just friends?" he asked.

"You make friendship sound like a *bad* thing."

"It is when you want more."

"It's not when you know in your heart that more won't work and might destroy what could be something beautiful and lifelong. And let's just say I'm . . . I'm *trusting* my feelings." Maybe it was time for Lamar to learn a new role—friend.

"Well, I'd rather have you in my life as my friend than not at all. So, we're friends?" he said, his eyes betraying his disappointment.

"Friends."

Forty-Five

Forty and Fabulous

The day started off like any other, even though it turned out to be anything but. I woke up and examined my face in the bathroom mirror for twenty minutes, checking for new wrinkles or crow's feet that had waited until this cursed occasion to emerge. I lifted my head up to expose my neck and ran my hand down my throat. *Thank God, no chicken neck.*

What's that? A new gray hair? I thought, while combing my fingers through my mane to unearth any evidence that might give away my dreaded milestone. *Naaah, false alarm.*

Each year, I'd selected a birthday theme song. Last year, I'd picked "I'm Every Woman" by Chaka Khan. My fortieth birthday tune was a smidge less upbeat—the theme song from *Dragnet.*

Dum-de-dum-dum, Dum-de-dum-dum-duuumm.

How appropriate. The song portended doom and gloom which is what I expected my day to consist of. I'd had lofty dreams for my life and thought I'd at least be married with two-and-a-half kids by forty. No such luck. I had no kids and no husband, but at least things weren't entirely bleak on the man front. Dwayne had promised to take me to the Sky Dome for dinner that evening. If he came through, I thought it might top my "all-time favorite date" list, bumping my first night out with Lamar to number two.

Lamar gave "*good date,*" even though he turned out to be a player.

I'd been lingering in my closet for an hour trying to find a little black dress to wear for the evening before my cell phone rang. Not a single one of the nine numbers that I owned screamed, "I'm forty and fabulous." Rather, they whispered, "You're not really going to try and squeeze your fat ass in me, are you?" I snatched the phone off my nightstand and plunked down on my bed in frustration.

"What is it?" I snapped.

"Happy fortieth birthday to you!" Nisey sang. "You know, the 'happy' in happy birthday isn't decoration. You're *supposed to be* happy."

"I'm sorry. Thanks, girl."

"What's got your panties in a bunch? The day just started."

"Where do I begin? I hate my life. I don't have a husband, no two-and-a-half kids. I've had more cheaters in my life than all the poker tables in Vegas—ever. And to top it off, I've got a real date for the first time since Jesus was a carpenter, and none of my little black dresses look cute on my big, black ass. I'll be sitting in the Sky Dome tonight, and my ass will cause a lunar eclipse"

"Rissey, you're such a damn drama queen. Why is everything so glass half-empty with you?" she asked, sounding exasperated. "Walk back to reality with me, and let's take a quick inventory of your life. You're beautiful, one of the funniest, coolest women I've ever known. You own a home the size of a small country and car I'd jack you for if I didn't know you. You have a dream career that you love and a loving family. They're a little nutso, but they love you. So, yeah, you're right. Your life is a complete bust. Why don't you end it here?"

"Nisey, I—"

"No, no, no. You can have a pity party if you want, but I'm not throwing it, okay? My mother always said 'Better to turn forty than die at the age of thirty-nine.' Now, wash your ass and put some clothes on. I'm on my way to pick you up."

"Pick me up? Where are we going?"

"European Beaute. We've got a spa appointment."

***

Nisey to the rescue again and right on time no less. She helped me avert yet another major meltdown. When we walked in the spa, I was reminded of the day I spent with Sean's wife. What a day. I'd moved forward and taken my life to a new level, especially since the New Year. Nisey had made a good point earlier. I needed to view my life as glass half full, not half empty. We sat at adjacent manicurists and dished while spunky Korean women did our nails.

"We haven't talked about Dwayne in a while, how are things going?" Nisey asked. "And don't give me the bullshit 'we're okay' answer. I want to know how you guys are *for real* doing."

"I don't know, Nisey. He's nice. You remember, he called everyday while I was taking care of my mom. He seems to go through great lengths to keep me in his life, what I don't understand is why? And trust me, this isn't one of those 'I don't think I'm worthy' issues. There's more."

"Well, what's ringing your alarm bells?"

"For starters, he slipped muscle relaxers in my Sleepytime tea."

"He did what!" Nisey yelled. Our manicurists went dead silent. My manicurist eventually blathered something to Nisey's manicurist in Korean; I knew they were talking about me.

"Yeah, right after my car accident. I'd been refusing to take any medication. He said he gave it to me so I wouldn't wake up in pain."

"I've been in an accident before, so I know what he's talking about. I only question why he wouldn't just try to convince you. Why slip it in your tea? Doesn't make sense."

"I know. It's not like he stole anything from me, nothing was missing. But I did catch him using my computer without asking. When I confronted him, he told me self-employed people don't get time off, and he wanted to get some work done."

"Makes sense, I guess. So, why do you still have doubts?"

"I guess . . . I don't know. He makes me feel uneasy, like he's pretending to be perfect because he has an angle. I haven't a clue about what the angle is though. I may never know. But when he's kind, I ask myself, 'What if I'm wrong?'"

"Hmmm . . . I can see why you're so torn. All I can say is be careful and keep your eyes open. If he has some hidden agenda, it will come to light in time. In the meantime, let him spoil you tonight. Today is your special day. Enjoy yourself for a change, you deserve it. Okay?"

***

After getting our nails done, Nisey and I went to Lord & Taylor where I found the perfect outfit. I'd returned home, washed my worries down the shower drain, got dolled up in my new threads, splashed on some

Donna Karan cologne, and waited for my dream date to commence. And waited. And waited.

Dwayne arrived—an hour late.

"I was beginning to think you weren't going to show."

"Yes, I know. I'm sorry. I've been dealing with client issues all day long. My phone has been ringing off the hook. If today weren't your birthday, I'd have cancelled, but I couldn't let you down."

"If you have to work, we can do this another ti—"

"Don't even say it. We're going to enjoy ourselves tonight," Dwayne interrupted, adamant and determined to keep his word. "Oh, I forgot something. Here's a little gift too."

He reached in his pocket and pulled out a small gift box. I opened it to find a gold chain with a small key dangling from it.

"Awwww, look at this, a real estate agent key. This is very sweet of you, but you didn't need to do this."

"You're welcome, but it's not a real estate agent key."

"It's not?"

"No, it's the key to my heart."

If bullshit were pennies, he'd be a billionaire.

***

The maitre de seated us at our table, and we soaked in magnificent, panoramic views of D.C. as the restaurant rotated above the roof of the Doubletree. The monument and airport lights illuminated clusters of the city like mini galaxies of stars. The scenery was perfect, however, my date? Not so much. His phone rang every thirty seconds, and he'd been distracted the entire night.

"Thank you so much for bringing me here, Dwayne. The scenery and the restaurant are lovely. But if you want to cut the evening short, we can go."

"I'll tell you what. Let me step outside and make a couple of calls, and then I'll turn it off so we can enjoy our dinner."

"Okay, that's a deal. Please, go ahead and take care of your business."

I stared outside, wondering why I'd even bothered to come. I'd never felt comfortable with Dwayne, like I could let go and just. . . *be.* I turned to watch some couples dance, so lost in each other's eyes, as if flashing beams of love through their pupils. The realization at my lack of fulfillment left a hollow pit in my stomach. I stood up to find Dwayne and ask him to take me home when I felt a tap on my shoulder.

"May I have this dance?" a familiar voice asked.

"Oh my God, Kevin? What are you doing here?"

"Hi, Charisse. I'm actually waiting on, uhhh, someone to show up. I'm sitting over there," he said, pointing to a table behind me on the other side of the room. No wonder I didn't see him. "It's such a coincidence to see you here . . . alone."

"Ohhh, I'm not alone. Dwayne is here . . . somewhere. He brought me for my birthday, left to make a few calls."

"Well, happy birthday! I won't ask how old you are."

"Thanks, I appreciate that."

"Well, since you're alone right now and I'm still waiting, will you honor me with a birthday dance?" he said, holding his hand out to me. I hesitated. "C'mon, a dance will help pass the time until he gets back, only one song."

I thought about how Dwayne might react to see me dancing with another man—and let the thought go as fast as it came. *It's my birthday. It's just one dance. It's not like it means anything, right?* I thought, trying to convince myself that I meant it. *I'm so confused.*

He led me to the floor and placed his hand on my waist when "So Close," my favorite ballad by John McLaughlin, began to play. The lyrics I could never forget.

You're in my arms, and all the world is gone...

And there I was, in Kevin's arms, and all the world was gone. I'd melded into his arms as the melody made my sadness, fears, and doubts about my future vanish into nothingness. A softness in his eyes warmed me with inexplicable comfort. I'd been drawn to him by a force I could neither define nor understand. How could this be? Kevin was a stranger. I didn't know anything about him, and he didn't know me, but our lives seemed intertwined in twisted warps of fate that kept throwing us together. The song drew to its end, and Kevin's lips moved closer and closer to mine.

"Excuse me, may I cut in?" Dwayne's voice said, jerking me out of my heavenly daze.

"Dwayne . . . you're back," I said, stepping away from Kevin and taking a second to gather my thoughts so I could offer him an explanation.

"This is Kevin. He's the one who ran into my car. He happened upon me sitting alone and asked me to dance."

"How you doin' man?" Kevin said, visibly uncomfortable. "Nice to meet you."

"You look familiar. Do I know you from somewhere?" Dwayne said.

"No, I don't think so," Kevin answered nervously. "But, uhhh, let me let you get back to your beautiful date. It was nice to see you again, Charisse. You're a lucky man, Dwayne."

"I know," Dwayne replied, sounding a bit agitated. "I'll take her from here."

I stood dumbfounded and silent as Kevin paced back to his table. As he sat down, his girlfriend strolled in looking like a black Jessica Rabbit, wearing a dress that hugged every curve on her body. Kevin stood up to pull out her chair and, for a brief moment, I wished I was her—evil attitude and all.

We hate her.

Some nondescript song started to play, and Dwayne rested his arm on my waist as he and I danced. I didn't hear the music playing, but I noticed one of Dwayne's sideburns was shorter than the other, and a stray hair had begun to dangle from inside his nose. Kevin didn't have any dangly nose hairs . . . just Witch Bitchy.

"What was that all about? Looked like you guys were getting a little *too* cozy," Dwayne asked.

"Cozy? I don't think so," I said. *Mmmm, so cozy.* "Besides, didn't you see his girlfriend walking in here looking like Naomi Campbell with junk in her trunk? Anyway, did you get your business taken care of?" I said, trying to change the subject.

"Yes, baby. I'm all yours," Dwayne said.

All mine?

Forty-Six

Bamboozled

Monday rolled around pretty quickly. Dwayne's big closing day. Settlement was scheduled for eleven, and the nine o'clock hour approached quickly.

I pulled a classic, black Jones New York suit from my closet and slipped into the shower. This would be one of the biggest single commissions I'd earned in nearly a year. I had so many things I needed to take care of, bills to pay, and thirty thousand dollars would come in handy. I could take care of my obligations and add a little padding to my safety cushion.

I arrived at the settlement company, and the receptionist escorted me into a large conference room. The seller and his agent were already seated. Dwayne was gazing out the window. His brow appeared wrinkled, and he was in deep thought. I decided to introduce myself and say my hellos before finding out what the problem was.

"Good morning, everyone," I said, approaching the other suited woman in the room, whom I rightly assumed to be the seller's agent. "I'm Charrise Tyson, Mr. Gibson's agent. How is everyone this morning?"

"Hi, I'm Katie Harper, the agent for the seller," she responded as she extended her hand. "It's nice to meet you. This is my client, Mr. Davidson."

I shook his hand. He was tall—at least six-foot three—gorgeous beyond words. He sported a suit that fit him like a glove, had to be tailored. He was also sporting a big platinum wedding band . . . moving on!

As I walked over to Dwayne, he turned to me with an "I'm-screwed" look on his face. His expression spelled trouble, with a capital "T" and that rhymed with "C" and it stood for "*con* artist."

"Can I speak with you outside for a minute?" he asked.

"Sure, what's going on?" I asked, walking toward the conference door.

"I'm a little short," he said.

"No, you're not. Six-foot one is pretty tall for a man," I said in blissful ignorance.

"No, that's not what I'm saying. I mean, I don't have quite enough money to close today."

Here we go.

"Jesus, why didn't you tell me before? How much do you need?"

"A few thousand."

"Define 'a few'?" I asked.

"About nine thousand . . . eight hundred, twenty-nine dollars," he said as his voice trailed off.

"About?"

Jackass.

I continued, "Well, it looks like we'll need to postpone the closing until you get the money. I'll go let the settlement attorney know. So what, do you think it's going to be a few days?"

"No, listen, that's what I wanted to talk to you about. We've got the seller here, everyone is ready to go. I was actually wondering if maybe you'd mind loaning it to me, from your commission. I'll pay you back next week, as soon as I get the deposit from my next client."

A vision of stop signs, red flashing lights blinked wildly through my mind. Suddenly, the words he spoke in my office after he slipped me the mickey replayed in my head, "It'll be like taking candy from a baby."

All I could think was, *Goo, Goo, Gaa, Gaa.*

"I'm sorry. You're asking me to give up *a third* of my commission?"

"I swear, Charisse, it's just a loan. I'll pay you back next week. I told you cash has been pretty tight, but business will be picking up soon. The thing is, if we don't close today, no one will get paid anything."

He had a point. Most of my commission was better than no commission, even if he didn't have the decency to pay me back—which I somehow didn't think he would. There we were, mere moments from settlement, the seller and the agent came prepared to close this deal, and its fate lay with me and my commission.

"Okay, I'll loan it to you," I said.

"I'll pay it back. Trust me."

Trust me? I didn't trust that 'bama any further than I could throw him, but the sooner the deal was over, the sooner "we" could be over. And as long as he owed me money, he wouldn't bring his dawg ass back sniffing around me.

***

Nearly two weeks passed, and I still hadn't heard one little peep from Dwayne. Now, there was a shocker. I'd pretty much given up on hearing from him again, and although I knew where he lived, I had no desire to try to collect the money he owed me. *Good riddance to bad trash*, I thought. The nine-thousand dollars was well spent; it would save me gallons of tears, months of aggravation, and at least fifty pounds on my ass.

I was working in my home office when the doorbell rang. It was a courier.

"Letter for Ms. Tyson?"

"Yes, I'm Ms. Tyson."

"Sign here, please."

I opened the package, and pulled out a check for twelve thousand dollars and a note from Dwayne that read, "Your money with interest. Still interested?"

I closed my eyes and shook my head. The jury might still be out, but a hung jury didn't equate to innocence—only a judgment deferred.

***

Later that night, I realized that, although I'd resolved things with Lee, emotional healing wasn't a sprint but a marathon. Each leg was just one step in a continual commitment that I needed to renew everyday. I wasn't the same woman I was when my journey began and I'd made progress. If I met Dwayne—or any of my boyfriends—after my North Carolina trip, my love history would read more like the Sunday comics than *Gone With the Wind*. Most of those relationships would have ended before they started.

233

I pulled another journal from underneath my bed. Alas, I'd come to Marcus—the man whose cheating ways helped set me on my journey. Who'd have guessed the man who broke my heart in a million pieces would lead me to the path of lasting happiness?

Forty-Seven

The Super Ego

J *une 8, 2005*
Nisey's trying to set me up with some guy she met at the restaurant and I'm a little afraid. The last date she hooked me up with looked like Mr. Ed—only Mr. Ed had better teeth. On the upside, apples are cheap. On the downside, even if he's hung like Mr. Ed, I'd still have to get past his face.

***

My relationship with Marcus was the longest and most disappointing of my life . . . because I put *a lot* of faith in him. On the surface, our union seemed like a no-brainer. It should've been easy and probably would've been easy if Marcus wasn't . . . well . . . Marcus.

And if I wasn't . . . well . . . me.

Nisey introduced us at her then-boyfriend's restaurant. He hailed from Montego Bay, Jamaica, and sold the best Caribbean food in town. Nisey used to host bi-monthly client appreciation parties, her clients brought their friends (preferably friends in the market for houses) and Nisey supplied the food—one of her better marketing strategies. One client didn't "get it" and brought Marcus—a real estate agent. But greedy ass Marcus kept coming back for the food. Nisey, the *worst* matchmaker in the *world*, noticed he was always alone, so she spoke to him one day and told him she had a friend he should meet—me. Nisey told me he was *foine* and a

Realtor. So, I figured he had a Web site I could check to see his picture. She got that one right. He *was* fine.

She gave him my number and he called me about a week later. During that conversation, I was "introduced" to his children. That I ever answered his phone calls again should've kept him faithful to me for eternity.

"Charisse? Hi, this is Marcus. Your friend Denise gave me your phone number. I hope this phone call isn't a surprise."

"No, she told me you'd be calling. It's nice to finally hear from you."

"So, how are you doing? Mikey—Mark—we do not put peanut butter in the VCR!"

"Uhhh, I'm doing pretty well," I said, a bit hesitant. "You've got kids?"

"Yeah, three boys: Michael, Mark, and Malik. Michael and Mark are twins. They're quite a handful."

"Sounds like it. I can understand if you're busy, you can just call me another—"

"No, no I'm not busy. Malik untie your brothers. You're cutting off their circulation!"

"So, I understand you're an agent," I said.

"Yeah, I've been in real estate for about ten years now. I love it."

"Me too, I got my license before undergrad. For some yet unknown reason, I majored in Economics, at least I finished though."

"Yeah, I know what you mean. I majored in psychology. Doesn't help you sell real estate, but it's helpful with understanding crazy clients—and crazy kids. Mikey get that marble out of your nose . . . now!"

"Sounds like your kids keep you busy."

"They do indeed, never a dull moment. So from, what Denise tells me about you, you sound great, you're successful. Not seeing anyone?"

"No, I'm recently divorced, so I am just taking my time before I get into another relationship."

"Well, we should definitely get together then and go out sometime. What do you like to do? Marky, that fishing rod is for the pond not the fish tank! Keep it up and you're going to time out!"

Time out? Sounded like they should be serving time, like five to ten in the state prison.

Marcus stayed distracted during our entire conversation. I thought maybe he forgot to give the kids their Ritalin for the day. So, I figured I could say just about anything, and he wouldn't notice.

"Oh, I'm open to just about anything, hot butt-naked sex, sky diving, drinking and driving, whatever you want."

"I'm sorry. Did you say something?" he asked after I heard what sounded like a few smacks on hands and a choir of moaning and tears in the background.

"No, no nothing at all," I said. "Well, I should let you go. Maybe we can talk another time when you're not so busy."

"Okay, so we're on for a date tomorrow? Say seven o'clock?"

"Sure, that sounds good."

"So what's it gonna be, hot butt-naked sex or drinking and driving?"

"Oh, you were listening," I said, laughing as I pressed the palm of my hand against my forehead. "Why don't we try dinner first? Maggiano's? We can save the other activities for our second date."

"Ohhhh, Italian food, perfect. See you tomorrow."

We met at Maggiano's for dinner as scheduled the next night, and it was love at first sight. Our eyes locked as we carefully forked our manicotti to avoid dropping food on our laps. I could tell by the way he chewed with his mouth closed, he was the next *"the one."* Marcus's quick-witted sense of humor sucked me in; he had the best of any man I'd been involved with. He always made me laugh, made me think. Marcus not only laughed heartily at my jokes, he tolerated my non-stop sarcasm, a quality that tended to annoy most men I dated. Our first outing played like a championship mental ping-pong match.

"This is so refreshing," Marcus said as he pulled the cloth napkin from his lap, wiped his mouth, and laid it on the table beside his empty plate. "You know, you're the first woman I've dated in a long time who ate more than a salad on the first date. I'm glad I stopped by the ATM machine on my way in."

"Well, aren't I the lucky one? You're the first man I've dated in some time who had enough money in the bank to make an actual ATM withdrawal. I was only going to order one dessert, but now I can order two—keep my diet balanced," I said, waving the waiter over. "Yes, I'd like the cheesecake and cannoli, please."

"Yeah, we wouldn't want one of your lovely hips getting bigger than the other."

"That's true. And you have such small hands, I'm not sure that you can handle them anyway."

"Well, I wear a size fourteen shoe, and you know what they say about men with big feet, don't you?"

"Yeah . . . they wear big shoes," I retorted, both of us laughing hysterically. The waiter placed the desserts on the table, and we fed each other as we continued our friendly banter.

"So, let me ask you a question. If you were stranded on a deserted island and could only take three things with you, what would you take?"

I thought, *This must be a test to see what I value.* I could've given a serious answer, but why? It would be against my character.

"I would bring a generator, a deep freezer, and a lifetime supply of Ben & Jerry's," I answered as he shook his head and chuckled.

"You're funny," he said. "You're not like most women who have answered that question. They usually try to get all intellectual, try to impress me, you know."

"Well, fortunately for you, I already know that I'm too good for you. So, I don't feel the need to impress you," I said, flashing a wide smile. "I've got a question for you. If you were stranded on a deserted island and could only bring three things to read, which would you bring?"

"That's easy: Playboy, Hustler, and Penthouse. They're all, shall we say, *very stimulating* reading."

"Uh huh, stimulating," I responded. "You know most of those women are lesbians, right?"

And we went on and on, for three hours. There was no question he had the whole package. I mean he had the clothes, the look, and he was intelligent. We had the same job—both of us were pretty successful at it—and he had three bad assed but loveable kids to boot.

I always wanted boys, never wanted girls. Why? Because I'd had a recurrent nightmare since the age of thirty in which my thirteen-year-old daughter comes home and tells me she's pregnant. Plus, I didn't know how to do hair. I'd been going to the hairdresser since I was eleven. I was only adept enough to make lopsided afro-puffs.

It didn't take long to realize Marcus had a pretty big ego. Most of the time, it arrived in the room about five minutes before he did. He threw money around like a Rockefeller, never let me help with anything. He wanted to be the man, and he wanted me to worship him as such. I was down with that and willingly stepped aside and let him be the man for the first two years of our relationship. We were blissfully happy because I took the backseat and let him drive.

Men didn't understand women didn't want to be controlling or superwomen; we didn't *want* to do it all. We did it all because we *had* to. We're consummate jugglers; we'd been keeping the balls in the air since the beginning of time. We demanded equality, but somehow the scales got tipped to the other side. Now, we have over-equality, and men don't want their part back.

I, like many women, would've gladly given up the "steering wheel" to a man, but Marcus didn't understand that he had to build up his credibility, you know, demonstrate to me that he was a safe and reliable "driver." As long as I saw him consistently keeping the car (think relationship) properly maintained, fueled up—and he was leading us to a positive place—I sat zip-lipped in the passenger seat and let him drive his little heart out. But he couldn't just tell me "Trust me, I got this" as I watched in horror as the car lurched toward the backend of a semi, with no attempt to hit the brakes.

As time went on, Marcus started losing clients, and his business started to tank. In his mind, his manhood was tied to his wallet, his ability to provide. He felt emasculated by my continued success, and when I bought the house in high-and-mightyville *without* his help—the house I bought to share with him—well . . .

He never said anything, but I think that's where our trouble really began.

Forty-Eight

Cold Busted

I n the world according to Marcus, not only was I supposed to let him drive, but it was against the Man's Rule Book for me to say "Ummm, dear, slow down" when our relationship careened toward a brick wall. To declare, "Marcus, I think we lost our transmission about a mile back"— out of the question. And I couldn't tell him "the car" was breaking down, running out of fuel, or that we needed to stop for directions because we were getting a little bit lost. I was supposed to keep my trap shut, assume he knew we had a problem, assume he'd identified what the problem was, assume he knew how to fix it, and then assume he'd get around to fixing the problem on his own without prompting from me. And all this "assuming" was *completely* against the Woman's Rule Book.

"You said we were going to start spending a little more quality time together, Marcus. We haven't been on a real date in months."

"I told you, Charisse, I'm going to start making the effort."

"When? I mean, you're always working; you never make time for me anymore. If I'm not working, I'm babysitting your kids. I spend so much time with them that they're starting to call *me* Daddy."

"Fine, if you don't want to babysit them anymore, I'll hire someone else to do it."

Classic Marcus. When he didn't want to deal with the real issue, he always deflected by making an issue out of something that wasn't an issue.

"Are you even listening to me? That's not the point. All I am saying is that I want us to spend more time together. I want to go dancing and go out to dinner like we used to do."

"You know business is slow, and I'm trying to get things going again. I don't feel good about going out when I'm worried about where my next check is coming from. Don't you understand that?"

"Yeah, I understand. We're in the same business, remember? I keep telling you that you need to get your ass moving and work harder, meet more people, hand out more business cards, make more phone calls, and the business will eventually come. Sitting around *thinking* about what you need to do isn't going to get it done, and neglecting me in the process will only add to our problems."

"Thank you, Ms. Know-It-All, but if I need your advice I'll ask for it."

"I'm trying to help. I'm in this relationship too, Marcus. Despite what you may think, my feelings matter."

"The only things that matter to you are your feelings, you know. What I'm going through doesn't matter, right! You want, what you want, when you want it. All you do is nag, nag, nag."

Oh, no he didn't use the "N" word with me. At that point, I could very well have de-escalated the situation, told him that he was right, given us a moment cool down, and talked it out rationally at a later time. But I didn't do that. No, the "N" word set me off. And if he wanted to take it there, I was going there too . . . *express.*

I rolled my head ghetto-style and said, "Oh I'm a naaaag now, huh? I'm not a nag when you want me to babysit your kids. I'm not a nag when I'm doing your laundry or taking your clothes to the cleaners. I'm not a nag when I'm cooking dinner or sucking your *little* dick. But I'm a nag if I ask for a *little* time and attention, right? Is that how it works? If I'm such a nag, why don't we end this? Maybe you can go out and find someone who'll do all the shit that I do for you and won't expect anything in return."

Yup, I'd said it. Within the span of thirty seconds, I'd broken six commandments from the Man's Rule Book, not the least of which was call his dick *little.* I'd told him the car had a problem, told him we lost the transmission a mile back, told him he might want to get that fixed, and even recommended a mechanic. And I'd told him that if he didn't like it, he could go out and find another ride. After that, I may as well have been Charlie Brown's teacher because all he heard was, "Wah, wah, wah, wah, wah."

Well, except for the 'go out and find someone else' part. That much he heard as clear as day.

"If that's the way you want it, that's the way it'll be."

I suspected Marcus might be seeing someone else about two months after our blow out. He started working a lot more and a lot later but wasn't making one penny more than before. He claimed he took my advice, started getting out there, talked to more people, handed out more business cards. What he *didn't* say is that he was hooking up with the women he met.

Rumors floated about the water cooler. The realtor community in our area was pretty small and well connected. Bad news spread like a wildfire during a summer drought. When I confronted him, he would always deny it, of course. As usual, Nisey had the real skinny.

"Rissey, I've been debating about whether I should talk to you about this, but I've been hearing rumors Marcus is seeing another woman, one of his clients. I heard her tits are so big she could knock herself out on a treadmill, right after she tripped over her super-extended weave."

"You and apparently everyone else in the office. I've heard, Nisey. I've asked him about it, but of course he denied it. I asked him if he wanted to break up, and he gave me an unequivocal no. I don't know what to say except if he's doing something, I don't think it's serious."

"You're not putting up with this shit, are you?"

"Nisey, I've been with the man nearly three years. I know that he loves me. I don't believe he'd do anything like that to me. If anything, his ego's a little bruised and he's maybe flirting more than he should, but I don't believe he's sleeping around."

"Can I have some?"

"Some what?"

"Some of those drugs you're taking. They must be the bomb if they have you so brainwashed that you'd even consider putting up with that bullshit from him, especially given the kind of woman you've been to him and his little raggedy-ass kids."

Nisey was right, but I didn't want to hear it. I didn't want to acknowledge that I could give nearly three years of my life to that man, take care of his children like my own, invite them into my home like it was their home, play the part of his virtual wife, and he could run around behind my back. I couldn't fathom it, especially as the holidays neared. One day, just before Christmas, I woke up determined to nudge us back on the right track and make our holiday the best yet.

"Marcus," I said as I rolled next to him in bed and rubbed his back, "I want to make this work. I love you, baby. I don't want to lose you."

He rolled over, wrapped his arms around me and pulled me to his chest. "Come here, I'm sorry I've been such an ass lately. I'm just under a lot of stress. But I want us to have a happy holiday together. We're family, and you're everything to me."

"I'm so happy to hear you say that; I really needed to hear it. Listen, I was wondering if I could borrow the Sequoia this afternoon, and you can take my car. I wanted to take the kids out to let them do their shopping, and we'll need more trunk space."

"You're a brave woman. You want to take all three of them in the mall . . . together?"

"Those are my babies. Plus, I'm carrying a switch with me just in case. I'll leave part of it sticking out of my purse as a constant reminder. I think we'll be fine."

"Which mall are you guys going to?"

"I dunno, I thought we'd ride out to Rockville, so I can take them to Dave and Busters afterward."

"Okay, baby. That's cool. I'm just going in the office to take care of a little paperwork, and I'll see you back here later. But, uhhh, can Santa get some cookies right now before you go?"

"What Santa wants, Santa gets."

We made love twice that morning, the second time was for good measure. I later jumped in my clothes, gathered the kids in the truck, and we headed for Tysons Galleria instead of Rockville. I didn't want to drive quite that far and Tyson's was closer.

The kids behaved well all day; the portable switch turned out to be highly effective. We'd been shopping several hours—without tears—before we ran out of steam and needed a little nourishment. I wasn't in the mood for Maggiano's, but I thought we could go to The Corner Bakery, a little eatery just outside of Maggiano's. We drove through the parking lot in search of a space when I passed what looked like my car. I stopped and backed up; indeed, it *was* my car. Marcus and some bitch were kissing in the front seat.

The Bum Magnet

The oldest son Malik said, "Charisse, isn't that Daddy?"

Forty-Nine

Where's the Beemer?

I couldn't believe that bastard took her to our restaurant and kissed her in my damn car. He didn't even know about that place before he met me. His idea of fine dining used to be eating pizza with a knife and fork.

Fortunately, the twins were fully engaged in *Finding Nemo* on the DVD screen in the back seat. They missed the whole scene. Malik, on the other hand, looked at me intently, as if he hoped I would explain it away. So, I tried.

"I, uhhh, I don't think so baby. It sure looked a lot like him though, didn't it?"

"Yeah, that looked like your car too."

"It sure did, baby, it sure did. But there are a lot of cars like that in this area," I said insincerely as I searched my mind for something to distract them. "I'll tell you what. How would you boys like to go to Chucky E. Cheese instead?"

A choir sounded, "Yeah, yeah, yeah, we want to go to Chuck E. Cheese."

"Okay, well, give me a few minutes. I'm going to call Aunt Nisey and let her take you to Chuck E. Cheese for a little bit, while I go shop for your Christmas presents. That way my present to you guys will be a *big* surprise."

"Yaaay, Auntie Nisey," the choir rejoiced.

Fortunately, Nisey hadn't long before left the mall and just started home when I called. When she arrived, I stood outside the car and told her what I'd seen. Not fifteen minutes later, she whisked the kids away so I could have a moment to figure out what I was going to do about Marcus and his little fifi.

My mind reran our morning together over and over and over again. The man that I made love to that morning and the man kissing this woman in my car could not be one and the same. They just couldn't be. Why he would jump from between my legs to find shelter between the legs of another woman—in the same day? Weren't there unwritten rules? People shouldn't be *allowed* to do that kind of thing, let alone get away with it. I wanted to kill him, but death would be too good for him, too easy. No, I thought he should have to suffer and that exact moment would not be too soon.

I waited for them to walk inside, and then I took my car, parked it around the corner and laid in wait for him and his little Kimora Lee Simmons-wannabe to emerge. As I stalked, my anger boiled like a cauldron, and my mind's eye replayed every sordid detail of our entire relationship, the long work days, late nights hanging out with the "boys," etc.

Now, it all makes sense.

For two hours, I sat on a park bench across the street, just beyond line-of-sight to the restaurant entrance, waiting to glimpse them approaching the exit. Finally, they'd started for the door. As Marcus spun through the circular doorway, I studied each movement in his face so that I could identify the precise moment that he realized my car was missing from the spot where he'd left it.

At first he appeared confused; he rubbed his chin and wrinkled his brow. I thought, *Yeah sucker that's the right spot.* Panic stricken, his eyes widened like he was getting a glaucoma test, then they rolled in the back of his head as his chin dropped to his chest. I read her lips, "What is it honey?" His read, "Someone stole the car."

I often wondered if his alarmed expression reflected the shock that someone stole the car or the fear of realizing he'd have to report the whole incident to the police . . . and then to me. He couldn't show up at my house and say, "Oh, *that* BMW? I misplaced it at the mall." I, of course, would not let my scheme go that far. The police had far more important work to do than answer bogus car theft calls. So, when he reached in his pocket to retrieve his Blackberry, I moved in.

As I trudged toward them, she detected me approaching Marcus, but any desire to quiz me was likely quelled by my "don't-fuck-with-me" expression. I tapped his shoulder, crossed my arms, and waited for the moment Marcus set eyes on my face. The initial relief he felt at realizing he was out of the frying pan would rapidly dissipate at the realization he was smoldering in the fire.

"Hi, Marcus, looking for something?"

He froze. His fight or flight instinct kicked in, "Should I run like hell or talk shit?" After a few seconds, he opted for the latter.

"Charisse?" he asked. "What . . . what are you doing here? Where are the boys?"

"No, I think the question is what are *you* doing here? And after Malik saw you sucking face with Miss Thang over here, I sent them to Chuck E. Cheese with Nisey."

Silence.

"Oh, I'm sorry, we haven't been formally introduced," I said as I turned to Miss Weave-A-lot. "I'm Marcus' soon-to-be ex-girlfriend—of three years. And you are?"

She scowled at Marcus but remained silent. Smarter than she looked.

"Don't worry. I don't blame you," I said, eyeing her hair to check for weave tracks. "I blame this lying, cheating, son of a bitch." I turned my attention back to Marcus. "And you, you brought her to our restaurant in my goddamned car."

"Listen, Charisse, I can explain."

"You can explain what? How you betrayed my trust? How you humiliated me in front of your children? Or would you rather explain how you've been humping around like a dog in heat behind my back, lying, cheating, and sneaking, making a complete fool of me? Which part would you like to explain first, huh? Go ahead, pick one. I'm all ears!"

"I... I..."

"I... I... that's what I thought. Save it! I loved you. I was there for you whenever you needed me. I was practically a second mother to your kids and this is how you treat me? You ungrateful bastard," I said as I turned toward the new fool. "Honey, you can have him. I know exactly what you're getting. The question is, *do you*?"

"Listen, I didn't know about you. I didn't know he had a girlfriend," she said.

"Bastard," I yelled. If my eyes could fire darts, he'd have looked like he was getting acupunctured. "That was for the both of us."

I stomped to my car, got inside, slammed the door, and drove home. Thankfully, the kids weren't around to see me in my current state. *What the hell am I talking about? He crushed me and I'm worried about his kids.* I drove home, pulled into my garage, and called the one person I knew was crazy enough to make me laugh.

"Mommy?"

"Hi, Charisse, what's wrong?" she asked, sensing the sadness in my voice.

"It's Marcus, I caught him kissing another woman in my car . . . in front of our restaurant," I said as I eased my grip on the steering wheel and sat back in my seat.

"Sweet Jesus, almighty. Are you okay, baby?"

"No, I'm not. I believed in him, and he let me down. I feel like such a fool, you know. I just feel like such a fool," I said, releasing sob after sob.

"Baby, what I been telling you since you were a teenager? There ain't no such thing as a good man. Men are what they are and they do what they do. Ain't no need in you falling apart over it. Nuh uhh, don't get sad, get even."

"Get even?"

"Want me to come up there? I'll take care of him for you. Give him the ass whoopin' of his life."

I laughed hysterically.

"What you laughin' at? I'm serious. I'll beat him like he stole somethin'. Make him run home cryin' to his mama. And if *she* says somethin' out the way, I'll kick her ass too."

I burst out laughing. I could picture my mom knocking Marcus out. "Do you ever think I'm going to find someone decent?"

"Well, of course you will baby, but *that* ain't your problem. Your problem is that you still haven't learned to love yourself first. Every time you get involved with somebody you make their life your life and you lose yourself. And baby, ain't nobody gonna look out for you, like you'll look out for yourself. It's okay to be selfish sometimes. It is okay to protect yourself sometimes. And it's okay to love yourself first sometimes. You understand me?"

"Yes ma'am, I understand."

"Now, you know he's gon' be over there tomorrow—if not tonight—trying to get you back. He ain't gonna let someone like you go that easy."

Boy, she'd said a mouthful right there.

"I know, Mommy."

"He's gonna be full of I'm sorries and I'll never do it agains. Trust me, your mama done heard it all before."

"Believe me, I know."

"So what are you going to do?"

"I don't know."

"Well, I can't tell you what to do. You have to live your own life. I will say one thing though—if you don't know what to do, stand still. The right answer will come to you in time."

"Okay, Mom. Well, I'm going in the house now. I'm still sitting in the garage."

"Try to get some rest tonight. Everything will look better in the morning."

Fifty

The Rissey Rip

After a few minutes, I walked in the house and headed straight to the bar, grabbed a shot glass, filled it three-quarters with Patron, and chucked it down. My pulse and breathing slowed. I caught a glimpse of myself in a mirror, my hair was still looking tight, but my mascara had run down my face. I looked like The Joker from Batman.

I took a deep breath, reached in the pantry for two lawn and leaf bags, and headed for my bedroom. Marcus kept about half of his wardrobe in my closet because he stayed overnight so often. I stepped in the "his" side of my his-and-her walk-in closets and filled the bags with all of his best friends—Kenneth Cole, Versace, Armani, Ralph Lauren, and Hugo Boss, shoes, suits, pants, shirts, ties, everything; I filled the second bag with his underwear, socks, and t-shirts. I only kept one thing, my favorite oversized Redskins sweatshirt I used to wear to the grocery store on Sunday mornings before we watched Fox NFL Sunday.

I dragged the bags downstairs to the family room next to the chaise, walked into the laundry room, grabbed a jug of Clorox, and grabbed a second shot of Patron from the bar. I returned to the chaise and unscrewed the cap on the Clorox when the phone rang. The caller ID read "Nisey."

"Marcus picked up the kids a few minutes ago. If looks could kill, he'd be worm food. I kept watching for y'all on the six o'clock news but I didn't hear anything, so I thought I'd better call and make sure you're okay. How'd everything go?"

"Well, I mean, it's over. What could he possibly say at that point? He was cold busted. I feel . . . like someone kicked me in the stomach. I supported him, sexed him, and took care of his little snot-nosed brats. I mean what else could I do?"

"Rissey, you know I'm your girl but you guys haven't been happy for a long time. Well, let me put it this way. *You* haven't been happy for a long time. He had a maid, a wife, a mother, and ass whenever he wanted it, and you didn't demand anything for it. So, he was happy as hell . . . but at what cost to you? Right now, your heart may be aching and you may feel betrayed, but in a few days or maybe months from now, you'll see this for the blessing that it is. I mean, think about it, what are the chances that you would see them at that moment?"

She had a point and a good one. And I'd be grateful for it in a few days, but at that moment, I wanted to remain fully immersed in my rage.

"You're right, I know you're right Nisey. But still . . ."

"So, what are you doing right now?"

"I'm getting ready to soak his clothes in Clorox."

"For real?"

"Yup."

She laughed. "Do you really think that's going to make you feel better? One splash and it's all over. It's all so *Waiting to Exhale.*"

"Nisey, I don't know if it's going to make me feel better, but I know it's gonna piss him the hell off which is all I can really ask for right now."

"Well, hold up a minute. I'm coming over. I've got a much better idea," she said.

An hour later Nisey showed up with two odd little tools in her hands.

"What are those?" I asked.

"Seam rippers, they're used to pull the hems out of clothes when you're sewing."

"Nisey, have I ever told you I love you like a sister?"

"Not nearly often enough."

"You're a *genius.*"

"Wouldn't hurt you to say that more often too," she said as she grabbed a seat on the sofa.

We pulled the thread from every seam and hem we could find, and when we finished, four hours and four margaritas later, the floor was filled with scraps of fabric that used to be high fashion; my rage vanished. She was the best friend a girl could ask for.

***

December 24, 2007
I caught that son of a bitch Marcus with a woman today, in my car no less—Merry Christmas to me. That's the story of my life. My sad, couldn't find a good man if my existence depended on it life. I feel so depressed and heartbroken. Men do this to me every time and I'm scared. I'm beginning to think that my problem doesn't lie with them. Maybe it's me.

***

Marcus arrived at my house early the next day as expected. Unfortunately, he still had a key. I'd planned to rectify that situation as soon as possible. If he didn't give them to me willingly, I had a locksmith ready and waiting to install a new one. That was one of the benefits of working in the real estate industry. I had service people ready to step in at a moment's notice; they'd do anything for a good referral source.

When I heard his car pull up in the driveway, I peeked downstairs to watch as he walked in. He cautiously poked his head inside, no doubt to ensure I hadn't set up a guillotine for him in the doorway. He walked in, closed the door behind him, and yelled upstairs for me.

"Charisse, are you home?"

"I'm upstairs," I yelled back. "I'll be down in a minute. Have a seat."

Have a drink too, I mumbled to myself. *You're gonna need it when I'm done with you.*

I grabbed the bag containing what used to be his wardrobe, brought them with me downstairs, and sat them next to the front door. That would be his next stop.

"What do you want, Marcus? I really don't have anything more that I need to say to you. So, say what you have to say. I want to get this over with," I said as I sat on the arm of the sofa and prepared to be bombarded by a bullshit storm.

"Listen, Charisse, I want to tell you how deeply sorry I am for what I did. I know how you must—" he started before I abruptly interrupted.

"Stop right there," I yelled. I stood up and gave him The Hand. "Don't even go there with me Marcus because you *don't* know. You *don't know* how it made me feel to have Malik turn to me while you were kissing another woman and ask 'Charisse, is that Daddy?' You have *no* idea! So please start somewhere other than 'I know how you must '. You don't know *shit* about 'how I must'."

"I'm sorry," he pleaded as he tried to approach me. He got The Hand again.

"I think we've *thoroughly* established that."

"I want to make things right between us."

"And how do you propose to do *that*?" I said, cocking my head to the side and hanging my hands on my hips.

"What if I ask you to marry me?"

"You must be out of your mind. You act like marrying you is some kind of fucking *bonus*. The way I feel at this moment, I wouldn't even *attend* someone else's wedding with you. Let alone stand up before God, family, and friends and marry your ass myself."

"For what it's worth, I broke it off with her, and I swear to you I never had sex with her. We kissed and that was it, nothing else. I just met her a few weeks ago. We had drinks, lunch, maybe a couple of dinners and that was it."

"So, let me get this straight because I just want to make sure that I understand everything perfectly clear. For months, I, your girlfriend of nearly three years, practically beg you to spend time with me, practically beg you to take me out on a date, and you all but gave me The Hand. Told me you don't have time, you're busy working, while I was babysitting your kids and taking care of home. Meanwhile, all the time, you were running around behind my back 'dating' this bitch. Why? Because I hurt your feelings by having the audacity to suggest we needed to work on our relationship? Or because I told you if you wanted to get more business you needed to get up off your ass and get some? For that, I deserved this knife in my back. That's what you're saying, right?"

"You know, Charisse, if you want the truth, sometimes the problem isn't *what* you say, it's *how* you say it. And you were being condescending, at least I felt like you were."

He was probably right about that. Sometimes, I'm less aware of *how* I say things than *what* I'm saying. But was I crazy in thinking the right thing to do was to *talk* to me about it, not screw around?

"If you felt that way, you should've come to me. Do you remember the kind of woman that I was to you for the first two years of our relationship? I let you be the man. I never encroached on your territory, not until I saw things were starting to fall apart and you weren't doing anything to save us, at least not that I could tell. I didn't want to lose you."

"I didn't want to lose you either, Charisse," he said with a modicum of sincerity.

"Well, what did you think would happen when you started seeing this woman? For weeks, I've endured rumors about you running around with someone else, and I told everyone it wasn't true. Now I look like a complete idiot."

"*You* don't look like the idiot, Charisse. *I* look like the idiot. I ran around on you, yet I'm here begging you not to leave me. I know you've got your pride, but I need you. No matter what you say, I won't let go. I won't."

"Did you break it off with her or did she break it off with you? She probably left your ass, and that's the only reason you came here trying to salvage what little is left of our relationship," I said as I looked at the front door ready for him to walk out of it. "Speaking of leftovers, please give me the key to my door and my car, and pick up your shit by the door."

"Don't do this, baby, please. We can work it out."

"I need you to go. I need some time away from you. I need time to see if I can forgive you. Right now, I don't know if I can. And while we're talking about forgiving, I hope you'll forgive me for what's in the bag next to the door. A good tailor should be able to piece them together again."

"What are you talking about?"

"You'll see."

Thus began Marcus's amnesia era.

From that day forward, Marcus acted like the entire incident never happened. I remember hearing it said once that a lie can become the truth if one believes it. Well, I think that's what happened with Marcus. His way of coping with what happened, his way of holding on to me, was to wipe the whole incident from his mind and refuse to acknowledge that the woman ever existed or that I ever caught him with her. And I believe that worked well for *him*, but unfortunately for him, *my* memory was long, steady, and completely unforgiving. I hadn't forgotten a *damn* thing, nor would I. Marcus, however, was not *at all* fazed by this reality. No, he continued on with his half of the relationship like we'd never lost a beat.

His way of coaxing me to stay was to feed me every chance he got, and when he stopped feeding me, he took me shopping or on dates. I wanted to tell him if he'd done that beforehand, we'd probably be married.

Thank *God* he didn't!

Fifty-One

Not-So-Jolly Holi-Daze

Filled with Christmas cheer, I thought I'd finally reached the first holiday season in nearly five years I wouldn't have to spend alone. Marcus and I usually spent the holidays apart, either because we were fighting like cats and dogs and couldn't stand the sight of each other — or because we made separate plans with our families.

But this year was different. I had bubbly to pop, confetti to throw, and a love to kiss at midnight's stroke (well maybe not a *love*, but a *like*). Nisey and I decided to do some late-afternoon shopping, so we kicked off our spree at the Nordstroms in Tyson's Galleria Mall.

Nisey wanted the new Marc Jacobs Stella bag, and I had planned to watch her buy it. A grand was still more than I'd part with for a handbag, that is, until I held one in my own hands. With rich, butter-soft, calfskin leather, the Stella bag screamed "I've arrived!" Conveniently, the $975 I laid down for the camel-colored piece of heaven allowed me to reason that I needed to spend an additional hundred dollars on the coordinating wallet. I mean, I couldn't use my old Coach wallet; that would constitute designer handbag blasphemy. So I took the plunge and all was right with the world.

We meandered in and out of a few stores before we decided to split up; Nisey headed toward Bloomingdale's to buy some perfume for her mom, and I went to Brookstone to scope out a massage chair Dwayne eyed during our last visit. I thought it would be perfect for his master bedroom or basement. Brookstone was one of my top five favorite stores because I lusted for gadgets as much as home décor. If Brookstone had a gadget for sale, in my estimation, it was a gadget worth buying. Didn't matter what minor feat it performed, or whether I could actually use it, it just needed the "nifty" factor.

When I walked in, my eye immediately turned toward a display of "$50 and under" gifts. The Holy Grail of all gadgets called to me, and by happenstance, I *needed* it too—a key finder. I could attach my keys to a special device armed with a screaming alarm if they got lost. I misplaced my keys at least once a day and always spent thirty minutes to an hour looking for them. It'd be a well-spent fifty bucks. As I reached to grab it from the shelf, a masculine brown hand brushed mine.

"Excuse me, this is mi—" I started.

"Hi, Charisse," a familiar voice said. I turned around.

"Marcus," I said as the edges of my mouth curled upward. He looked the same but different, like the man I remembered from our first date, not the man I'd caught making out in my Beemer. "What are you up to?"

"I'm doing a little shopping for the kids. Wow, you look as beautiful as always. How have you been?"

Who was that man or who inhabited his body? He only called me beautiful once, after he had his pupils dilated.

"I'm good, good, just doing some Christmas shopping," I responded.

He grabbed the key finder from my hand. "I know this must be for you. You never could keep track of your keys, drove me nuts. Between the two of us, we must've spent the equivalent of two weeks a year looking for them."

I chuckled. "Yeah, you're probably right about that. How have you been? You're looking good. And how are my . . . I mean, the boys?"

"I'm feeling pretty good. The boys are doing well. I've been focusing on the kids a little more and *a little less* on me, the way it's supposed to be. Even started taking them to church . . . almost every Sunday."

"*You've* been going to church? When you walked in, did the doors ignite?"

He laughed. "Ha, ha, very funny."

"I'm kidding. You know me, silly to the end."

"One of the many things I loved about you. Do you think we could do lunch? Maggiano's? Catch up a little bit, you know, as friends."

"I'd love to, but I'm here with Nisey. I've got to *catch up* with her soon."

"Okay, well it's so good seeing you again."

"You too, Marcus . . . sincerely."

I wandered around the store a bit longer before I decided on four NBA bar stools rather than the massage chair. I'd just spent a grand on my Stella bag; sixteen hundred dollars for a chair would definitely stretch my Christmas budget. When I reached the sales counter to pay for my key finder and Dwayne's stools, the store clerk said, "Hello, ma'am. You're Charisse Tyson, correct?"

"Yes, I am."

"A gentleman told me to give this to you before you completed your order," he said as he handed me a small Brookstone shopping bag. I looked inside to find my key finder, and Marcus had scribbled "I still love you" on the back of the receipt. I smiled and shook my head; Marcus certainly had his moments. As I walked out of the store, my phone rang.

"Charisse, I need you to haul ass over to Bloomingdales, pronto!" Nisey ordered.

"What's going on?"

"Dwayne's here, with some woman. I don't want him to see us, at least not yet. So don't pass the Bailey, Banks, and Biddle."

Bailey, Banks, and Biddle was a high-end jeweler. I thought he was probably buying someone a Christmas gift, but I didn't know who the woman could be.

"I'm on my way."

I jetted to Bloomingdales at lighting speed, didn't know my big ass could move that fast. I spotted Nisey standing adjacent to the doorway where she could spy on Dwayne without getting caught. When I arrived, I saw Dwayne standing next to a beautiful woman, with my build and skin tone. She toted a tiny infant in a baby carrier; the baby couldn't be any more than two or three months old. I paused for a moment then a wave of relief came over me when I realized it must be his sister.

"Nisey, I think she's his sister, remember? She would've had the baby about two or three months ago," I whispered, still slightly out of breath.

"Why are you whispering?" she asked in plain voice.

"Because we're being sneaky, and you're supposed to whisper when you're being sneaky," I whispered in response.

"Girl, please, don't make me hurt you. This is serious."

"So, what's going on?" I asked in a more discernable tone. Nisey might've taken a swing at me if I didn't.

"Well, they've been looking at rings. Do you think he's buying it for you?"

"Jesus, I don't know. You think?" *A ring for me?*

"Let's do this. Call him and see what he says. If he says he's shopping with his sister, no harm, no foul."

My hands trembled slightly as I pulled my cell phone from my pocket in nervous anticipation of Dwayne's response; I pressed his speed dial number because I couldn't dial the whole thing. It rang once, it rang twice. I watched Dwayne take the phone from his coat pocket and glance at the display. He saw my number, stepped away a few feet, turned his back toward the woman, and answered the phone.

"Hey, what's up?" he said in a semi-hushed tone.

"Hi, baaaabyyyy," I sang. "I just called to see what you're up to. I hadn't spoken with you today."

"Hey, let me call you back shortly. I'm just leaving the gym. I'm going to get cleaned up and call you back this evening."

I paused as the reality set in that the woman was *not* his sister. "Okay, you do that," I snapped, wishing I could slam a cell phone.

"What did he say?" Nisey asked.

"He said he was leaving the gym, and he'll call me back later," I said as my pulse began to race. *Here I go a-goddamned-gain!* My life had become a really bad one-episode rerun . . . in twenty *long ass* years of syndication.

I glanced back into the jewelry store and watched. The woman dangled her hand in Dwayne's face to flaunt her ring while nodding in excited acceptance; she'd solidified her selection. He turned to her and lodged his tongue squarely in her throat. It resembled The Exorcist kiss I'd remembered from our first date, but it wasn't quite the same. Mine didn't come with baby and a diamond ring—a sobering realization to say the least.

"Okay, Rissey, she definitely ain't his sister."

Fifty-Two

Bugs and Windshields

My stubborn tears dangled in the corners of my eyes, refusing to be wasted on the likes of him. I started to walk away but enough was enough. Dwayne would pay for his dirty deeds and those of all the men before him. I'd been on an emotional roller coaster for months, trying to determine what kind of man he really was. Well, the truth had found me. The only question was what to do next.

I wanted revenge in the worst way, revenge for being lied to and deceived again, revenge for my wasted time and broken heart. I'd worked up some good hate rage when, out of nowhere, Nisey said the unimaginable.

"Now, you can run over there and make a fool of yourself *and him*, I know that's your first instinct, but why? He's not coming back, not that you'd even *want* his sorry ass back, and you can't un-waste your time. Charisse, sometimes the Lord reveals things to us that he wants us to see when He's ready. I think He's ready for you to see that Dwayne is the dawg you feared he is. If I know my God, the way I know my God, the reason is because something better is around the bend."

I looked at her like she'd turned Japanese. "Okay, who are you and what've you done with Nisey?"

"I know . . . this coming from Ms. Seam Ripper, right? Well, I've learned the hard way sometimes it's better to stand still and let God move when He's ready, let the vengeance be His. And trust me, you can't do a fraction of what God could do. Let Him do His job, He's usually pretty good at it."

Those words reverberated through my entire being. I hated it when she got all biblical on me, especially when I wanted to be in a rage. She was right, though. If I ran over there, the only one who would look like the fool is me, and I already looked like a fool right where I was standing. So, after some thought, I did the only thing I could do.

"Okay, I guess I'll stand still. But can we get out of here, please, before I change my mind?"

"Let's go," Nisey responded. "Move it, move it."

About five minutes after we got in our cars to leave, I came to my senses. Forget this *"be still"* shit! I was going *Color Purple*. I wanted to kill him and deal with God later. I seethed because I'd let him off the hook without so much as a kiss my ass. The heat from my anger swelled, and I could hear my heart thump in my ears. The tension in my jaw tightened, and my teeth grinded. Once again, I was the most dangerous person in the world—a woman scorned.

We drove back to my house and copped a squat in my family room while I made us a couple of drinks. Nisey decided to monitor me closely to make sure I didn't do anything stupid. Easily distracted by shiny objects, she went through my shopping bags.

"Oooh, a key finder! This is awesome. Where did you get this?"

"Marcus bought it for me. I ran into him in Brookstone," I said.

"Is that right? That's *damn* coincidental. How's he doing?"

"He's doing fine, looks even better. I didn't even know he bought it for me. He paid for it and left it at the register."

"Hmmm . . . interesting. A pretty nice thing to do, wouldn't you say?"

"Yeah, pretty nice," I said, still distracted by my thoughts. I couldn't shake the picture of the woman holding the ring up to Dwayne's face, but my anger subsided long enough for me to grin. I never thought the day would come when my only happy thought involved Marcus. Life sure lobbed some curve balls, and the Dwayne curve ball had caught me square in the head

Well, not really.

I'd had concerns about Dwayne since the first day he walked butt-naked in front of me, and those fears never subsided. I just didn't trust my intuition. As I flashed back over all my relationships, one notion really sank in: one person in my life truly deserved my trust but never received it—me. I'd never learned to trust my intuition even though it was almost always right. I was right about Lamar . . . and Jason . . . and Sean and all the others, including Dwayne. I wasn't a bum magnet because I trusted them; I was a bum magnet because I didn't trust myself.

Nisey was right—for a change. No matter how hurt I felt by what Dwayne had done, my satisfaction from revenge would be fleeting and no doubt followed by remorse. Despite my hurt, I'd made too much progress in my life to do anything I might feel sorry about later. In the long run, I'd be better off leaving him alone. Indeed, revenge would be a waste of time.

***

Dwayne called me later that evening. I didn't want to talk to him then, but would there ever be a good time? I'd decided to confront him another day, so I waited a week before I accepted his too-late phone call. Once we spoke, I gave it to him straight with no chaser; I was in no mood for games.

"Hey, baby," he said. "I've been calling you all week. What's going on? Why aren't you talking to me?"

"I hear congratulations are in order."

"Congratulations? For what?"

You won the Prick of the Year award, that's what!

"Your pending nuptials," I said. "You must be excited, a new wife, a new baby . . ."

He said nothing, waited to see what else I'd reveal—all for naught. I knew I'd said enough.

"Charisse, I don't know what you're talking about. I—"

"Stop okay, stop. Don't you ever get tired, Dwayne? Keeping up with all these bullshit lies must be exhausting. All I want to know is why? Why me? Why for so long?"

"How'd you find out?"

"Don't worry about that. Why don't you try telling me the truth for a change. It's time to stop living this le, don't you think?"

To save a little face, Dwayne took the offensive. "Look, don't play the victim with me, okay? I ain't the one. I did what I needed to do to take care of me and mine. I never told you that I loved you or that I wanted to marry you, did I? No, I didn't *mislead* you. You misled yourself. All I can say

265

is, you know what happens when you *assume,* except in this case there's only one ass—and it ain't *me.* Is it my fault you didn't know? With that said, let me say, Charisse, the sex was the bomb. I ain't gon' lie! But you got yours and I got mine. If this is any consolation, I am sorry you found out before *I* had a chance to break up. I would've at least lied to make it a little easier than knowing the truth. For that I'm sorry."

"You have some fucking nerve. Please, Dwayne, don't feel sorry for me, feel sorry for *yourself.* You're a human curse as long as you walk around with that attitude. You think you got away with something? You didn't get away with anything. It's only a matter of time before it all catches up with you, and I just pray that I'm somewhere to witness it."

"*Whatever.* I got what I needed from you. I don't need you any-more. So, I'm glad I can stop fakin'."

"Got what you needed? What does that mean?" I asked confused.

"Let's say I'm glad you're such a good real estate agent. My family will be comfortable for a long time thanks to you. Now, if you'll excuse me, my fiancé and my baby are waiting for me. I should be getting back to them."

Comfortable? Thanks to me?

"Yeah, you do that. Enjoy them while you can. Oh, by the way, does she know you're not divorced and can't marry her yet?" I asked.

"Don't worry about what she knows."

"I won't, but you should," I threatened.

His words were harsh, nearly cruel. What did I expect from a man who'd proven to be so dishonest and scheming? And what was he talking about? He got what he needed from me?

My resolve not to take revenge on Dwayne vanished. I sat for hours thinking of how I might inform his fiancé-baby's mama she couldn't marry Dwayne anytime soon unless she wanted to be his co-wife. I was sure she didn't know. My heart filled with disgust and hurt until I was bursting at the seams. No amount of Grey Goose, Godiva, or Doritos could bring me consolation. I realized there was only one thing that could.

I trudged up to my bedroom, knelt by my bed, and prayed.

Dear Lord, I know I don't do this as often as I should. I mean, I know I talk to you throughout my day, every day, but sometimes, I forget the importance of just praying. Anyway Lord, I'm sure

you saw what happened today. You knew it was coming way be-
fore I did. The thing is, I don't want to hate him and I don't want
to hurt because of him or anyone, not anymore. At first, I wanted
to ask you to run his car into the Potomac River, after you struck it
with lighting and set it on fire, but I realized that nothing I could
ask for would match what Your will is for him if he is the horrible
wretch he seems to be at this moment. So Lord, my only prayer for
him is that he gets everything that he deserves. Only You know
what's in his heart and whether my prayer for him is a blessing or
a curse. Amen.

And just like that I let the pain go, knowing I'd placed it in good hands. I'd survived worse than the likes of Dwayne. I crowned him bum of all bums. They were all a pesky bunch of blood-sucking insects—but I, as luck would have it, was a windshield. And God was my windshield wiper.

***

As I headed to bed, my cell phone rang. It was my client, Mr. Thomas; he'd become a first-time homebuyer at the ripe old age of sixty. I'd never in my career seen anyone so excited to hold a house key. He'd been saving fifteen years to buy a fifty-year-old, two-level ranch house in a neighborhood where the houses were dwarfed by the surrounding acreage. It was a handyman special but a bargain for the price.

"Mr. Thomas, how are you?" I asked.

"Hey, Charisse, I've been better. I wanted to let you know that you may not want to refer that contractor, Mr. Gibson, anymore. I hired him to work on my basement, and his work has been crap to say the least," he responded, sounding deflated from his typical bubbly personality.

"Mr. Gibson? I never referred him to you or anyone," I insisted.

"You didn't? Well, he said he came highly recommended by you; that's the only reason I hired him."

"How'd he get your phone number?" I asked.

"He said he got it from you."

"No, I never gave anyone your phone number and never would. This is upsetting," I said as I pressed my hand against my forehead in frustration.

"Upsetting isn't the word for it. He came by last week and picked up a twelve thousand dollar deposit. He dropped off some materials, pulled down some drywall, and I haven't seen or heard from him since."

Twelve thousand dollars? It probably wasn't a coincidence that's how much he repaid me for the money I loaned him. *That motherfu—*

"Well, Mr. Thomas, I cannot even begin to tell you how sorry I am about all of this. Please know that first thing tomorrow I will give Mr. Gibson a call and find out what is going on. I never referred him, and I don't know how he got your phone number, but I will get to the bottom of it. I promise you."

"Well, I would appreciate any help you can give me. You know my income is limited; I can't afford to give away twelve thousand dollars."

"No one can. I'll give you a call tomorrow and let you know what I find out. Okay?"

"Okay, thank you, Charisse. Take care."

What the hell is going on? I wondered. *How in hell did he get my client's phone number?* I sat on my bed in complete disbelief. That was low, even for *that* snake. I planned to curse his ass out until I made his eardrums bleed, but I was spent. Oh, I'd ream his ass out alright, but it would have to wait until the next morning.

Fifty-Three

Loving Bruno

As the sun peered through my window, I relished the new day and then remembered I had no reason to be happy. Another New Year's Eve approached, and I'd arrived back to square one—sort of. I had everything but a love to kiss at midnight's stroke, the one gift I really wanted. And from the looks of it, conniving, son-of-a-bitch Dwayne had scammed my client, using my good name. But at least this year all the goldfish were still alive. I could feel the tension tighten in my neck and shoulders. I never drank in the morning, but I was tempted to down a shot to calm my nerves before I called Dwayne to find out what the hell he was doing. Otherwise, my end of the conversation might consist of high-pitched squeals.

I decided to soak in a hot whirlpool bath to soothe my nerves when the phone started to ring. At first, I figured I'd take my bath and call whoever back, that is until my house phone and cell phone started ringing off the hook all at once.

I thought, *Sheesh what's going on? All hell must be breaking loose.*

I grabbed the house line because it was closest. It was Nisey.

"Charisse! Turn on the news quick! You are not going to believe this. Hurry up before the commercial goes off!"

"What is it?"

"Just go!"

I ran downstairs; juggling the telephone as I grabbed remote control and turned on the plasma.

"What channel?"

"Channel 4! Hurry, it's coming back on."

"What the hell is it, Nisey?"

"Just watch! Just watch!"

My favorite anchorwoman, Stacy Smith, led in with the story.

Virginia home contractor Dwayne Gibson faces as many as twenty years in prison for his involvement in a home improvement scam that defrauded one hundred twenty homeowners of more than eight million dollars over ten years. Seventy-five victims were from Virginia, fifteen were from Washington D.C., and the remaining were from Maryland. The victims allege Gibson made fraudulent statements to induce them to contract with his company and make payment installments on work he was supposed to complete in their homes, including false claims that he possessed a contractor's licenses in D.C., Maryland, and Virginia. Gibson would complete the minimum amount of work necessary to collect payments and eventually abandoned the projects, resulting in numerous Better Business Bureau claims. FBI Agent Kevin Douglass, who headed the case, stated Gibson's arrest is the culmination of a year-long investigation by the FBI and U.S. Attorney's offices in D.C., Maryland, and Virginia. Calls to his wife for an interview were not returned.

"Oh my God, Nisey! Did you see that?"

"Yeah, I saw it," she answered.

"Did you . . . did you catch the name of the FBI agent? That was Kevin, my Kevin! You know, the one that ran into me and kept mysteriously appearing everywhere I went. You don't think—"

"Yeah, I think," she interrupted.

"I need to sit down," I said. "Oh my God, poor Mr. Thomas! He called me yesterday and told me that Dwayne used my name to get his business. He took a twelve thousand dollar deposit and never did the work."

"That bastard! I can't even believe this. You must be livid," Nisey said.

"Livid? That is the understatement of the century."

"Well, listen. I hate to go, but I have a few errands to run. I 'm going to call you later when I get home. You gonna be okay?"

"Yeah, I'll be fine. I just can't believe this."

My phone rang off the hook for the rest of the morning, but I didn't want to talk to anyone. I watched the local news shows over and over until the story finally sank in. I thought about the night that Dwayne had slipped the medicine in my tea. He wasn't spoiling me; he was stealing my clients' information from my computer. My stomach twisted in knots.

Then it dawned on me that Dwayne had been *arrested*; he was in jail without the bail. God had me on that one! I couldn't have dreamed that scenario if I tried. The lightning-induced car accident into the Potomac River I prayed for *paled* in comparison to twenty years in jail and Dwayne's becoming a man-whore for some six-foot-eight guy named Bruno with an affinity for men in terry towel. I didn't know whether to laugh or die laughing when the significance settled in.

The doorbell rang. I figured Nisey dropped by but wondered how she got to my house so quickly. When I opened the door, I was stunned at who I saw standing before me.

"Marcus? What are you doing here?"

"I saw the news. I've been calling you, but you didn't answer. Can I come in?"

"Sure," I said, hesitating momentarily before I stepped back and let him in.

Has Marcus come to be supportive? Has he changed that much? I asked myself as I hung his jacket in the coat closet. My disdain for him had waned when he bought me the key finder, such a nice gesture. I thought maybe his visit would be the perfect time to determine whether our paths might be leading back to one another.

"So, uhhh, I saw your boy on the news. Are you doing okay?" he said, flopping on the couch and putting his feet up on my coffee table like he owned the place.

My boy?

"I'm doing as well as can be expected under the circumstances I suppose. What brings you here?" I asked as I stood in the entry way just in case I needed to help him find the door. I didn't like where the conversation was headed.

"Well, given everything that happened, I thought you might be ready to talk, I mean, about us."

"Talk about what?" I asked.

"I figured you probably had some regrets about ending our relationship now, maybe you're thinking you made the wrong choice. So, I wanted to tell you that, even though you acted shitty when you met dude, I'll take you back. We can start right where we left off."

The part where you cheated? No, thanks!

"Is that right?" I asked

"Yes, you don't have to thank me now. Why don't you make us a couple of drinks, and you can make it up to me *upstairs . . .* in your *bedroom.*"

Oh, no he didn't!

"Marcus, I have a much better idea," I said as I stomped over to the bar. I grabbed an empty pilsner and shot glass and shoved them in his hands. "You thirsty? Here! Have a tall glass of shut the fuck up, with a kiss my ass chaser. Drink up!"

I walked to the closet, yanked his jacket off the hanger, threw it in his face, and continued my rant, "I can't believe this shit. Thank you! Thank you for being the jackass I always believed you were. You are one of the sorriest men I've ever met in my life, which says a lot given the bums I seem to attract. I want you out of my house and don't *ever* bring your *monkey ass* back. Now, you ain't got to go home, but you've got to get the hellll out of here," I yelled (borrowing my favorite Morris Day and the Time quote).

"It's your loss," he said as he placed the empty glasses on the bar and sauntered out the door.

"Damn right, it's my loss. Hallelujah!" I rejoiced and slammed the door behind him, hoping the doorknob would catch him in the ass.

I collapsed on my chaise and let the moment soak in. It was over between me and Marcus, finally and forever. So, I laughed and laughed. From the core of my healing soul, I laughed. Closure felt good, real good.

Fifty-Four

Expect the Unexpected

Life had a funny way of going full circle. Another New Year's Eve arrived, and I was alone (again), but I'd kicked Marcus to the curb for good and found the strength to empty some of my very hefty and painful emotional baggage. Lee's and my relationship would never be the same, but I forgave him and let that shit go. By moving that unwieldy mess out of my life, for the first time, I thought my life might have enough space for the right man, whenever he did come along. I was no longer full of pain; I was full of hope.

As I dressed in my most elegant pair of flannel feetie pajamas to bring in the New Year, my phone rang; it was my mother. After coming so close to losing her, I vowed to enthusiastically answer all of her phone calls forever—or until the guilt wore off—whichever came first.

"Hi, baby, ready for the new year?"

"Oh, I'm definitely ready. I'm just going to stay in tonight, put my pajamas on, and watch the ball fall at midnight. This has been one hell of a year."

"Yeah, with hell being the operative word, huh?" she responded.

"You can say that again. And, uhhh, I have a little news," I said, pausing to grasp what I was about to say. It still hadn't sunk in. "Dwayne, the guy I was seeing, he's in jail. But, before you say anything, I'm sure it was harder on his fiancé and new baby than it was on me."

"What! Jail? For what?" she asked. "Wait a minute, did you say fiancé and baby? Where the hell they come from?"

"Chicago. Apparently, he'd been seeing another woman all along, got her pregnant. As for the jail part, I heard on the news that the FBI arrested him for defrauding a bunch people out of millions of dollars in a home improvement scam. The FBI had been investigating him for a year, and I had no idea."

"Sweet Jesus almighty. Ain't that nothin'? Well, you always told me you suspected something wasn't right about him. Now you know why. Girl, you got the best instincts of anyone I know. Ever since you was a wee little child, you knew people before they knew themselves. That's a God-given gift, girl. No doubt about it."

"Really? I didn't know that."

"That's right, absolutely right," she said, pausing for a moment.

"Is something wrong, Mommy? You okay?"

"Oh no, I'm fine, baby, couldn't be better, but my heart is aching a little bit. Me and your Aunt Jackie had a long talk this morning."

I gasped because I sensed what she'd say next. She was going to find out eventually, but I thought I'd be the one to tell her once she was finished with rehab.

"She told you?"

"Yes, baby, she told me. And I have to tell you, at first, I was so angry that you didn't tell me that I couldn't hardly see straight. You're my baby, and I'm s'posed to know. But after I thought long and hard about it, I realize we didn't make it easy for you, everybody treatin' Lee like he was the best thing to happen since Michael Jackson. It couldn't have been easy."

"No ma'am. So many times I wanted to tell you but couldn't bring myself to do it."

"Well, we can't do anything about it now, that's the past. But, in this moment, I want you to listen to what I say and don't you ever forget it. I am your *mother*. There ain't a soul on this earth more important to me than you, not a single soul. And there ain't nothing that you can't share with me that will ever change how I feel about you. Don't you know, baby? There is no love like a mother's love. It ain't always perfect 'cause we ain't always perfect, but it will always be there. Don't you forget that, you hear me?"

I got choked up.

"Yes, Mommy," I said as cleansing tears poured down my face.

"Don't cry baby. It's gonna be okay . . . you're gonna be okay. You know, I'm sorry I ever told you 'bout Santa Claus, tryin' so hard to save you from my disappointments that I didn't realize I was blockin' your blessings by makin' you afraid to believe someone could love you. But you gotta live your own life. Disappointments will come, but they'll only make you that much stronger and smarter. I believe the Lord has a lot of good in store for you next year. I believe it in my heart. You'll see."

"I hope so," I responded.

"No, don't hope . . . believe."

***

I placed a bottle of Moet in the overpriced stainless steel ice bucket I bought from Crate & Barrel and assumed the position on my chaise. I planned to watch one of the many New Year's celebrations on television; my all-time favorite was *Dick Clark's New Year's Rockin' Eve*. I had no love to kiss at midnight's stroke, but I was going to toast myself. Just as I got comfortable, my doorbell rang.

Marcus!

Thought he might've returned, so I grabbed the bottle of Moet like I was gripping a baseball bat just in case I needed to knock him over the head with it.

"Kevin?"

"Hi, Charisse, I'm sure you've heard the news, huh? It's been crazy. Can I come in?"

"Sure, what brings you here on New Year's Eve? And where's your girlfriend?" I said as a rush of butterflies attacked my stomach.

"Well, I needed to talk to you and figured you'd be home alone since Dwayne's in federal custody. I took a chance. Is it okay? Or would you rather I leave?"

"No, no, please come in and have a seat. Make yourself comfortable."

"What's with the bottle?" he asked as I lowered the bottle from its strike position and led him to the family room.

"Oh, I thought you were someone else, brought it with me in case I needed to put someone to sleep."

Kevin trekked toward the fireplace, while I perched on my favorite chaise and watched him flinch. I wasn't upset with him (although I'm sure he thought I was). He didn't know, but he answered my prayer.

"Okay. So, you're wondering why I'm here, right?"

275

"Uhhhhh, yeah, the thought had crossed my mind."

"Well, there are some things I wanted you to know, about the investigation . . . and about me. Obviously, there are certain things I can't share with you, but I thought you deserved to hear some things from the horse's mouth, so to speak."

"Okay, I'm listening."

"Well, I guess I'll start with Dwayne. We've had him under investigation for some time now, since before our accident. You were under surveillance at the time."

"Wait a minute, *I* was under surveillance? Why me?"

"Well, part of Dwayne's operation was to recruit real estate agents who referred clients to him. Sometimes they were paid thousands of dollars for their client lists and referrals, and other times he stole them and told the clients the agent referred him. In your case, based on conversations that you had with him, we determined that he stole your client list."

"Shit, I remember a few months ago I caught him using my computer; he put something on a disk. He even slipped some of my back pain medication in my tea to make me sleep . . . but wait a minute, you said something about our conversation. My phone was tapped?"

"I'm afraid so," Kevin responded.

"Oh my God. So, you guys heard everything I said? For how long?" I asked, searching my memory to ensure I hadn't engaged in any embarrassing phone sex.

"I can't give you an exact date but it would be safe to say it's possible anytime during your relationship with Dwayne."

I froze. "You didn't listen yourself, did you?"

"No, my partner read most of the transcripts though," he answered.

"Your partner?"

"Yeah, Kristen. She's an FBI agent too."

"But I thought she was—"

"My girlfriend?" he interrupted. "No, she isn't. Just seemed easier to let you believe that she's my girlfriend than find another explanation. She's actually married with two kids . . . well separated. She's going through a difficult divorce now so she hasn't quite been herself."

"So you're—"

"Single? Yes."

Hallelujah!

"Whew, can I sit down for a second?" I said, already sitting down.

He chuckled. "Sure, I know this is a lot to take in."

"So, that's how you guys showed up everywhere I went, at church, the doctor's office . . . wait a sec, my cell phone was tapped too?"

"Technically speaking, yes."

"So, the reason you'd been popping up everywhere was because of *the case?*" I asked.

"No, that's not true. There's more to the story, more to us than you realize."

"I . . . I'm not sure what you mean by that?"

Kevin resumed pacing in front of the fireplace. "I know that you don't . . . well . . . this is something you really may want to sit down for."

Fifty-five

Full Circle

"**I** 'm already sitting, Kevin. How much further down can I get?"

"Oh yeah, I forgot. Well, maybe *I* need to sit down," he said, fidgeting as he searched for an explanation. "Well, I told you that I was from North Carolina, remember?"

"Yeah, I remember," I responded, waiting anxiously for the punch line.

"Well, what I didn't tell you is that I'm from Winston Salem. I know your cousin Lee, personally. Very personally."

"Well, you told me you played football against him."

"I know, but there's more," he said. He stood still and turned his head to look me in the eyes. "He and I were acquaintances in high school; we both played football, although I went to a different school. Anyway . . . I hosted the party . . . the party that you went to . . . *that night* . . . in Buena Vista."

My heartbeat raced and I lost my breath as the reason for Kevin's nervousness became clear. He knew, but . . .

"You were there? But, I don't rememb—"

"I was the one burst into the room and threw him off of you. I sat with you and took you home," he interrupted. "You were a little too distraught to remember me, but I never forgot you."

"That was you?" I said. Chills raced through every crevice of my body as tears welled in my eyes. *Kevin.*

"Yes, it was me. You have to know I didn't know what was going to happen, I swear I didn't. I only heard from some of the guys talking about it and ran as fast I could to find you, to see if you were okay. I was also the reason for Lee's swollen eyes; I kicked his ass and the other guy's ass too. Lee's your cousin, your family. I couldn't believe he would let that happen to you. What kind of man—" he said, stopping himself. There was no need to say more; we both knew the answer.

"Oh my God. Oh my God. Oh my God," I said. "You fought them . . . for me?"

My knight in shining armor, I thought. *What he did for me all those years ago; what he did for me yesterday without even knowing . . . or did he?* I looked at him in a heavy silence. Finally, he spoke.

"What? What is it?" he asked, sounding concerned.

"You didn't by any chance read the transcripts from my conversation with Dwayne yesterday, did you?"

"And Mr. Thomas. I arrested him shortly thereafter . . . not because of you—although it certainly made the arrest more enjoyable. You see, once I was assigned to the case and realized you were the Charisse Tyson involved, I started following you on my own. I couldn't believe the girl I sat with that night would defraud innocent people. So, at first, I set out to find out if you were a con artist. When it became clear you weren't involved, I was determined to prove you were innocent. Those conversations gave me what I needed to prove you had nothing to do with his scheme. So we moved in and locked him up."

Ain't God good?!

He continued, "He posted bail and tried to run, but his fiancé turned him in—"

"Shut up!" I interrupted.

"Yeah, the news reports were the first she'd heard of *his wife.*"

"Well, I'll be damned!" I said, chuckling. "And the accident? Hell, if I knew the FBI was behind it, I wouldn't have settled for so little."

"No, no, that was a bona fide accident. What can I say? I always thought you were beautiful. I was so busy looking at your reflection in your rear view mirror that I accidentally hit the gas instead of the brake."

"You think *I'm* beautiful?"

"It's hard to explain my feelings, Charisse. You've been a part of me for twenty-seven years. I'd always felt like a little part of me was missing . . . until I met you again," he said. "There's something else I want you to know too."

"What's that?"

"What happened with you all those years ago is what inspired me to become an FBI agent. Being there for you, it changed something inside me. I wanted to protect and help people. You touched my life in ways you never knew. It's crazy to think that what you inspired me to do with my life is what brought you back into mine."

"Wow."

"And when this is all over, I hope that maybe we can go out sometime, you know, get to know one another better."

"With everything you know about my past, you're still interested?"

"Why wouldn't I be? I don't know what world *you* live in, but in my world nobody's perfect. We've all got our shit to deal with. If you stick around me long enough, I'm sure that you'll find out more about me than you ever wanted to know. But that's what dating is about, isn't it? Finding someone who can love us unconditionally enough to tolerate us," he said as he walked over and slid next to me on the chaise.

The moment was surreal.

Fate, destiny, or mere coincidence, he reappeared into my life for a reason, I was certain of it, like I was certain neither Creed nor the Commodores would ever get back together. For the first time in my life, I just knew. I didn't question how or why. I laughed to myself when I remembered his was the face that came to mind when Lamar asked me to search my feelings for a man I had a good feeling about—the irony. But still . . .

I didn't want our relationship to start out like a July 4th fireworks show, just to fizzle out like a wet sparkler later down the road. On the other hand, his irresistibility intensified with each passing second. Would I make a return trip to the sex rodeo for an inconsequential, short-lived bull-ride, or was I going to take things easy and slow?

"Wow, they've started the countdown. It's almost New Year's Day. Under the circumstances I think we've got just one last thing to do . . .," he said as he gazed into my eyes and covered my lips with his. As we came up for air the countdown continued, "Five, four, three, two, one, Happy New Year!!!" the plasma echoed.

"Happy New Year, Special Agent Douglass."

"Happy New Year, Ms. Tyson."

"Kevin, I hope you don't mind, but there is something special I always wanted to do with a man on New Year's. I have to tell you, I've never done this with any other man before. But I think if we ended our night this way, it would be absolutely perfect. Are you game?"

"Hell yeah, I'm game."

"Alright, come on up to my bedroom . . . *if you dare.*"

***

I looked down at my watch and shook my head in disbelief. "Can you believe this? We've been at it all night?"

I shifted my position, my leg was falling asleep.

"Ouch, Charisse, that hurt. How can you stick it to me like that?"

"Oh, don't be such a baby. It'll feel better when you do it to me. Now, stop stalling and move your ass, so I can get what's coming to me," I said as I grabbed the bottle of Hershey's chocolate syrup. "Do you want me to put some chocolate on it?"

"No, no more chocolate, baby. I'm gonna get a stomach ache," he whined.

Big baby.

"Okay, okay, I'm moving my ass. You happy now?" he continued. "Back to the business at hand, though. I wouldn't treat you that way. I'm nice. I'm a gentleman, remember?"

"There's no room for a gentleman on this bed. There's only room for a real man—a real man with real money. I bet you never thought four inches could cause you so much pain. Now, pay up!" I shouted with excitement. "I own Boardwalk with three houses and a hotel. You owe me thirty-four hundred dollars!"

Kevin shook his head, feigning disappointment and looking dejected. "Well, that does it for me. I'm bankrupt! I don't have any money left. I guess that means . . . you win."

"I win, I win, I win, I win," I said, joking as I broke out in the Cabbage Patch dance, laughing hysterically. "Don't feel bad Kevin. You didn't actually think you could beat a real estate agent in Monopoly, *did you*?"

"Yes, but I guess I should have known better," he said. He rolled on his back and stared at the ceiling.

"It's almost five in the morning, we just finished our third ice cream sundae, and I *creamed* you in Monopoly. I have to say this is absolutely the best New Year's I've ever had in my entire life. Honestly, Kevin, thank you for staying."

He turned his head toward me and smiled. "Trust me, the pleasure was all mine, even though I lost."

"Next time, I'll let you win," I said as I rubbed his hand and poked my bottom lip out to fake pity. I put the game back in the box, slid it under my bed, and lay beside him staring at whatever we were staring at on the ceiling.

"No, next New Year's Eve *I'll* choose the game," he said.

"Oh, really? So, you think you're going to survive an entire year?" I asked, glancing at him out of corner of my eye.

"I'm counting on it, Ms. Tyson," he responded.

"So, uhh, what's *your* game?" I asked.

"Clue, you know, the mystery game."

"Clue? Ohhhhhhh, I get it, FBI Agent, murder mystery, so cliché," I said. "I'll take that bet though. You're on. And I'll warn you up front, I'm going to beat you at your own game."

"Care to wager a bet?" he said as he propped himself up on his elbow.

"Okay, since I'm now a gambling woman, what are the stakes?"

"Well, I can only think of one thing that I really, really want," he said as he took his free arm and nudged me close to him. The heat from his body warmed me.

"What's that?" I asked.

"Your heart," he said as he looked deeply into my eyes and kissed my lips.

Mmmmm. Kevin's kisses were the most magical of all. While the others may have warmed what's between my legs, Kevin's kisses warmed my heart. Nothing in this world could touch that.

"Oh, well, it looks like you're going to have to find something else to bet then."

"Why is that?" he asked with a hint of concern in his voice.

"Well, silly," I said as I caressed his contented face and gazed into his eyes, "you can't bet something you've already won."

***

Well, as it turned out, my mom was right. Good men are like Santa Claus. Believing in them feels really good, and once you relax and stop watching for them, they appear when you least expect it.

About the Author

K. L. Brady is a D.C. native and grew up in Prince George's County, Maryland, the setting of her debut novel. She discovered a love for reading and writing at the age of three, by her mother's accounts. Through the years, she has maintained diaries and journals, but it is the journals she wrote as an adult that provided the inspiration, of sorts, for *The Bum Magnet*.

When she hit her "tween" years, her mother packed the family and moved to Bellaire, Ohio, where she eventually graduated from Bellaire High School. She attended the University of Akron for a year and a half, where she pledged Sigma Gamma Rho Sorority, Inc., before moving back to the D.C. area.

A single mom, Brady lives just outside of D.C. in Cheltenham, Maryland, with her son, William. She's an editor for a government contracting firm and an active real estate agent with Exit Realty. Brady is also an alumnus of the University of the District of Columbia and University of Maryland University College, earning a B.A. in Economics and M.B.A., respectively.

Visit K.L. Bradys Web site at:
www.klbradywrites.com

Want more Nisey and Rissey?
Check out their "Get Off the Short Bus"
relationship blog at:

http://www.thebummagnet.blogspot.com

[i] Battaglia, Emily. Adapted from "Leave Your Emotional Baggage Behind," 26 Jan 2006, www.LifeScript.com. Copyrighted Material, All Rights Reserved. Permission Requested.

LaVergne, TN USA
01 July 2010
188110LV00004B/123/P